END OF MEN

SUZANNE STROBEL

PIVOT
PUBLISHING

Published in the United States by Pivot Publishing.

First edition 2020

Denver, Colorado, 80204

suzannestrobel.com

ISBN 978-1-7361345-0-4 (ebook)

ISBN 978-1-7361345-1-1 (paperback)

Quotes from Gloria Steinem and Valarie Kaur are reprinted with permission. Valarie Kaur, "'Breathe! Push!' Watch This Sikh Activist's Powerful Prayer for America," *Washington Post,* March 6, 2017.

Cover design by Milan Klusacek

For the boys and girls who struggle with anxiety, depression, fear, and doubt. You are not alone.

We've begun to raise our daughters more like sons...but few have the courage to raise our sons more like our daughters.

—Gloria Steinem

What if America is not dead, but a country that is waiting to be born? What if this is our nation's greatest transition?

—Valarie Kaur

PROLOGUE

IT'S STRANGE, looking back, that we didn't notice sooner. There were small signs, of course. Single women unable to find boyfriends, university courses crowded with females, Elizabeth Hatcher becoming president. The boys were fading into the background, but we were too distracted to notice. A million other things fought for our attention: climate change, food shortages, disease, the shattered economy—and, of course, the violence.

By then the mass attacks were a daily occurrence. We watched them play out like a twisted horror movie. On Monday, a twenty-year-old man in Willimantic bombed an office after being fired from his job. On Tuesday, a twelve-year-old boy awoke, brushed his teeth, and shot up the elementary school down the street. Every day was a new attack with a different twist. Once upon a time, they'd been designated "random acts of violence," but that had stopped years ago. Daily events couldn't be random.

Maybe you can understand, then, why news of the birth pattern didn't feel shocking at first. The mass of us had been numbed by a steady stream of bad news, lulled into a constant sense of discontent and dis-ease. The phenomenon was revealed in the middle of winter, and we leapt on it like the welcome distraction that it was. Across the nation, millions of babies were born, normal in all ways but one: every one of them was a girl.

The danger was distant enough that it was laced with curiosity, a thrilling mystery to enjoy with buttery popcorn and speculation. Would Mother Nature reverse the trend as abruptly as she'd started it? Could we harvest enough sperm to eliminate reliance on males? Would women find a way to not only survive but thrive on our own?

But I'm getting ahead of myself. Let's go back to the beginning: the day I learned about the End of Men.

PART I

WINTER

CHAPTER ONE

Marika and I stood in the entryway of my studio, waiting for our iCar. The ceiling panel over my head slid open and my bulletproof vest sprang down, dangling on an orange bungee.

I grabbed the vest and tugged it on, noticing the fibers were already coming loose. It was a charcoal-colored knockoff I'd hastily ordered over the summer, a new brand that promised to be "just as tough as Kevlar" at half the price. Marika wore a beautiful leopard print Wonderproof Hoodie, designer cut with a gleaming bronze zipper and thick gold stitching.

I zipped up my bargain armor, wincing as it pinched at my sides.

"Did this thing shrink?" I muttered.

"Yep, just like my jeans always do after four months of not exercising," Marika replied.

I smiled, grateful for her attempt to lighten the mood. It had been 124 days since I'd stepped outside. I'd gone into hiding after my dad was killed in the RDC Marathon shooting, so consumed by grief and guilt I couldn't work or think straight. Sometimes I could barely even breathe.

My Virtual Therapist (VT) promised the pain would ease with time, but my grief had morphed into post-traumatic stress disorder and agoraphobia, with a healthy dose of survivor's guilt mixed in. I'd been running in the marathon that day, too—six minutes behind my dad. Now I was what society referred to as a "shut-in," a person far more comfortable in isolation than in the outside world.

My dad would have been horrified. And that was the only reason I stood at the door: a desperate need to fight the thing that was growing in me, to do what my dad would have done and get back to work, to be courageous, useful, and strong. Work had always been my safe place—I'd inherited that from him. If he were there, he'd tell me to wipe away my tears, march out that door, and go find a story worth telling.

I certainly had plenty of stories to choose from. In a world where many citizens didn't leave their homes, media was as essential to life as air. People devoured our content over breakfast, lunch, and dinner. Some were hungry for a glimpse into the real world, others just wanted an escape.

The hall lights dimmed and my home's Envoy system announced in a friendly feminine voice: "Your iCar will arrive in ninety-four seconds, Charley. This morning's threat alert level is red. Please ensure that your vest is secured and prepare for departure."

My Envoy had no official name, but I called her Vanessa. She had a soothing tone that helped slow my racing heart, the same way a pill did in the dark of night.

"You ready for this, girl?" Marika handed me a stainless steel travel mug of coffee. I took it and sipped, but it was way too hot and burned my tongue.

"Ow," I said, frowning.

"It's hot, silly," Marika said with a laugh.

"You should have warned me."

"No, you should have known."

I peeled off the mug's lid and blew on the steaming liquid. A delicious heady aroma rose up around me and the fuzziness in my head shifted. I'd had too much wine the night before, attempting to numb my nerves by downing a bottle-and-a-half of cabernet. Of course, all I'd done was make the morning that much more difficult, piling a nasty hangover on top of my grief and anxiety.

Vanessa announced: "Sixty seconds to departure."

Marika grabbed my hand and squeezed it. "I'm proud of you. Your dad would be too."

I met Marika's gaze, wishing I could soak in some of her strength. Even at the crack of dawn, she looked confident and beautiful. Her curly black hair was still damp and, as usual, she didn't have an ounce of makeup on. She didn't need it. She had flawless light-brown skin, deep cheekbones, and huge eyes that changed from brown to black to gold, depending on the light.

For as long as I could remember, I'd wondered how it would feel to live in Marika's skin—so at ease with her natural self, no blemishes or flaws to cover up or hide. Growing up, she and her mom had lived in the apartment upstairs from my family. One time, she slept over on Halloween and we dressed up as each other. She carefully darkened my pale skin and thickened my thin eyebrows. I straightened her hair with a searing hot iron and caked thick white powder on her face. We giggled as we emerged from my bedroom, excited and proud of our costumes.

"Hello, I am Marika," I had announced, changing my tone to emulate her musical Indian accent. "And I'm Charlene, but y'all can call me Charley," Marika proclaimed in an exaggerated southern drawl that sounded nothing like my real voice.

My dad's eyes widened in surprise and my mother

shrieked, "You girls go scrub that off right now!" We stood at the sink and scrubbed our faces. My tears mixed with the water, chest burning with shame as I tried to understand what we'd done wrong. To make me laugh, Marika washed half her face clean and left the other half pasty white. "Look, now I'm me and you, all mixed together, different but the same."

Marika was the closest thing I had to a sister. I knew she missed my dad too, even though I'd yet to see her shed a tear since his death. That just wasn't her way.

"Well, thanks for the boiling hot coffee," I told her. "And thanks for not giving up on me these last few months."

Marika tucked an unruly curl of hair behind her ear.

"Give up on you? The thought never crossed my mind. Well, maybe that one night, when you made me sit through twelve hours of sappy romance movies."

"You loved it," I teased.

"Maybe a little," she replied with a wink.

I laughed and immediately felt a slap of guilt. How could I laugh when my dad was dead? I swallowed and tried to force the thought from my mind, remembering what my VT had told me: *Your father would want you to find joy in the world again.*

Behind Marika's head, a black spider scurried up the wall before disappearing into a crack in the white plaster. I scratched a sudden itch on my neck.

"Vanessa, please remind the cleaning bot to dust the ceilings," I requested.

Marika always teased me for talking to Vanessa as if she were a person, reminding me the system would fulfill my needs whether I was polite about it or not.

Vanessa replied, "Certainly, Charley. Have a safe day."

The front door slid open and together, Marika and I stepped outside. Drops of sweat formed on my chest, back, and armpits.

I'd forgotten how hot the world had gotten, our Februarys more like June. It was terrifying to be outside, but I also felt a thrill—a tiny but glistening piece of the freedom I'd lost or surrendered. The sun was blinding and I pulled dark sunglasses from my satchel, then put them on to survey the neighborhood.

The beastly apartment building across the street had finally been finished. It stood tall and stoic, bulletproof windows glistening in the sun. Next to it, my favorite old yellow Victorian looked tiny and vulnerable, shades drawn, porch light blazing despite the bright morning. A few weeks ago, a mother and her little boy had moved in. I'd perched in my studio's window seat watching the mother carry in pillows while the little boy clung to her hand. He was around six, a thin and gangly little thing with thick glasses and shaggy blond hair. *You should go say hello and welcome them to the neighborhood,* I told myself, knowing I wouldn't.

As if on cue, the front door of the Victorian burst open and the little boy bolted down the steps, dressed like Batman. His cape fluttered behind him as he ran in erratic circles around their front lawn, which was really just a patch of dirt thanks to the relentless sun. The boy leapt onto a stone pillar near the property's perimeter and stretched his arms out in front of him as if preparing for takeoff.

"Hi, lady!" he called out.

"Hello, Batman!" I responded, glad for the distraction.

His mother rushed out the door, face pinched with worry. "Milbert, get back inside! It's a red day!"

"But Mommy, I want to talk to those ladies," he said, pointing at me and Marika.

She looked over and her scowl softened. "Oh, hello." She flashed a quick wave before grasping Milbert around the waist and gently lifting him down from the pillar. "You can talk to them on a green day, honey. Right now, I need you to come inside."

"But Mommy, it's *never* green," he whined. His shoulders slumped as he trailed after her into the house.

My blue iCar zipped up to the curb, vibrating with sun-fueled energy, its soft hum now the only sound on the quiet street. Our destination flashed in neon letters on the side door's screen: *The Verge, 9467 Fayetteville Street, Raleigh, NC.* The iCars had been released two years earlier, a ground-breaking solution to greenhouse gas emissions, claustrophobic traffic, and deadly crashes. The circular pods were controlled by automated sensors that were far more capable of operating automobiles than humans ever were.

I lifted a thumb to the doorpad so it could confirm my identity. The side panel slid open and Marika slipped inside. I glanced back at the red front door of my brick building, feeling like Lot's wife. Did we really *have* to go? Couldn't I just make like a spider and crawl into a dark, safe place? But I owed it to my dad—and myself—to try. *The world needs your voice,* he'd say if he were there.

I sighed and slid into the iCar next to Marika, clasping the bottom of my mid-length skort as I bent. The hot leather on the beige wraparound seat burned my bare thighs.

"Ow!" I slid forward to perch on the edge of the seat and ran a hand across the back of my right leg. I knew I should have opted for neoprene pants.

"First your tongue, now your legs," Marika said in a teasing tone. "Guess you've got some adjusting to do."

Our seatbelts wrapped around us and a green light flashed to announce our departure. The iCar picked up speed and the windows darkened—another automatic setting. The system was measuring my pupils, heartrate, and a variety of other biometrics to determine whether I'd feel more comfortable looking out the window or enjoying seclusion. I relaxed as the outside world disappeared.

"Good morning, Charley," a familiar voice greeted. The iCars automatically matched our home system's preferences, which meant that Vanessa's soothing tone followed me everywhere. "You will arrive at your destination in eight minutes, thirty-six seconds."

I leaned back into the plush leather seat, which was now cooled to my preferred 68-degree setting, and sucked in the sweet scent of vanilla. The car's systems leveraged a library of rich passenger data to customize everything for our enjoyment —from the odors pumped through the air vents to the entertainment they played.

I swiveled to face Marika. "I need a distraction. Got anything good?"

She rubbed her hands together and grinned. "I have a speed date lined up for tomorrow morning!"

"A morning speed date? Has the dating world changed *that much* since I've been out there?"

"You have no idea. There's one eligible bachelor and six successful ladies. We get five minutes with each person to find the best match for our futures based on our personalities and life goals. And all of it is done blindly, so we won't know who we match with till afterward."

I laughed and lifted an eyebrow. "What happened to good old-fashioned 'boy meets girl'?"

"Pshhhh, that's so last century. I'll fill you in on all the juicy details tomorrow. Maybe you can join me on the next one!"

"Thanks, but that sounds horrible. And besides, who'd want to date me right now? I can barely make it two hours without a panic attack."

"Anyone with a brain, that's who."

I waved off her compliment. "Vanessa, please show me the news."

Vanessa's warm voice replied, "Here is the latest news, Charley. Please relax and enjoy your ride."

A holograph of Sloane Steele appeared on the iCar's west panel, glowing with my favorite rose-colored filter. She stood in front of the State Capitol in a red cotton dress that accented her flat stomach and molehill breasts. The iCar system had some learning to do, because I detested Sloane Steele and would hardly consider her coverage "news." Opinionated and untrustworthy, she pushed her agendas on others with the wave of a perfectly manicured hand. She was little more than a beautiful pseudo-celebrity, famous for being famous, without an ounce of empathy or objectivity in her petite body.

"Who the hell wears a tight red dress to a rally?" I asked, sneering at the holograph in disgust. She was probably in heels too. I could just see her sinking into the soft grass, hollering at her production assistant between takes.

Sloane smiled through a mile of perfect white teeth and said, "We're reporting live from the Capitol, where the Fear Fighters have organized yet another flash peace gathering. The latest research estimates the group now has more than two million members across the nation, and its numbers are rising daily."

The hologram flashed to a closer view of a crowd of Fear Fighters, huddled together under the hot blue sky. I swallowed a sip of my coffee, now cooled enough to drink, and leaned forward in interest. I'd been watching these activists on the Hub over the last several months. They were fighting for freedom of movement and the right to gather, among other things. They claimed the government's attempts to control and minimize public places were killing society more than the attacks were. I chewed my lip, wondering if they had a point.

Five months ago, the government had shut down airports and train stations. Then schools, shopping malls, and event venues. The RDC Marathon was one of the last crowded events the nation had seen. We still had a few opportunities for public entertainment—there were small restaurants, city-run bars, and well-secured Virtual Recreation Centers (VRCs) where we could take part in fully immersive sensory experiences. But every day, we had less and less reason to leave our homes. We ordered our groceries online and drones delivered them. More than three-quarters of employees worked from home instead of braving an office. We traveled less, talked less, shared less. Drank more.

The Fear Fighters had been organizing flash peace gatherings across the nation to protest the shutdowns. They must've had some type of secret signal or beacon, but the government couldn't crack the code. A crowd of them would converge upon a park, old stadium, or school like ants swarming on a lost sucker—strength in numbers, defiant and radiant.

"Look at all of them," Marika whispered in awe. "Your dad was right. How many did he predict there'd be by now?"

"Two million," I answered.

I watched as the camera zoomed in for a close-up. Their arms were wrapped around one another, faces full of passion as they chanted their three doctrines:

> *Build connections, not walls!*
> *Use words, not weapons!*
> *Seek freedom, not security!*

The camera's gaze shifted away from the demonstrators and returned to Sloane, who smoothed down her already-perfect chestnut hair.

"While some may empathize with the Fear Fighters' desire

for freedom, the fact remains that they're breaking the law. The capacity restrictions are intended for our protection, and they are deliberately ignoring them. What are they trying to prove? Who are they going to get killed next?"

The camera switched to an overhead drone view. Thousands of activists were packed on the Capitol's lawn, chanting and buzzing with energy. Thousands and thousands of people out in the open, where anything—anything—could happen.

I pressed my feet into the floor and struggled to breathe. The holograph blipped away from the Fear Fighters and was replaced by the shimmering 3D image of an athletic blonde woman. Her skin was dewy with joy, her hair glossy and clean, and she stood in a green pasture with snow-capped mountains rising behind her.

"Seeking a sense of security?" she asked in a musical voice. "Come live at Vista Haven, where safety is a given and worry is a thing of the past. Enjoy daily yoga and meditations in a community of women seeking connection and peace. All surrounded by a state-of-the-art Tesla shield for impenetrable defense and a comfortably cool climate."

The abrupt media change was a response to my rising anxiety and heartrate, an attempt to soothe me by showing me a safe place.

"Isn't that where your mom lives?" Marika asked. "We should go visit. That spa sure looks nice."

Guilt burned in my chest alongside my anxiety. I fixed my gaze on a tiny rip in the iCar's gray carpet, trying to focus my mind. Once I was triggered, I felt like I was on one of those old teacup rides, spinning round and round, faster and faster, a passenger with no control over the tipping, tilting earth. I looked back at the blonde hologram and her dewy face blurred. She'd probably never lost anyone she loved, never woken to a stranger's hollow eyes in the mirror. She probably wasn't even real, just a digital animation of peace and beauty that was no longer possible.

I dropped my head to my hands and dug my nails into my scalp, hoping a pinch of physical pain would distract me from my overwhelming emotions.

Marika's voice swam into the darkness. "Charley, are you okay? Envoy, turn it off."

Marika wrapped her arm around my shoulders and rubbed my arm. Usually I took comfort in her presence, but at that moment I wanted nothing more than to be alone. My studio might be dark and lonely, but it was safe. I could curl up in bed, drink and sleep until reality blurred into darkness.

I closed my eyes and tried to visualize happy things: snow-capped mountains, blue skies, birds soaring overhead. Images of the Fear Fighters flickered persistently, unwanted static. Their voices chanted in the silence: *Seek freedom, not security.*

I wanted to ask: what about the things I'll never be free of?

CHAPTER TWO

THE iCAR CAME to a stop and the door slid open. Marika gently nudged me and I got out, eyes on my silver boots as they landed on the red brick walkway. *One step at a time*, I told myself, practicing my VT's advice to count my breaths. *One, two, three. Breathe, breathe, breathe.*

We were in front of the Verge, the media network where Marika and I had worked for the last three years. Technically it was Clarion now, but the logistics of the merger were still settling into place. The building looked just as I remembered, a bulky and angular concrete monstrosity. The same square blue Verge logo hung crookedly above the entrance.

We rushed toward the front door, Marika quickly taking the lead with her long athletic legs. I wiped a bead of sweat from my hairline. It was barely nine a.m. and the temperature was already nearing 90 degrees. If this was winter, what would summer bring? We reached the entrance and positioned ourselves in front of the thick metal door for the pupil scan. A soothing tone like a harpsichord sounded.

"Hello, Marika Singh," the system greeted. "Hello, Charlene Tennyson."

Like all the nation's automated systems, the station used a feminine voice, though it wasn't nearly as charming as Vanessa's. The unfriendly tone was like an ice pick, each word landing with a stiff blow.

The door slid open and cool air swept over us, a welcome but artificial relief from the heat. We hurried inside and the door shut behind us with a loud *thwump*. Above our heads, a red digital counter beeped and logged our entrance: *18 people now present*. Once upon a time, our twelve-story building had been filled with hundreds of employees, but we were now capped at thirty on-site reporters and support crew—yet another preventive measure against the attacks.

The security guard, Sam, stood in his usual spot next to the metal detector, behind a tall desk enclosed in a divider of bulletproof glass. His white beard was just as bushy as ever and his blue uniform still bore the Verge's logo.

"Charley!" he bellowed, his face lighting up with a huge grin. "Pleasure to see your beautiful face again."

Sam had a big jolly voice that made me imagine him as Santa. Aside from his thick white beard, he also had a round belly and a contagious laugh that had brightened many of my mornings. For a moment, I could believe nothing had changed. I was just a reporter heading into work, Sam was simply a precaution, and the world was not falling apart.

Sam's smile slipped away and he lowered his voice. "I'm real sorry about your dad. How are you doing?"

"Thanks, Sam. I'm okay," I lied through a stiff smile.

No one ever knew what to say when death visited your family. Aside from my anxiety, the pity was another thing that made facing the public so hard. Everyone's eyes were full of sorrow and questions—though in reality, no one wanted to hear the honest answers.

How are you doing? Terribly, thank you. Last week was his birthday and I couldn't drag myself out of bed the entire day. *Do you need anything?* Drugs. Liquor. More sleep. A magical time travel contraption to whisk me away to somewhere, anywhere, besides the here and now.

Sam shook his head and sighed. "It's just not right, Charley, not right at all. But listen, you don't have to worry about a thing. Clarion upgraded all our security machines, and we got a five-star rating on last week's safety check."

He motioned to the metal detector and a new machine I didn't recognize. "See this tube? Just deposit your firearm there. We'll do a quick body scan and have you through here in a jiffy."

"I don't have a firearm, Sam."

I lifted my arms into cactus pose and walked through the metal detector, pausing as a silver wand swept in front of me to check my temperature and biometric signs in an infrared inspection. A beep indicated I'd been cleared.

"No firearm?" Sam asked, and lifted his bushy gray eyebrows in surprise.

President Hatcher had signed the "Guns for All" defense bill last month, her first major initiative after being re-elected. The government swore that arming as many citizens as possible was one of the best ways to defend against attacks in public spaces. We were flooded with charts and graphs proving that incidents went down in areas where citizens were armed and trained in self-defense.

The Fear Fighters disagreed. *Use words, not weapons,* they chanted at their rallies. But for too many people, words had become just another weapon in the arsenal, every discussion more vicious and polarizing than the last.

"You'd better believe I'm packing," Marika interrupted. She dropped her pistol in the tube and breezed through the metal detector, then retrieved the gun from the carousel and slipped it back into her holster.

I wished I felt comforted knowing Marika and Sam could protect me, but the sight of their guns just filled me with more prickly anxiety. The layers of security felt inept and wrong, like a Band-Aid to fix a fever. The world started to tip and twirl. How foolish I'd been to think a few weeks of VT sessions could prepare me for being back in public. As if PTSD was like a bad day, something you could shake off and forget.

"Bye, Sam," I said, eager to get out of the lobby.

I hurried down the west hallway toward the elevators, Marika close by my side. The black marble floors used to be covered in thick rugs but now stood bare and glistened under the harsh fluorescent lights. A strange painting hung on the east wall. It was of a jagged purple mountain range that cut through a fiery red sky. The brushstrokes were amateurish and childlike, with specks of white canvas showing through.

"That's new," I said, pointing.

"Isn't it ugly?" Marika asked with a smirk. "I swear, it must've been done by some Clarion big-wig's grandkid or something."

I shrugged. "It's not that bad. Looks better than what I could do."

"You've never even tried painting," Marika said.

"Do you always have to be so damn logical?" I asked.

We approached the elevator bay to find all three elevators standing empty, doors open as if waiting for us. We stepped into the middle one and Marika pressed the buttons for the third and fourth floors. I eased myself against the back elevator wall, comforted by the smooth, strong steel against my back. The doors slid shut and I felt a wisp of relief as we started rising. We were safe—for now. Three floors up, then sixty-four steps down the hallway and around the corner until I reached my desk. Sixty-four steps alone, with nowhere to hide.

The elevator glided to a stop and a warm feminine voice announced, "You have arrived." Unlike the voice at the entry, this one sounded soft and soothing, like a mother kissing her child's sweaty forehead after a bad dream. Another upgrade from Clarion?

The elevator doors slid open and I stepped out, carefully avoiding the crack. *One, two, three, breathe.*

"Good luck today," Marika said. "Try not to think about the Fear Fighters, or any of the other craziness out there. Just stay focused on what *you* need. You'll be great. Virtual Taekwondo tonight?"

"I can't, I have an appointment with my VT."

She held her finger on the open door button, using her other hand to reach into her satchel and pull out a small gold box. "Here, I got you this," she said in an off-handed tone.

I took the box from her and fingered the edges. "What is it?"

"You'll have to open it to find out, silly." She punched another button on the elevator panel and waved goodbye.

I clutched the box to my gut and hurried down the hall to the media room, keeping my head down as I rushed to my desk. I didn't want to talk to anyone yet. I needed to be alone, needed to sit, think, and remember how to breathe. I stepped inside my cubicle and pressed the button to seal me in, waiting anxiously until the clear glass dome clicked shut and the lights across the top flashed green.

"Work space secure," a melodic voice announced.

I unzipped my vest and sank into my chair. My heart was pounding. If just being out in public felt like an extreme act of bravery, how was I going to go back into the field?

I gazed down at the gold box Marika had given me and slowly lifted the lid. Inside was a silver necklace with a red ceramic pendant bearing an etching of a lotus. I touched the digital notecard on the lid's underside and a message appeared:

The lotus grows in muddy water, its petals shedding dirt as it rises above the murk to achieve beauty. You're stronger than you think, my beautiful friend.

I ran a finger across the necklace's ceramic etching, then opened the clasp and slipped it on. The pendant rested at the center of my chest, heavy and comforting.

My worksphere illuminated and I looked up to see a message from Frida, my production manager, on the side of the clear dome.

Glad you're here. On my way over.

Across the news pit, the door to Frida's office swung open and she stepped outside. She wore a loose white silk blouse with puffy shoulders and mint green culottes, looking tanned and fit as always. Her sandy brown hair was wavy today, which was usually a sign that she was in a good mood. She flashed a huge smile and strode toward me as if the news pit were a runway, chest out, head high.

A tall, lean guy trailed behind her, a white badge around his neck marking him as a newbie. He looked like he was from another decade, decked out in old-fashioned denim pants, a crisp white tee, and a blue baseball cap.

I pushed the button to unlock my worksphere. The green light along the top changed to yellow as the safety mechanisms released and the door slid open.

"Charley," Frida said. Her smile quivered and her eyes darted from left to right, flickering past me before resting squarely at the top of my head. She clasped her hands.

"We're so happy to have you back," she continued, stretching her smile bigger to reveal a tiny dot of red lipstick on her left incisor. "I'd like to introduce you to your new production assistant, David Vine. David, this is Charley Tennyson."

"Nice to meet you," I said with a curt nod.

"The pleasure's all mine, Charley. I'm a big fan of your work."

He extended his hand in greeting and I looked down at it in surprise. No one shook hands anymore. I paused before accepting, then slipped my hand into my pocket to wipe away the warm, tingly sensation of his firm grip.

I squinted at him. "A big fan, huh? What's been your favorite piece?"

He grinned and a dimple flashed in his left cheek. "Tough call, but I'd have to go with the story on Ganta's CEO and her quest for the Alzheimer's cure. That was really riveting."

Apparently Frida's hiring skills had improved since I'd been on leave. My last assistant, Carl, had barely been able to string together two sentences. Thinking and talking about work was already helping to ease my anxiety. The notion of getting back into the field sparked a rush of excitement. The positive emotion felt wrong, though, like opening a gift on someone else's birthday.

I smiled back at David and looked closer at his face. "When did you start? You look kind of familiar."

"This is day five," he replied. "I hear that a lot, I think I just have one of those faces. But we haven't met before. I'd remember."

He grinned and gave me a sly wink. Was he...*flirting* with me? I looked back at Frida.

"So, what's on tap for today?" I asked.

She tapped the gold Surge on her wrist. The thin wearable devices had been released in the late 20s, and now adorned nearly every citizen's arm. Young or old, free-moving or shut-in, most people rarely removed their Surges from their wrists. And why would we? The ultimate convenience, each bracelet was resilient, waterproof, and branded with our own unique code, making credit cards and identification unnecessary. With just a tap, we had instant access to the Hub and our personal payment systems, communications networks, holograph recordings, and transportation. It was a wonder people had ever survived without them.

Frida tapped her Surge again and a stream of information rose in a holograph before us. She scrolled through it, eyes riveted and focused, then stopped.

"There's a governor in Chatham County who's pushing to reopen a handful of local schools. Says she's developed a new security system that's 'foolproof' against mass attacks. You up for it?"

I lifted an eyebrow. I'd been hoping for less of a hot button topic to ease back into things. A celebrity divorce, maybe, or commentary on the promising new cancer vaccine.

David interrupted, "I heard there's a big Fear Fighters peace gathering at the Capitol. Do you already have someone on that?"

"It's taken care of," Frida said in a dismissive tone.

"Who's on it, Corinna or Trent?" I asked, curious.

When I'd taken my leave, the network's top two reporters had been dueling for coverage rights on the Fear Fighters, certain the small activist group was on the brink of major growth.

Frida paused before answering, "No one, actually. It's been banned."

I frowned. "What do you mean, banned? I saw Sloane Steele covering it on the way in."

"Yeah, well, that's Sentient. We're the Verge—excuse me, we're *Clarion*. A lot's changed since you've been gone, Charley."

The acquisition of our homegrown media network, the Verge, had officially gone through three months ago. Clarion was the nation's leading media conglomerate and the merger was a huge celebration. After years of struggling to survive, we'd finally have access to bigger budgets and the resources needed to pursue quality journalism. But based on Frida's sour expression, it seemed the cracks in that sweet little story were beginning to show.

"Hatcher sent out an executive 'request' to all the major networks," Frida explained. "She's worried showing coverage of the Fear Fighters gatherings will encourage more people to join. Sentient's still small and independent, so they can afford to ignore it. As for us? Corporate doesn't want us touching it."

Frida turned her attention back to her Surge and began flipping through its data stream again when suddenly, all the lights across the news pit flashed red. A red alert only meant one thing: another attack. We stared up at the big screen across the news pit and watched the details flood in.

Who: An eight-year-old boy named Elliot Monker.

What: Shot a group of Fear Fighters with a semiautomatic Glock 19 he'd stolen from his mother.

When: Ten minutes ago.

Where: the Capitol.

Why:

I had it all except the last one. A lump swelled in my throat, like a pill too big to swallow. Eight years old? How could a gunman be only eight years old?

"Goddammit," Frida said. She tapped a button on my worksphere and her voice broadcast across the news pit. "Everybody meet in the briefing room, now."

She bolted across the pit, David close at her heels. Heads popped up from cubicles as the masses followed the order and rushed to follow her. Amidst many unfamiliar faces, I spotted Corinna and Trent. Corinna saw me too and flashed a smile and a quick wave.

I waved back, then gripped the side of my worksphere and looked down at my feet. They were planted firmly but appeared to be rising and falling, swimming as the world tipped and twirled. My Surge vibrated and I looked down to see a warning:

HEARTRATE ELEVATED!

A tiny heart pounded on a jagged rising line as the heartrate counter pulsed upward. I ignored the numbers and watched the red heart beating, lulled by the steady *thump-thump-thump*. I took three slow breaths in and out, then another three, and another. Finally, the numbers descended and the pounding slowed.

I wrapped my arms around myself and went to be briefed on the next big story.

CHAPTER THREE

We gathered in the briefing room, just over a dozen of us. Frida stood up front near the screen. The other reporters and I sat around the oval conference table, while the production crew lined the back wall. I glanced over my shoulder and saw David blending right in, looking as if he'd worked there for five years rather than five days. He caught my eye and gave a quick nod before looking back at Frida, his expression somber and focused.

Frida turned on the Hub. Sloane and Sentient were already reporting from the scene.

"So far, we know there were three casualties," Sloane said with urgency and excitement. "Several others were injured and rushed to medical facilities. We'll share more details as they become available."

Photos of the victims flashed before us. Melina May, a freckled redhead, stood atop a rocky mountain, hands on her hips. Joseph Morrell, barely out of high school, wore a black graduation cap, yellow tassel dangling to the left. Carly Kimber embraced two toddlers whose black cornrow braids and gap-toothed smiles matched her own.

I remembered the cherished family photo the media had used in their stories after my dad was killed, how they'd turned it into a flag waved amidst the rubble. It was a picture of my parents and I huddled together in front of Cape Hatteras Lighthouse, on a rare vacation to the Outer Banks. The sky was golden with the sun's last rays, and a line of tall dune grasses rose behind us like nature's soldiers. We'd been laughing at some silly thing, and the photographer had snapped the photo at just the right moment. My mom had framed the photo and hung it in their hallway. I wondered if it now hung in her new Luxury Haven or if she, like me, could no longer stand to look at it.

A red banner flashed across the screen and a feminine voice said, "We interrupt this broadcast to bring you live commentary from the White House."

President Hatcher stood in the press briefing room, her face somber as she addressed the nation. She clasped her hands on the podium, exposing small sweat marks in the armpits of her electric blue silk blouse.

"Our thoughts and prayers are with the families of those who lost loved ones in today's attack. We believe today's incident was the result of an emerging epidemic our scientists have dubbed male-pattern violence, or MPV."

She paused and bit her lip as if fighting back tears. It was the first time I'd glimpsed the real woman behind the stoic public persona she usually presented.

"This rapidly spreading phenomenon causes young boys to experience and act upon violent urges resulting in injury to large groups of civilians. Early symptoms include increased aggression, sudden bursts of rage resembling temper tantrums, unusual mood swings, and impulsivity. We expect to have more information to share over the coming days and weeks as our scientists explore causes and treatment therapies."

The sea of reporters around her erupted with questions.

"Is it contagious?" one voice rang out.

"Can girls get it, too?" another bellowed.

President Hatcher held up a hand. "Please, hold your questions until the end. We are uncertain exactly how MPV is spread. It can affect females, though it is far more common in males. Boys and men aged eight to twenty-nine are most susceptible. One thing we know with utmost certainty is this: the impact of MPV can be dramatically reduced by adhering to the public safety guidelines we have laid out."

The holograph switched from Hatcher to a view of the CDC's official guidance. She narrated, "No more than thirty people may be gathered in public at any given time. Mass transit stations, schools, and entertainment venues will remain closed. Unnecessary travel is restricted. The fewer crowds we have, the fewer attacks there will be, and the fewer innocent people will die."

President Hatcher's face reclaimed the broadcast. She took several swallows of water, then refolded her hands and looked directly at the camera. Her empty water glass was now marked with a dark lipstick stain and fingerprints.

"I urge the public, everyone watching: let this be a reminder of how crucial it is to heed the capacity restrictions. To ensure the safety of the public, there will be punishment for those who break the laws. Vanyala Dawson, Fear Fighters, if you are watching: these 'flash peace gatherings' must stop. You are not fighting fear; you are creating the opportunity to spread it. Until we can better understand the early warning signs of MPV and begin to treat it, the only solution is to arm ourselves, restrict public gatherings, and remain vigilant."

The hologram feed of the Hub flickered and President

Hatcher disappeared. She was replaced by the digital avatar we'd come to recognize as a stand-in for Vanyala Dawson, the Fear Fighters' founder. Her cartoonish avatar sat in the same dark, mysterious cavern where all her broadcasts came from, her true identity hidden behind layers of visual and audio technological distortions.

Vanyala raised a fist and made a proclamation as if in direct response to Hatcher. "We mourn our fallen brothers and sisters, but this will not stop us from fighting. If anything, it has renewed our sense of purpose. Today's attack is why we gather. It is the reason we fight. We will not go quietly into the dark night!"

Behind me, Trent let out an exasperated sigh. I turned to look at him and he rolled his eyes. "She's so dramatic. Does she not realize fear has already won?"

He was right. More than 90,000 people had been killed in America last year. Mass shootings, bombs, grenades, stabbings. Before free driving was taken away, intentional crashes were the attack of choice. We lost an average of 250 people a day. 250 mothers, fathers, daughters, sons. International travel had been banned since the Great Separation but we saw other country's stories on the Hub, horrific tales that increasingly mirrored ours. Fear and death were everywhere, spreading like a contagion.

Vanyala continued, "President Hatcher and her legislation will attempt to scare you. They'll remind you that we've successfully hidden away through other pandemics, emerged shaking and restless but vaccinated and alive. What's happening today is different. This is not a contagious virus spread through the air. It exists only in the mind—and together, we can stop it. Young boys do not need to be vilified and extricated from society. They need to be nurtured and loved. All of us do."

Vanyala's holograph disappeared. We sat in silence for a moment before Frida took control of the room.

"Does anyone have a lead on Vanyala?" she asked.

As usual, no one answered. We—along with every other media outlet—had been trying to get an interview with her for nearly a year. She hacked the airwaves to give her public addresses. She was the face of the Fear Fighters, yet she never appeared in person. She was like the Wizard of Oz—endowed with almost magical powers, yet a complete mystery. Some had begun to speculate that she wasn't even a real person, just a computer-generated program.

"All right, everyone's going to cover a different aspect of this story," Frida continued. "Katiana and Zachariah, you're on this 'MPV' epidemic. Dig into the CDC's info, talk to doctors, researchers, anyone who has information about this thing. Corrina and Trent, keep up the work you're already doing to find Vanyala. Hold nothing back. Corporate has classified the hunt for Vanyala as a Tier 1 story, so you have unlimited budget and resources at your disposal. If you can find her, we'll have the biggest story of the year. Lucinda and Graver—tell the stories of today's victims and survivors. And Charley..."

The hardness on Frida's face softened as she looked at me. "I need you to interview Elliott Monker's family. If anyone can get them to talk, it's you."

I nodded, my voice strangled by fear and horror.

Frida clapped her hands. "All right, everyone. You have your assignments. Let's do this."

I watched the room empty out before I stood on shaky legs. In the old days, I'd have been flattered by Frida's confidence in my interview skills, but the idea of going to the Monkers was incomprehensible. Not that any of the other stories Frida had doled out seemed any better. All of the day's events felt way too painful and close to home.

David hovered at the back of the room.

"I need to make a quick call," he said quietly. "Can you give me three minutes?"

"Take all the time you need," I replied.

As he darted into the hallway, I sank into one of the chairs and checked my vest for the hundredth time. The teacups were spinning, round and round. And I had a feeling there was no getting off anytime soon.

CHAPTER FOUR

LESS THAN TEN MINUTES LATER, David and I sped toward the Monkers' in Mule 9, him in the driver's seat and me riding shotgun.

Media workers were among the "chosen few" who had maintained self-driving rights after the iCars had been released. Mules were tall, boxy vans loaded with resources. The rear held a small icebox packed with artificial food, a tiny block slab where we could eat, and hooked panels lined with recording equipment, sleeping bags, foraging tools, and other gear. While the iCars ran on programmed destinations and circuits, the Mules enabled us to change directions on the turn of a dime so we could pursue breaking stories anytime, anywhere.

David hung his left arm out the window and talked as we drove, but I wasn't in the mood for conversation. His words echoed around me like a movie playing in another room. I ran my fingertips across my harness, grateful for its ability to keep me from sliding into the dangerous world outside.

My Surge vibrated with a message from my mother: *Did*

*you see the news? Are you okay? I hope you're not still planning
to go back to work today.* A fresh wave of guilt swept over me as
I hit *Ignore.*

While I appreciated the convenience of our Surges, I often
wondered if we'd be better off without them. Sometimes I
dreamed of standing on a remote beach, sand in my toes,
wearing a yellow bikini instead of a heavy bulletproof vest. I'd
yank my Surge from my wrist, toss it into the deep blue ocean,
and listen to the waves crash and the seagulls call. The sun
would be shining instead of smothering, and I'd be free from
fear.

But that was just a dream.

"How many people do you think will be at the Monkers'
house?" I wondered aloud.

"Why, are you nervous?" David asked.

When I didn't respond he said, "Don't worry, they'll have
SWAT all over the place. I know it's been a while, but you'll do
great."

I glanced at him sharply, wondering how much he knew
about me. He kept his eyes straight ahead.

"Warning," a voice advised. "You are approaching an
endangered zone. More than 50 people are present. SWAT
teams are on hand and a security perimeter will be enforced. If
you must proceed, do so with caution and ensure that your
vests are secured."

We turned onto Westover Street and were assaulted by
chaos. Armies of reporters lined the road, fighting to catch a
killer's family on film. Helicopters swarmed overhead, the
steady hum of their blades chopping through the air. I
imagined the Monkers hunkered down inside, praying it was all
a nightmare—that any moment they'd wake up, sit down to
dinner, and ask their son how his day was. I could understand

the grief they felt, the desperate yearning to turn back time. I thought of my dad, the morning he'd headed into work, not knowing it would be the last time he'd kiss my mother goodbye.

That's why Frida had sent me—hoping I could turn my wounds into a weapon, a way inside. But as I looked around at the crowd of hungry reporters, my confidence ripped apart. What could I say to show the Monkers I was any different? If I were them, I wouldn't let me in.

David pulled up to the security clearance area. A SWAT team member approached our van and conducted a weapons check, then scanned our Surges and logged our identities.

"So much for the land of the free," I said as we drove through clearance.

"Same as it ever was," David replied.

"What do you mean? All this crap is new."

He shook his head. "There's nothing new under the sun."

David pulled onto the side of the road and we got out. I grabbed my neoprene satchel and gazed around at the other reporters, not feeling like one of them anymore. The energy, the adrenaline, the hunger—all of it was just like I remembered, but it felt so different now. "Getting the story" was no longer my goal. I just wanted to get through it.

I lifted my hand to the necklace Marika had given me, pulling it out so it lay on top of my vest. *You're stronger than you think.*

Together, David and I headed through the crowd. Flashing lights and buzzing voices filled the air as photographers took their shots and reporters angled for the best spin. David motioned for me to follow him and beelined toward the far right side of the crowd, closer to the trees, where the crowd was thinner. He stopped and held up his hands to frame the shot, then looked back at me.

"Okay, this is it," he said. "I'm thinking we start with you here, get the house and helicopters in the background. I want to get the crowd in there too—show the people, the chaos, all of it, with you way out in front. What do you think?"

My eyes darted toward the van. Maybe I could just make a run for it. Instead I nodded, knowing the best of my bad options was to go forward.

"Gimme two minutes," David said.

He tapped his Surge and a virtual videocam recorder arose. He tweaked the settings and I unzipped my satchel, reaching for my compact and a vial of red lipstick. I cringed at the face looking back at me. Circles and worry lines darkened my face and a handful of wiry grays screamed at my temple. I focused on my lips, lifting the vial with one shaking hand. Cover, shine, blot, repeat.

The last time I'd put on lipstick was for my dad's funeral. Memories of that day shoved their way in. I saw the purple casket my dad had insisted on, the birds flying overhead as he was lowered into the ground. I heard the officiant's nasal voice mispronouncing his name and talking about stupid stuff that didn't really matter, like his desire to help the homeless and the donations he made at church.

"All right, Tennyson, we're ready to roll," David said.

I stuffed my makeup back into my bag and tugged at my vest. The air felt used, dirty, smothering. Was I having a stroke? My head was foggy and my fingers had gone numb. A prickly discomfort spread through me, snaking through my veins as if it had a life of its own.

The crowd buzzed louder. Something was happening up ahead, you could feel the adrenaline rise a notch. I craned my neck to see a young boy being escorted through the crowd by cops.

"It's the older brother," a reporter next to me hissed. "Alexander."

Shouts rang out as everyone fought to get his attention. "Alexander! Alexander! What's it like, knowing your brother is a killer? Did you know what he was planning? Did he have MPV? Do you?"

The boy was hunched over like an old man, pain lining his face. My heart pounded and my breath grew shallow as the world around me grew blurry.

"I can't..."

And then I was running, the crowd's noise roaring in waves as I fled. My legs were weak but they carried me to the Mule. I crouched down beside the passenger door, buried my head in my arms, and wept. I wept for my dad and the Fear Fighters, for Elliott Monker and our lost boys. I wept for myself and the other family members who wished it had been them instead. I wept for our terrifying world and a future that felt more hopeless every day.

David appeared and knelt down beside me. "Tennyson, you okay?"

Embarrassment flashed through me as I wiped tears and snot from my face. I wanted to tell him to go away, leave me alone, but words escaped me.

"Here..." David reached into his pocket and pulled out a string of purple beads. "Rub these back and forth in your hands, then hold them up to your face and inhale. They're lavender-infused. They always stop my panic attacks."

He handed me the beads, then stood and walked to the back of the Mule. I was grateful for the space. No eyes full of pity, no worried questions, no pressure. I knelt on the pavement, rubbing the wooden beads between my palms and trying to catch my breath. The sharp, floral scent of lavender drifted up around me and I sucked in the air. Seconds ticked by, then minutes. Slowly, feeling returned to my fingers. Fresh air found its way back into my lungs. I could still hear the helicopters and reporters in the distance, but they were no longer crushing me. I had survived.

After a while, I stood up. "Thank you," I called out.

David turned and walked back to me. I handed him the string of beads but he closed my fingers around them.

"Keep 'em," he said. "I've got more at home."

"Thank you," I repeated. There was more to say, but I wasn't sure what. I cleared my throat. "You said this happens to you too?"

He nodded. "Ever since I lost my wife."

"Oh," I replied. Now I knew how people felt around me, when there was so much to say that nothing seemed appropriate. I couldn't stop from asking: "Was it...an attack?"

He nodded, tears glistening in his eyes. I didn't know why I was surprised. Lately, it seemed there were more of us victims than not. Things were getting worse and we seemed powerless to stop it. Those of us who weren't brave enough to be Fear Fighters or rich enough to flee to Luxury Havens just buried our pain and anxiety behind more layers and solitude, waiting for something, anything, to change.

"Should we get outta here?" David asked.

I nodded, eager to feel walls around me again.

He unlocked the Mule and I got in, watching him as he walked around to the driver's side. I didn't know how I hadn't seen it before. It was in his walk, the long steps he took as if he were trying to escape something. It was in his chest, the way he held it up with pride that was a thin shield against pain. It was in the lines around his eyes, the crinkles at the sides of his mouth. David had all the signs of a man who had been torn apart and put back together.

He opened the door and slid in next to me. "Back to the station?" he asked.

I imagined having to face Frida, telling her I'd lost my nerve, admitting I was a failure. I wasn't ready to face the consequences of letting her and the network down. I shook my head. "I just want to go home."

"I can understand that," David said. "But you shouldn't be alone. Why don't we go somewhere and talk?"

"I don't know..." I said. My VT had been suggesting group therapy ever since I'd started working with her. I kept turning her down, not wanting any real people to see how crazy and lost I was. Now, I wondered if there was some wisdom to be gleaned from talking to another survivor. *Survivor.* The word echoed with pain. Was I still a survivor if I was barely surviving?

"How did you move past your wife's death?" I asked. I wanted a secret antidote, something to make life seem worth living again. Anything besides the canned response of *time.* I stuck my hand in my pocket and fingered the prayer beads David had given me, restraining from the urge to hold them up to my face and inhale the soothing lavender again.

"Let's go get a drink and I'll tell you about it," David said. "I have an idea that might help."

I tapped my Surge. It was 11:05 a.m. "Isn't it a little early for a drink?"

"Does it *feel* too early for a drink?" David shot back.

I laughed in spite of myself. "A drink actually sounds really good."

I sent Frida a short message: *Can someone else cover the Monkers? I couldn't do it. I'm so sorry.* Then I turned off incoming calls. I'd deal with the mess I'd made later.

David flipped a switch on the side of the Mule and I knew without asking: We were going off the grid. I thought again of the Fear Fighters gathered together at the Capitol, willing to die for what they believed in. Did I have that kind of strength in me?

Marika's words floated into my head unbidden: *You're stronger than you think.*

Maybe one day, I'd believe them.

CHAPTER FIVE

As WE DROVE AWAY, I looked in my side mirror at the chaos we were leaving behind. Part of me expected to see it all crumble like a pillar of salt, but it was still there—the reporters and armed forces, the helicopters and flashing cameras. When did the world become so insane? I looked up at the sun beating down on us, searching for God, but all I could see were clouds and questions.

David turned right, and then left, and then right again. After a while, I lost track of the way and thought he might have too. Just when I was about to ask if he was lost, he pulled onto a dirt road surrounded by pine trees.

It appeared out of nowhere: an old-fashioned, off-the-grid tavern. I'd heard about these places. Unlike the city bars, this place wasn't authorized by the government. It didn't have the machines, layers of security, or strict capacity limits. You had to be personally invited and you couldn't divulge the location to anyone. Even if you did obtain the coordinates, you still had to figure out how to get there. The iCars couldn't take you—the taverns didn't show up on their navigation systems.

I leaned forward in my seat. "How'd you find out about this place?"

"My mom built it."

"Seriously?"

I gazed at the rustic wooden shack in awe. It was made of beetle-kill pine, black swirling across tan like the most beautiful kind of death. I could still see the axe marks in the wood. I thought of my own mother—afraid to step outside, urging me to come live with her at Vista Haven, ridden with worry if I was anywhere besides safe at home. She'd been like that ever since I was a child, even before we'd lost my father, before society had broken and crumbled. Sometimes I wondered if her paranoia had somehow created the world we lived in, her worst fears so vivid they'd been brought to life.

"Your childhood must've been a lot different from mine," I said.

He chuckled. "My childhood was a lot different from most people's. But that's a story for another day."

David pulled to the side of the dirt road, expertly guiding the Mule into a tiny spot between two tall pine trees. As soon as we got out, a feeling of peace enveloped me. It wasn't just that it was quiet—there was a sense of mystery that hung in the air. No one knew where we were. No one could find us. I couldn't remember the last time I'd felt so unattached to the world's chaos.

A hot wind rushed past us, sending leaves whirling through the air. We approached the entrance with crackling footsteps. David slid the wooden barn-style door open and we stepped into a long, quiet, barren room. There were three other people in the bar and none of them had their vests on. David looked at me and smiled, stripping off his Kevlar. I followed his lead and took mine off too, a pang of fear mixing with the elation of freedom.

We walked up to the bar and the bartender strolled over to us, an old grandfatherly man in overalls. He had silver hair and deep laugh lines around his eyes and mouth.

"Hey, David. How ya doin?" His southern accent reminded me of the country music my dad used to play. Sweet, nostalgic.

"Hey, Moe, this is my colleague, Charley."

"What can I get ya, Charley?"

"Double bourbon and ginger, shot of Jameson on the side please."

I smiled and tried to hide my discomfort at not wearing my vest—and my shock at the fact that they still made overalls.

David lifted an eyebrow at me. "So when you said it was too early for a drink, what you really meant was that we should start with *three* drinks?"

I shrugged. "My dad always said, go big or go home."

David laughed and turned to Moe. "I'll have the same."

Once our drinks came, David headed for a table in the far corner of the room. I followed him and he gestured for me to sit down first. The tables were made of wood and the seats looked like old church pews, vintage walnut polished to a shine.

I picked the seat facing the door and slid in. The wood was cool on my thighs, a welcome surprise after the stifling heat outside. David slid in across from me and we sat in awkward silence. Usually I rushed to fill voids in conversations, but I let myself sit with the quiet, curious to see what David would say.

"How are you feeling?" he asked.

"I'll be fine," I replied with a shrug. My gaze wandered down to my drink.

David took the unspoken queue and lifted his shot glass toward me. "Here's to new stories. *Better* stories."

We tossed back our shots and the Jameson burned my throat in a sweet, delicious way. I set my glass down before he did and quickly reached for my bourbon and ginger to chase it down.

"That was a rough scene back there," David said, his voice raspy from the liquor. "I hope you don't feel bad about leaving. The story didn't feel right to me either."

I shrugged again. The truth was, I felt like a failure. I'd had my first chance to rejoin the world, to stand up and fight like my dad would have, and I'd run away. We sat in awkward silence until David broke it.

"How long's it been?" he asked quietly.

I knew what he meant without him saying the words. Since the attack that killed my dad, my life had split into "before" and "after."

"A little over four months," I replied. "You?"

"Almost three years. Thirty-four months. One thousand thirty-one days."

I gave him a sad smile. "You don't ever stop counting, huh?"

He shook his head. "Not yet. And, sorry to break it to you, but birthdays and holidays don't get any easier either."

"What about the regular days? When do those get better?"

David spun his glass in his right hand. "After Stefania died, I was insane with grief for at least a year. I couldn't breathe, couldn't think straight, wanted to die myself. I sat in meetings with no idea what was being said. One day, I saw a dead pigeon in the road and just started sobbing."

He paused to take a sip of his drink and I did the same. He set his glass down and continued spinning it in his hand, the liquid coming dangerously close to the rim as the ice cubes rattled against each other.

David continued, "My VT told me that when you lose a loved one, you heal the same way an amputee does. The raw, bleeding stump heals, and you learn to live with the loss. You rebuild your life around it, and in some ways, it makes you who you become. But you always have that aching reminder of what you've lost. And sometimes you still get this shooting pain in your phantom limb that takes you right back to day one."

The analogy was comforting and haunting at the same time.

"My VT is big on analogies," I told him. "She says that when the grief comes, I should let it rush over me like a wave. Don't try to fight it, just ride it out."

"Sounds like good advice," David said. "Though I'm sure that sometimes, it feels like you'll drown before the wave passes."

I nodded. "Like today."

"Give yourself some credit, Tennyson. You were brave to go there in the first place, after all you've been through."

I frowned, thinking of his comment earlier. *I know it's been a while, but you'll do great.* How much did he know about me? I filed the question away to be addressed later and instead asked, "You said you had an idea that might help me move past it?"

He nodded. "I found that the best way to move past Stefania's death was to start rebuilding my life around something else." He glanced over his shoulder before leaning closer to me and continuing. "I have a lead on a huge story. It's perfect for you."

I frowned. "Why do you keep saying things like that, as if you know me?"

"I may not know you, but I know your work. I also know your father's work."

I gripped my drink tighter. The glass was slippery but I could still throw it at him if things took a turn, could still make a run for the door. But then what?

"What do you mean?" I asked.

"Sorry, that probably sounded creepy. After I lost my wife, I was obsessed with finding a reason for the attacks, a reason for her death. I became fascinated by some research your father was doing. Did he ever talk to you about something called 'The Y Factor'?"

I shook my head. My dad had been a clinical research scientist. He loved what he did and spent most evenings in his study, reading and developing hypotheses for his latest projects. My mother joked that work was his mistress, the thing that made his heart light up and gave him a spring in his step. It wasn't really a joke, of course—even as a young child, I could see how passionate and devoted he was to his career. He used to tell me, "If you love what you do, you'll never have to work a day in your life."

I frowned at David. "So *how* exactly do you know about my dad's work?"

David glanced over his shoulder before looking back at me and leaning forward. "I'm a Fear Fighter," he said quietly. "Your dad was working on a study we sponsored."

"You're a *Fear Fighter*?"

For some reason, the revelation made me see him in an entirely different light, like when your eyes adjust to discover a hidden 3D image and you can't unsee it afterward. Before, David had seemed charming, easygoing, kind, quirky. Now he seemed intriguing but dangerous. I glanced down at my vest on the seat next to me, then back at the entrance. Less than a dozen long steps and I'd be back outside.

David shook his glass and a big clump of ice cubes hit the side, then broke apart.

"Why do you sound so shocked?" he asked. "There are lots of us now."

I shrugged. "Between Vanyala Dawson being ultra secretive and the big mass gatherings—the Fear Fighters just seem like such rebels. My mom would freak out if she knew I was here."

He laughed. "Your mom? How old are you, ten?"

"I *wish* I were ten again. But Frida would also freak out, and so would a lot of other people. You heard Hatcher earlier. You guys are basically being branded as outlaws."

He rolled his eyes. "The media loves to focus on our flash peace gatherings and acts of so-called 'civil disobedience,' but that's a tiny fraction of the group's focus. We do a ton of work with researchers, government officials, and other activist groups developing solutions to stop the attacks. 'The Y Factor' was a study we sponsored and your dad was the lead researcher."

I took a sip of my drink. "Go on."

"Your dad had a compelling hypothesis that the increasing violence was linked to a mutation in the Y chromosome. The group just came across a new piece of information we think is related."

David leaned forward and lowered his voice. "Have you heard of a sex ratio?"

I shook my head. David tapped his Surge and a hologram of a line graph appeared before us.

"The sex ratio is the ratio of male births to female births," he explained in a low voice. "In most sexually reproducing species, the ratio tends to be right around 1:1, with a slight tendency toward more males. So for humans, approximately 125 males are born for every 100 females."

He pointed to a steady line charting the ratio of male births to female births through history. "This is the global sex ratio through the 1800s, 1900s. You see? It's so stable, some people even consider it proof that there's a Divine Being."

I briefly glanced at the chart before redirecting my attention to my drink. The only thing less appealing than line graphs was a discussion on the existence of God. I took a big gulp and was pleased to find Moe's drinks were as strong as his accent, and getting stronger by the moment.

"The global sex ratio is quite stable, but it's not uncommon to see small, local deviations," David explained. "Sex ratios at birth can be skewed by a range of factors, including exposure to environmental contaminants, the age of the mother at birth, sex-selective abortion, even climate and temperature. The Fear Fighters uncovered information showing something much more mysterious—a steady decline in the sex ratio in the United States that started in the early 2000s."

He flipped to another chart showing the sex ratio in the U.S.

"You see that dip there? The number of boys born plummeted before starting to rise again a couple years later."

I took another sip of my drink. The alcohol softened my discomfort and eased the remnants of my hangover. My glass wasn't empty yet but I was already craving another.

David zoomed in on the graph and pointed to an extreme dip followed by a flat line along the y axis.

"See that? That was two days ago."

I squinted at the graph and tried to absorb some of his excitement. Mathematics had always been my least favorite topic in school—the numbers and rows of data were so dry, with nothing left to question or chance.

"It looks like this is saying no boys have been born at all," I said.

"Exactly."

I frowned and looked closer, tracing my finger along the line. "None at all for two days? That's kind of weird, isn't it?"

"It's more than weird—it's statistically impossible. Even one day without any male births would be alarming. Two whole days is unimaginable. But according to government birth data, that's what happened. What's *happening*."

I examined the bottom of the hologram, looking for a

source. "Why haven't I heard about this? Where did you get this?"

"The National Center for Health Statistics—NCHS. They're part of the CDC, responsible for charting all the nation's birth data. Want to hear another interesting bit of information? The birth data they've been reporting on their website doesn't match up with the raw birth data on the secret web. The day after we got access to the raw file, I went back to the public site to compare it, just to make sure. All the data's gone and the website's now 'under construction.'"

He swiped away the holograph and leaned back, hands clasped in front of him as if resting his case. "Something fishy is going on, I can feel it in my gut."

I shifted uncomfortably. The wooden seat had been cool when I sat down, but it was now slick with sweat from my thighs. A distant memory niggled at the back of my mind as I thought about the birth data and the research he claimed my dad was working on.

"You should talk to my friend Marika," I told him. "She was always geeking out with my dad about his latest theories. I bet he talked to her about this Y chromosome thing. Now that I think about it, it does sound vaguely familiar. She works at the station too."

David's face lit up with excitement. "Perfect! Can you introduce us? Maybe we can all work on the story together. I bet Frida will eat it up."

A sharp ray of sun sliced through the dark room as the door opened, and a woman walked in. David glanced over his shoulder and watched her for a moment before turning back to me. I held my gaze on the woman, watching as she approached the bar and ordered a drink. My heart started to race. Why did David keep looking around so nervously? Was that woman a Fear Fighter too? What had led her to get a forbidden drink

alone in the woods in the middle of the day? When David and I
had first come in, I'd felt like we were miles away from the
world and all its chaos. Now, it felt like chaos was edging closer
and closer, ready to take over.

I emptied my glass in one big swallow. My head was
starting to spin and I felt a sudden longing to escape.

"I can introduce you, but I actually don't think this story is
up my alley," I said. "You probably want to find someone a little
more *intellectual*. Maybe Trent. He loves conspiracy theories."

"Tennyson, are you crazy? This is the kind of story that
would not only make your career, but change the world! And
it's a perfect tie-in with the research your dad was doing."

I glanced at David's drink, which was mostly untouched.
Condensation dripped down the sides of the glass. I restrained
from the urge to reach over and finish it for him.

I sighed. "Honestly, I'm not sure I'm ready to work on
something my dad was working on."

The desire to leave was suddenly overwhelming. I lifted my
wrist to check the time on my Surge and saw a reminder for my
VT appointment.

"Shoot, I have to go," I told him, even though the
appointment was still five hours away.

I grabbed my vest and stood up, feeling comforted as I
pulled it on. David rose and touched my arm, his face lined
with concern.

"Will you just think about what I told you? I know you're
scared and hurt, but I also know you can do this."

I pulled my arm away and took a step backward. Despite
the fact that he barely knew me, David's eyes were full of
conviction.

"Sure, I'll think about it." I turned and headed for the door,
eyes on my silver boots.

I slipped outside and filled my lungs with fresh air. We'd

been inside the tavern for less than an hour, yet everything felt different now. The sun was high in the sky and the forest was stifling hot, even with the shade of the trees. The peace that had enveloped me earlier was replaced with a familiar anxiety. The oaks hovered over me, their twisted branches reaching out to grab me. *Hurry home*, a voice inside warned.

I rushed to the Mule, leaves crackling under my feet as my mind spun toward the future. I'd go home, lock the doors, pull the shades, take a hot bath. Have some wine. Maybe I'd watch a movie after my VT appointment.

We got into the Mule, and David pressed the start button. The harness slid around me, tight and secure. I gazed up at the sun flashing through the trees as we drove away, squinting at its bright rays. It didn't seem to realize that no matter how relentlessly it shined, darkness was always on the way.

CHAPTER SIX

When I got home, the building's weekly robotic cleaning service had been completed. The dirty dishes and piles of clutter were replaced with sparkling surfaces and the clean smell of citrus and pine. They'd even gotten rid of the spiderweb by the front door.

"Welcome home, Charley," Vanessa greeted. "Here is your relaxation playlist. Would you like me to start a bath?"

"Yes, please."

I stripped off my heavy vest, hung it on its bungee, and gave it a quick tug to send it springing back into the ceiling compartment. My black t-shirt was drenched in sweat so I peeled that off too, dropping it into the empty laundry pod by the door. The air conditioning tickled my sweaty skin as I wandered into the kitchen, where an open bottle of my favorite pinot noir was waiting alongside a bouquet of fresh wildflowers. I poured a generous glass and took a big sip, then topped it off and headed to the bathroom.

The tub was already half full, thanks to Vanessa's connection to my Chroma home spa. Steam hung heavy in the air and the lights were dimmed to emulate candlelight. I dangled my fingers to test the bubbly bathwater. It was extra hot, just the way I liked it.

"Thank you, Vanessa," I said.

"Relax and enjoy your bath," Vanessa encouraged.

I stripped off the rest of my clothes and slipped into the hot water. The day flickered in my head, noisy and sharp. I could still see and feel the crowds, the Fear Fighters, the pictures of the shooting victims, the boy at the Monkers. I tipped the container of rose-scented relaxation minerals to add extra crystals.

My Surge vibrated. I warily lifted my wrist, expecting a warning about my increased heartrate. Instead it was a new message from my mother. *You didn't go back to work today, did you? I wish you'd just come stay with me for a while.*

"Vanessa, please turn up the music."

The tinkling of jazz filled the steamy air and I plunged my entire body underwater. Moments later, my Surge vibrated again. This time, it was a live call from Frida. My stomach turned. How was I going to explain my failure? She might fire me for not finishing my assignment. A not-so-small part of me was glad at the thought. Maybe escaping to my mother's Luxury Haven wasn't such a bad idea.

I reluctantly switched my Surge to voice-only mode and answered.

"Hello, Frida."

"Charley. What happened today?"

I sank back against the tub's smooth porcelain. "I just...I couldn't do it. There were so many people there, I panicked."

My excuse sounded lame, even to me. I adjusted the bubbles to cover my bare chest.

She snapped, "Well, corporate is pissed. We had to rework the whole lineup to accommodate for your missing segment."

"I'm sorry."

The water jets pounded harder against my back, hitting the exact spot where my muscles were starting to tense up. *Thank you, Vanessa*, I mouthed silently.

Frida sighed. "I knew coming back would be hard, but you can't just disappear like that. I've decided to move you to the entertainment beat. We have an opening that needs to be filled."

Her swift tone made it clear the move was not up for discussion.

After we hung up, I sat in the tub for more than an hour, hugging my knees to my chest. I'd been demoted and I deserved it. I was a failure, a fraud. Vanessa continually circulated the water to maintain my preferred 112-degree setting, pumping in fresh bubbles and adjusting the jets, but none of it helped.

By the time I dragged myself out of the tub, the sun was going down and shadows slipped through the house. I refilled my wine and trudged into the study for my VT appointment. At the bookshelf, I pulled down a tattered old book my dad had read to me as a child. The cover was a watercolor drawing of a man in a green shirt marching through tall grass, a tiny blonde child perched on his shoulders.

I opened the book and ran my fingers across the words as if they were written in braille.

> *We're going on a bear hunt.*
> *We're going to catch a big one.*
> *What a beautiful day!*
> *We're not scared.*

I could almost hear my dad's voice, excitedly reading me the lines and pausing as I recited them back. I flipped the pages, not bothering to wipe away the tears as they streamed down my cheeks. Despite all my dad's bravery, the bear had gotten him. Why couldn't we have just stayed in the swishy swashy grass and splashed in the deep cold river? If I hadn't been such a slow runner, he wouldn't have been waiting at that bend. He'd have already been at the finish line, far away from the sniper's bullet. It wasn't fair. None of it was fair.

The lights dimmed and the holograph system flickered on.

"Hello, Charlene," my VT's voice greeted. "Are you ready for our session?"

As part of the survivor system, the National Center for Mental Health assigned free virtual therapists to all families and victims. The VTs were computer-simulated programs, trained in human cognitive behavior and generated from eons of research and data. At first, I had rejected the sessions. The idea that a machine could help me heal seemed ridiculous and downright creepy. I finally gave in—mostly due to Marika's badgering, but also out of sheer desperation. I completed a short questionnaire with a few details about my dad's death and my upbringing, values, and beliefs. The next day, a free VT simulation was crafted to fit my needs.

I clutched the children's book to my chest and hurried to my purple velvet chaise. I sat, legs curled under me, and wiped my face.

"Yes, I'm ready."

"How was your first day back at work, Charlene?" my VT asked with a kind, soft smile.

After a month of our weekly sessions, I was still amazed by how lifelike she looked and sounded. She bore a striking resemblance to Amelia Earhart—plain face, rosy cheeks, and a crooked nose dabbled with freckles. Her short hair was perpetually windblown and she always wore the same weathered brown leather jacket.

"It was horrible," I confessed. I told her about the Fear

Fighters attack, my breakdown at the Monkers, my demotion, and my longing to give up.

"Everything you're describing is completely normal, Charlene. Most survivors have a mix of all these symptoms. You finally made your way back into the world and you were immediately confronted with the danger and reality of what's happening out there. It would be surprising if your survival instinct had *not* flared up. What we must figure out is how to give you a more approachable route back into the world."

Her soothing words gave me hope. I closed my eyes and leaned back on the chaise, trying to embrace the idea that I wouldn't always feel this way.

She continued, "You may not be ready for stories like talking to an attacker's family in a crowd of people, but that doesn't mean you need to go back into hiding. What *are* you ready for?"

I chewed on my fingernail, a terrible habit I'd had since I was a kid. "Well, my boss moved me back into entertainment reporting, which definitely sounds less terrifying. I'm sure I can manage to cover a celebrity breakup or movie review. But does that make me a coward?"

"It makes you human."

"And what would *you* know about that?" I joked.

She laughed. She always laughed at my jokes, even the dumb ones. The truth was, it felt like she understood me better than many of the human beings in my life. She always knew just what to say—when to comfort me, when to push me, when to just listen. We talked for an hour and planned my coping strategy for the week. The next time I felt afraid I would breathe through it and use positive symbols to maintain my energy and strength. I had Marika's necklace, David's lavender beads, my dad's book—there were hopeful signs everywhere, she explained. I just had to keep looking.

After the session, I poured the last of the wine into my glass, sank onto the couch, and flipped on the Hub. I scanned Clarion's coverage from the day and caught up on the Fear Fighters attack. Elliott Monker had killed himself after the shooting, and no one had been able to get commentary from his family. I flicked from stream to stream and all the coverage was the same. Hatcher's warning and Vanyala's response played on repeat, along with photos of the victims, personal information about Elliott Monker, and swirling questions about MPV.

I paused when I landed on Sloane Steele. She sat in an armchair across from a bare-faced woman with curly brown hair and glasses. Her interviewee's identifying caption read: *Gloria Fenway, Sociologist: Modern men pose threat to society.*

"Vanessa, please switch to holograph mode," I requested.

A 3D holograph of Sloane and Gloria hovered in the air before me, lifelike aside from a flicker every few seconds due to bandwidth issues.

Gloria gestured wildly as she spoke in an authoritative and crisp tone.

"As females have gained power over the years, males have been faltering. American women now earn more college degrees than men. Women now comprise the majority of our workforce. In the average married couple, the woman's income is 1.8 times greater than the man's. I believe the societal shift toward women's empowerment has caused young males to suffer a crisis of purpose that has led them to violence and despair. Unless something changes, this dramatic power imbalance will continue to wreak havoc on our nation."

Sloane flashed a smile and turned away from Gloria to face me. "Viewers, please tune in on Friday for my full interview with Gloria. We'll explore pressing questions like whether today's independent woman even *need* men to survive.

Personally, I haven't been on a date in two years, and I can say with certainty that I've never been happier."

My skin prickled. How could she smile like that when she'd been at the scene of a shooting that morning? And did she really just take a serious discussion about violence among young boys and turn it into a discussion on her dating life?

I frowned, wondering if David had gone to Sloane with what he knew. The story sounded strangely connected, but it wasn't quite the same. David had hypothesized that my dad's study on the Y chromosome was linked to MPV and an alarming new decline in male births. What if it *was* all connected?

The more I thought about it, the more intrigued I became. Snippets of a dinner conversation between Marika and my dad hovered at the edge of my memory. They'd been talking excitedly about his scientific research and I'd largely tuned them out, feeling excluded and disinterested. *Evolutionary genetics...mutating Y chromosome...type of accelerant.*

Was it possible Marika held some of the knowledge that could give us a jump start on the story? I tapped my Surge to call her and she answered on the second ring, breathless.

"Nice timing, I just finished Taekwondo. You missed a great one tonight. How was your VT session?"

"It was...illuminating. Listen, do you have a few minutes? Something weird is happening."

I quickly got her up to speed on the drop in male births and the potential connection to my dad's research on violence in males. I was barely done explaining when she jumped in.

"Charley, your dad did more than tell me about his research on the Y chromosome. He left me the hard drive where he kept his files. I just haven't had the courage to dive into it yet. I kept telling myself I would...someday."

I reached up to touch the pendant on my necklace. The

wine slid through my blood, causing my anxiety to feel slippery and faraway. Marika and I hurriedly made a plan to meet and I called Frida back before I lost my nerve.

"I have a lead on something," I told her. "I think it's going to be really big."

I didn't even make it through summarizing the data David had shown me before Frida interrupted.

"This sounds riveting—and urgent. Corporate may want a different journalist after the stunt you pulled today, but I'm willing to give you another chance. *One.* Get me something concrete by tomorrow."

"Thanks, Frida. I won't let you down this time."

I messaged David and invited him to join Marika and me for a working session over dinner. It was time to discover the secret world my dad had left behind.

CHAPTER SEVEN

I PULLED open the heavy oak door to Luigi's, a tiny secluded Italian bistro that Marika and I loved. After a heated debate about where to meet, she'd convinced me that Luigi's would be safe.

As one of the few restaurants left standing, they'd used the funds from a recent crowdfunding campaign to install a top-of-the-line security system, complete with bulletproof and soundproof privacy shields around each booth. While I was still nervous, I couldn't argue with the grumbling in my stomach and my own bare cupboards.

I stepped into the security clearance area. David was already there, arms stretched out at his sides as he waited for the weapons scan. He tipped his chin toward me and smiled.

"Hey, Tennyson. Long time, no see."

I smiled back. Despite my mixed feelings about David being a Fear Fighter, he had a light demeanor that put me at ease.

"You are cleared for entry, David Vine," an automated voice said. David walked through the clearance area and turned to wait for me. I stepped under the scanner and looked up at the video surveillance camera. A green light flashed as it scanned my retinas and completed the MM wave imaging.

"You are cleared for entry, Charlene Tennyson," the system announced.

"Charlene, huh?" David asked.

"Don't even think about it. No one calls me by full name except virtual programs and my mother."

I glanced down at the weapons check, realizing David hadn't retrieved a gun. "You don't carry a firearm either?" I asked.

He shook his head. "My mom raised me pretty strictly under the doctrines of the Fear Fighters. You know, the whole 'use words, not weapons' thing? I'm basically a modern-day hippy. I've been trying to get them to add, 'Make love, not war' to their doctrines since I can remember."

I laughed. Something told me David practiced making 'love not war' quite often. He was good looking, charming, and easygoing—an increasingly rare combination.

The glass door in front of us slid open and we stepped inside the restaurant. Thankfully, despite the modern security upgrade, the heart of Luigi's had retained its cozy, old-fashioned feel. The tables were covered in red-and-white checkered cloth, and the exposed brick walls were decorated with black-and-white photos of sweeping hillsides and well-fed Italians.

Marika and I used to drop by Luigi's every Wednesday night after our virtual Taekwondo class, putting back on the calories we'd burned off. We'd devour homemade spaghetti noodles drenched in marinara, cheesy garlic bread, tiramisu, and wine, asking each other why the things we loved had to be so bad for us.

"I love this place already," David said as I led him toward

the back booth I'd pre-reserved. The tiny restaurant had space for a dozen patrons, but we appeared to be the only ones there.

"Just wait until you try the spaghetti. Marika and I have vowed that if they ever shut down, we'll locate the culinary staff and hire them as our own personal chefs. She should be here soon, by the way."

We slid into our booth and the shield closed around us. It was a clear orb with the option to add one-way or two-way shading for complete privacy. I left it clear so Marika would spot us when she arrived.

As soon as the orb clicked shut, a digital menu appeared on the table in front of us. David briefly glanced down at it, then flicked it away with a brush of his hand.

"I'll have what you're having," he said.

I laughed. "You don't even want to look at the menu?"

"I trust you."

I tapped the screen and punched in our order: three plates of spaghetti and meatballs, extra marinara, a carafe of chianti.

David pulled off his Kevlar vest and placed it on the booth next to him, leaning back and looking completely relaxed. My eyes flickered upward to confirm the orb was completely sealed before I took off my own vest. I leaned back in the booth, trying to emulate David's relaxed posture.

"So what changed your mind about doing the story?" he asked.

"My VT made me do it," I said jokingly.

An orange light flashed to indicate someone else had entered the restaurant. I looked up to see Marika exiting the security clearance area. She looked casual and comfortable in a yellow neoprene shirt and sneakers, lightweight black athletic pants, and the same leopard print Wonderproof Hoodie she'd worn earlier. Her curly hair was pulled into a messy bun. She lifted her hand in greeting and headed toward us, shifting the bulging satchel on her shoulder.

David opened the orb and stood up to greet her. "Marika?" he asked with a smile as she approached, extending his hand in greeting. "It's a pleasure to meet you, I've heard so much about you."

She smiled back and shook his hand, a warm glow in her eyes. "All good, I hope?"

"Absolutely," he answered. "Not only from Charley, but everyone I talked with during my job interviews. They all say that when it comes to research, you're the best there is."

"That's so nice to hear. Remind me of your name again?"

"David. David Vine."

Marika looked him up and down before replying smoothly, "Well, David, I cannot tell you how lovely it is to meet you. Truly. Any friend of Charley's..."

They both sat down, Marika next to me and David across from us. The orb clicked shut and we added the two-way shade so it was just the three of us in our own little world.

Marika wrapped her arm around my shoulders. "How are you doing, honey?"

She knew what a big deal the day had been for me—facing the real world, work, resuming the responsibilities and routines I'd left behind. Going back to work was like admitting that all of it had happened, acknowledging that I had to go on living despite the grief.

"I'm okay," I answered. "Though I still can't believe what a failure I was at the Monkers."

She shook her head, anger flashing in her eyes.

"I don't know what Frida was thinking, sending you there. That was the wrong story for you. It's too raw."

I shrugged. "I should've just said no, but I thought I could do it."

Marika knew me well enough to know I was beating myself up inside. She reached out to touch the lotus necklace she'd given me, which hung perfectly in the deep V of my silver blouse.

"It looks good," she acknowledged with a smile. She stripped off her vest and tossed it across the booth next to mine.

The red serving light at the center of the table flashed and its flaps opened. We watched as our wine was lifted from the conveyor belt below.

"Thank God, I was hoping you'd gone ahead and ordered," Marika said. She grabbed the carafe from its claw-like attachment and filled the three glasses—first mine, then her own, then David's. The table flaps closed and she set the carafe down before picking up her wine glass and raising it toward me in a toast.

"To being stronger than you think."

I raised my glass and clinked with hers, then reached my glass across toward David's.

"Cheers to that," he toasted back. He clinked my glass and then went to toast Marika. She blinked as if she'd forgotten he was there and then repositioned her body to face him.

David took a sip of his wine and settled his gaze on Marika. "So where should we start? Charley said she got you up to speed. Did you have a chance to look into any of the data yet?"

Marika laughed and rubbed her hands together, clearly savoring the anticipation. I'd sent her more details on what David had discovered to give her a head start, and from the look on her face, she'd already gotten a ton done. She was not only the best researcher I knew, but also the fastest.

"I sure did. But before we dig into the birth data, why don't we start with a little refresher course. How much do you remember about biology?"

"I nearly flunked every science class I ever took," he admitted. "I was always more into the arts."

I chimed in, "Don't feel bad, David. I didn't know the difference between biology and physics until Marika explained it to me."

"Those are different?" he asked jokingly.

Marika laughed. "Well in that case, why don't we take things from the top? Are you familiar with Darwin's theory of evolution by natural selection?"

"That one I know," David replied. "The idea that organisms evolve over time, and that the weakest of any species will be weeded out."

"You got it. Darwin hypothesized that population growth would lead to a 'struggle for existence' in which favorable variations would prevail as others perished. And as it turns out..." Marika paused and swirled the wine in her glass for emphasis. "...Darwin wasn't the only one who believed in an 'inferior' species being weeded out."

I often wondered how I was the one in front of the camera and not Marika. She knew just how to take center stage—how to add suspense, create drama, and draw out the intrigue, often without even trying.

Marika lifted her wrist. "But instead of telling you, why don't I show you?"

She tapped her Surge and suddenly, a man in a white lab coat was sitting at the table with us in the form of a hologram replay.

"Courtesy of Papa Tennyson's files, allow me to introduce you to Simon Sykes," she said. "Professor of Human Genetics at Duke E-University."

The man's light brown complexion was similar to Marika's. He had deep brown eyes and thin, straight brown hair that was slicked down. The pocket of his lab coat was full of stylus pens and a God-awful tie peeked out from his collar—puke green with orange polka-dots.

Marika hit play and the man's voice filled the air.

"The Y chromosome contains a large number of genes whose purposes have not previously been understood. However, our research team has successfully deconstructed one of those genes and discovered something astounding. We have discovered a gene which is the source of extreme rage and aggression. You might say we've traced the origins of violence— and it is rooted in the Y chromosome."

"See, this sounds just like what Hatcher mentioned today," David mused. "What they're now calling MPV."

"Shhhh," Marika said. "Just wait."

Simon tapped his chin and continued. "Based on our deconstruction of the Y chromosome, we believe the extinction of the male species is likely to occur within the next five million years. In fact, it may have already begun. Not only is the number of genes in the male chromosome rapidly dwindling, but a recent study found that the number of live male births has been declining in the United States. An increasing proportion of fetuses that die are also male."

Simon pulled a stylus pen out of his pocket and waved it for emphasis. "You see, we believe that a defect in the Y chromosome is leading to increased instability and an ultimate demise of the male human. And while this, this—gender evolution, as some might call it—could lead to the extinction of the human species altogether, I believe it is more likely to lead to the evolution of a new hominid species that does not require a Y chromosome to survive. It will be an extraordinary example of survival of the fittest, Darwin's theory of natural selection come to life in modern times."

Simon put the stylus pen back in his pocket and clasped his hands in front of him. "If the human reproductive process can evolve to become asexual the way some other species have, we will no longer require men at all. In a few eons, the male species will be gone."

Marika pressed the pause button and Simon Sykes hung there, speechless, his face twisted into a look of deep focus and concentration.

"Holy moly!" David exclaimed.

"Holy *moly?*" Marika repeated with a smirk. "You can say 'shit' around us, David."

David laughed. "Oops. Guess my Midwest roots are coming out."

I glanced back and forth between Marika and David. They gazed at each other and laughed. *Make love not war,* I heard David saying, blue eyes twinkling. A strange twist of jealousy coiled in my gut.

"All right, let's just stay focused, shall we?" I asked.

Marika nodded. "David, walk me through the sex ratio data you told Charley about."

David pulled up the line graph and explained it the same way he'd done with me. She listened closely as he pointed to the dramatic decrease in the number of boys born in the early 2000s, the subsequent rise a couple decades later, and the most dramatic phenomenon: two days ago, when boys had stopped being born.

Marika frowned. "These shifts seem way too abrupt to be natural selection like what Simon described. Not to mention, it's happening way too soon. Simon was pretty radical in his claims, and even *he* predicted this wouldn't happen for centuries. Eons, to be exact. Something had to have accelerated it."

"Or *someone,*" David added.

I chewed on my thumbnail. "Wait, you think someone could have deliberately caused this?"

David lifted an eyebrow. "Remember how I told you that the birth data vanished from the CDC's public website? That's a pretty good indicator someone knows about what's going on."

Marika nodded in agreement. "The drop in the sex ratio *has* to be linked to the Y chromosome defect Simon told your dad about. And probably to MPV too." She rubbed her hands together and burst out in a huge smile. "This story is going to be huge."

Our red serving light lit up and the table's flaps opened. A large platter ascended, holding three plates piled high with thickly coiled spaghetti noodles, rich glistening marinara, and giant meatballs. My wine glass was almost empty and I reached for the carafe to refill it, topping off David and Marika's glasses afterward.

"This looks delicious," David said. He passed plates to me and Marika, then took the last plate and picked up his fork.

We dug into dinner and began chatting excitedly, moving past the research and story ideas to discuss lighter topics. Before long, we were talking about next week's big game—the nation's first ever virtual Super Bowl. Ticketholders would log into a secure digital arena where they'd sit in a virtual crowd, able to cheer on their team without worrying about the stadium being bombed.

"Wait a minute, you're a *Patriots* fan?" Marika asked, her voice full of disapproval.

There were only two NFL teams left and the intense rivalry split the country in half. Like most of our region, Marika was an avid Isotopes fan. I could care less about either team, especially now that sports had been reduced to virtual reality games.

David shrugged. "Blame my mom. I have four brothers and she raised us all as Patriot fans. She likes to do things the hard way. Root for the underdog and all that."

Marika crossed her arms and shook her head as she leaned back against the booth. "*Patriots*. You seemed so nice and normal until now."

"Normal people don't say 'holy moly,'" I reminded her.

"Good point." She wagged a finger at David. "I've got my eye on you."

We all laughed. After months of grief and seclusion, it felt so good to smile again, to be normal, to connect over topics like football—mundane, ordinary things that weren't weighted with life and death. Sitting there at Luigi's, eating spaghetti and drinking wine and joking with our new friend, I felt the first flutter of hope I'd felt in a long time. I could hardly wait to get started on the story the next day. Maybe the world wasn't coming to an end after all.

Maybe, just maybe, everything would be okay.

CHAPTER EIGHT

THE NEXT MORNING at half past seven, David and I sped toward Duke University Hospital.

After an early morning briefing with Frida, we'd decided the fastest way to confirm the latest birth data was to pay a visit to a local hospital's birthing center. Duke was the Research Triangle's largest medical facility and had a huge maternity ward. David and I would interview medical professionals while Marika tried to get ahold of Simon and find someone at the CDC to address the data discrepancies.

The hospital rose in the distance, an enormous concrete building surrounded by a dual electromagnetic shield. The government had identified medical facilities as critical to the public's well-being and turned each one into a virtual Fort Knox.

We passed through the first layer of security: a four-lane tunnel where machines performed a full scan of our vehicle and its contents. Ambulances raced past us in the emergency lane, red lights and sirens flashing. After we completed the mobile clearance, we sped toward the lot reserved for media.

David pulled into a charging station near the ER and docked the Mule.

We got out of the van and made our way to the security vault for RF identification and pathogen detection. I glanced around and tried to take comfort in the enclosure, the layers of security, the absence of people in the near vicinity. The surveillance camera scanned my retinas and completed the MM wave imaging. A green light flashed and my Surge vibrated with an automated confirmation message: *Sector 406 clearance granted.*

"Charlene Tennyson and David Vine, you are cleared for entry," the system announced.

The wall at the end of the security vault opened and we stepped into the ER. Although the maternity ward was our end destination, we knew the ER entrance would provide the fastest access to the building.

Staggered rows of plastic blue chairs held people in varying states of shock and grief. I zoned in on a little girl and a woman sitting closest to us. The woman's eyes were closed, but her worried face indicated she was far from sleep. The little girl played with the long braid trailing down her shoulder, twisting it in her fingers. She swung her legs back and forth as if she were on a swing, pumping to go higher and faster.

I'd sat in a chair like that too, holding my mom's hand, waiting to hear if my dad would survive the gunshot wound to his chest. I closed my eyes to block out the memory.

David poked my arm and pointed to the right. "Main access center is that way."

I nodded, grateful to escape the ER. We rushed down a long climate-controlled concourse and reached the elevator bay, where a sign informed us the birthing station was on the fifth floor.

We stepped inside an empty elevator and the doors slid

shut. As we began to rise, I stood at the back wall and pressed my sweaty palms against the cold steel. My mind was stuck on my memory of the ER, replaying it like a glitch. I remembered the ticking of the clock as my mother and I waited for an update from the surgeon. The smell of burned coffee and stale, sleepless breath. The handful of crying people looking anywhere but at each other, afraid our faces would convey the hidden truth: *If anyone dies, I hope it's your loved one and not mine.*

My mom had leaned her head on my shoulder. I could still feel the hardness of her skull, the softness of her cheek. I'd sat there, eyes on the ticking clock, numb with the realization that even if my dad miraculously pulled through, there would come a day when my parents would actually die. And one when I would too.

"You okay?" David asked.

I looked down at my feet, unable to muster a convincing response. When would everyone realize the truth? I wasn't okay. None of us were. We were fragile, human, doomed.

David and I stood in silence until the operating system's voice chimed in: "You have arrived."

The elevator doors opened to reveal a stark, white room with a circular nurse's station at the far end, surrounded by a clear shield. A woman in yellow scrubs stood behind the tall bulky counter, hunched over and watching something on a screen. As we approached, I could see it was footage of yesterday's Fear Fighter attack.

She looked up, face ashen. A flicker of recognition flashed in her eyes.

"Aren't you Charley Tennyson?" she asked.

Pride swelled in my chest. I never understood how celebrities got tired of being recognized. No matter how many times it happened, it always made me feel special.

"Yes, that's me," I answered with a small smile.

She pointed in the direction we'd just come from. "The ER's downstairs, on the east side of the first floor. This is the birthing center."

"This is exactly where we want to be. Do you have a few minutes to talk with us?"

She lifted her eyebrows in surprise and nodded, then came around the divider to join us. Her frizzy hair was pulled back in a red scrunchie and her bloodshot eyes were puffy. She was mousy and frail, her face full of ordinary features except one: her eyes. They were big and buggy like a cartoon character's, in a lovely shade of gray that resembled the sky after a storm.

"What's your name?" I asked, even though I could see her nametag. Part of my job was to establish rapport.

"Beatrice," she answered with a nervous smile. "Beatrice Thompson."

"It's so nice to meet you, Beatrice."

"You can call me Betty. You have no idea what an honor it is to meet you. I'm such a big fan."

Her voice quivered and her huge eyes widened even further.

David extended a hand and flashed a dazzling smile. "Hi Betty, I'm David Vine, Charley's production assistant."

Betty looked down at his hand with surprise before tentatively reaching out and shaking it. I might've been a local celebrity, but I could already tell: David was the kind of guy people fell in love with instantly. It was that down-to-earth, old-fashioned charm—a quality I'd only seen in classic romance movies from far happier times.

I cleared my throat. "Betty, we're doing a story on some recent births. Something positive to break up all the horrible news. We may take a 'circle of life' angle, remind our viewers that even though terrible deaths are occurring, new life is blessing our world too."

The lie fell easily from my lips and I wished it were true. If only I had enough hope in humanity to believe an optimistic story like that could make any difference.

David played along perfectly. "Would you have some time to show us around? I've got our media credentials right here."

He tapped his Surge and a holographic badge hovered above his wrist.

Betty's eyes glimmered as if we'd just invited her on a trip to the moon. She looked back at me. "I'd be thrilled to show you around! Would you like to see the nursery?"

"That would be perfect," I replied.

She turned and led us toward the birthing center, her orange clogs squeaking with every step. We walked through a VR tunnel, where digital photos of happy families and babies flashed around us. I stopped to look at one, a blonde woman holding a sleeping baby in her arms, gazing down at its face with love. In another, a family of six stood in front of a Christmas tree wearing matching red shirts. The mother was poised in the center, cradling an infant dressed in pure white. The caption read: "It's a girl! Please welcome baby Genesis!"

We exited the tunnel and arrived at the nursery. Betty gestured to the glass, eyes glimmering. "Meet our angels."

We gazed through the thick pane of bulletproof glass. The room looked as secure as a metal bank vault, screens and monitors covering every square inch of the yellow walls. More than a dozen infants were assembled, two full rows of six with a few stragglers in the back, all nestled in incubated protective capsules. Each capsule was covered in a clear dome and connected to a machine showing the baby's name, sex, inoculation stats, and vitals. I admired a few tiny sleeping faces before scanning the information on each capsule. It was true: they were all girls.

"Aren't they beautiful?" Betty gushed. Pride swept across her face as if she'd been the one to birth them. "They're nestled away in the vault seconds after being born. It takes a week to do all the vaccinations and clearances, then they're whisked back to their parents. You'd be amazed how much comfort they take in each other's presence. It's almost like they form a language all their own."

I frowned. "Isn't the first week after birth a difficult time to keep a baby from its parents?"

"The immunizations are crucial to their health," Betty explained. "And it all happens so quickly, they don't even notice the difference between their new cocoons and their mother's womb. We pipe in the sound of their mother's voices and heartbeats to make it a seamless transition. The days they spend here are the safest and happiest of their lives."

I nodded, creeped out by her explanation. I wanted to take them all in my arms, whisk them away to some faraway place where none of this was happening. Somewhere they could grow outside, play, laugh, be free. They were so innocent, so vulnerable.

My blood vibrated with a sudden rush of anxiety and I looked away, searching for something to calm me. My gaze settled on Betty's red scrunchie. I let myself imagine her wrapping it into her hair that morning, fingers wrestling to smooth down the frizz and untangle the knots, carefully turning chaos into order. I glanced at David and realized he was watching me. Could he see the anxiety mounting in my eyes?

David looked back at Betty. "So which one's your favorite?" he asked, giving her a conspiring wink. I could tell he was warming her up with small talk. He was good at it, too.

Betty pointed to a red-faced infant on the far left.

"We're not supposed to have favorites, but see that one? Her name's Alesia. She's a fighter, put her poor mother through 29 hours of labor. She wailed for hours through the night, her little face purple as a plum, until I figured out the secret. We piped in a looped recording of her mom humming 'Itsy Bitsy Spider' and she went out like a light."

"I can tell you love your job," I said.

Betty smiled with pride. "It's hard work, but it's the only thing I ever wanted to do. At the end of every shift, I stop right here to remind myself what matters. Looking at all of them together, so peaceful and safe...it makes me feel a little less tired."

"Really?" I asked. "Looking at all of them together makes *me* feel exhausted."

She laughed and the gentle sound cleared the fog in my head.

"They're all girls," I said casually, as if just noticing. "Is that unusual?"

"It is, actually. We haven't had a boy born in a while. Must be something in the water," she joked.

"When you say, 'in a while,' how long has it been exactly?" I asked.

Betty's eyes darted from me to David and back again. Neither of us were laughing.

"I'd have to double-check the records, but I think it's been about three or four days," she said. "I help process all the birth certificates and I don't remember any boys being born since late last week."

She paused and bit her lip, looking suddenly uneasy. "What did you say your story would be about again?"

"Actually, that's the story," I told her. "We've received reports of an unusual decrease in male births."

Betty's gray eyes widened with curiosity. "Wow, that sure is interesting. You should talk to Dr. Wakefield while you're here."

"Who's Dr. Wakefield?"

"One of our top medical researchers. She's been working on a project exploring the ability to create an embryo using two eggs."

It turned out Betty was not just a nurse; she was an angel.

"Do you think she'd be willing to talk to us?" I asked.

"You bet, the researchers love to get publicity on their studies. It helps us secure funding to keep their work going. I can call her from the nurse's station if you'd like."

"That would be wonderful. Can we meet you there in five or ten minutes? We have a few items to cover here." I flashed my biggest smile.

"That should be okay, as long as you sync your media credentials to me. You know—for our files."

David stepped forward and tapped his Surge, then held his wrist against hers to complete the data sync. She glanced down and smiled at the badge with satisfaction.

"Okay, I'll be back in a jiffy!"

David and I watched her walk away, her orange clogs squeaking into the distance. As soon as she was out of sight, we turned to look at each other, faces glowing. I gestured to the rows of babies in the nursery.

"We should film a test segment right here," I said. "It could end up being the perfect spot for our intro."

"I'm right there with you, Tennyson. Give me two minutes."

David ran some lighting tests while I pulled out my pocket mirror and applied a fresh layer of red lipstick. It was hard to believe how much had happened in the last twenty-four hours. It was even harder to imagine what the next few hours might hold. I felt the tug of purpose, the rush that came from having an important job to do.

"All right, Tennyson. Let's roll."

I turned to face the waiting eye of the camera as David began filming. My old routine came back to me without even thinking about it. I imagined I was poised at the edge of a diving board, ready to make a perfect dive into the water. I took a deep breath, smiled, and began.

"I'm Charley Tennyson, reporting for the Verge."

I stopped and shook my head, then started again.

"I'm Charley Tennyson, reporting for Clarion. We're here in the newborn nursery at Duke University Hospital, where a baby girl named Alesia was born just a few hours ago. And she's not the only one. Alesia is the latest in a series of births connected to startling new phenomenon: all female births. We have obtained exclusive new birth data which indicates the number of male births has plummeted across the nation, with only females born over the last several days. Early reports indicate this trend is likely to continue, raising serious questions about the survival of humankind. What's causing the phenomenon? Can we stop it? Does the end of men mean the extinction of humanity, or can women find a way to survive on their own? We're on a quest for answers, and you can find them here, first."

I gave David a sign to stop filming. He captured some B-roll footage of the nursery while I tapped my Surge and hunted for information. Betty's comments had gotten me thinking: Why would Dr. Wakefield be experimenting to have two eggs form an embryo if she hadn't known about this? Was such a thing even genetically possible? I looked it up: two eggs reproducing. What had Betty called it again? There it was in the search results: Parthenogenesis. I tapped to read the Wiki and became riveted.

"Hey David, listen to this," I said, reading aloud from the article. "The whiptail lizard is one of several species that evolved to become asexual. These all-lady lizards need a male even less than a fish needs a bicycle. They produce well-bred offspring without the aid of male fertilization through a unique hybridization process. Although asexual reproduction might seem like a bore, it has multiple benefits. A female that is capable of parthenogenesis has an extreme sociological advantage. Her independence gives her the power to survive and multiply freely, without requiring a mate."

I glanced up from the article and realized David was still filming. I paused, flustered that he'd caught me on camera without me realizing it.

He smiled, the dimple in his cheek flashing. "Asexual reproduction? I agree with the 'sounds like a bore' part."

I shook my head. "Seriously? Talk about a one-track mind. Stay with me here."

I scrolled to the next part of the article and continued reading. "In 2028, the U.S. government issued a national call for research to determine if the phenomenon could be replicated in other species. In 2030, a research team in Des Moines created a fatherless pig named Adamina. However, by and large, they have been unable to force parthenogenesis in larger mammals without it resulting in abnormal development and genetic vulnerability."

A squeaking sound came from down the hallway. Betty emerged from the VR tunnel, a look of concern on her face.

"Hey," she whispered as she approached, furtively glancing behind her. "The obstetrics manager is on her way over. She says I can't talk to you anymore. And Dr. Wakefield won't be able to speak with you either."

"What's the obstetric manager's name?" I asked. "We're happy to talk with her about what we're covering."

"Her name's Hilda. But trust me, you won't be happy to talk with her. She's...difficult."

Down the hall behind Betty, a tall figure appeared. As the figure got closer I could see that it was a muscular woman with a chiseled jaw and steely black eyes. Hilda. Her name was a perfect fit. If Betty squeaked, Hilda thundered, her heavy footsteps pounding down the tunnel like an elephant.

Hilda held her gaze on me as she approached and kept walking beyond the point I thought she'd stop, getting so close I could smell onions on her breath.

"You need to leave," she commanded.

I choked down my nausea over her bad breath and took a step backward, flashing my best smile. I pulled a move from David's playbook and generously extended my hand.

"Hi there, you must be Hilda. I'm Charley Tennyson."

Hilda looked down at my hand as if it were covered in crap.

"You can't be here, lady. Filming these babies is a violation of code 4582. I need you to hand over your recording."

David stepped forward, close enough to Hilda that she took a step backward.

"Hilda? I'm David Vine. You may not have heard, but Code 4582 does not apply if the recording is related to a public health concern, which this story most certainly is. You'll need a judge's order to erase this recording—and I assure you, no judge in this county is going to give you one based on the evidence we've gathered thus far."

I looked at David in shock. He was an uncanny combination of scholar, superhero, and guy next door. I blinked at him, almost wondering if he'd disappear. But there he stood, looking Hilda in the eye, full of grit and determination.

Hilda ignored David and returned her attention to me. "Lady, you heard me. You two need to surrender your recording and leave the premises or I will call state patrol."

"You think the police don't have better things to do?" David interjected again. "Or did you miss the news? After yesterday's Fear Fighters attack, and the millions of attacks and protests going on everywhere, do you really think the police want to come down here to fight for a recording of some newborns?"

Wow. I hoped I never had to get into a debate with David. Even Hilda—steely, black-eyed Hilda—was withering like a dying weed. She reminded me of the wicked witch, melting before our eyes. Betty just stood there in wide-eyed shock, her red scrunchied ponytail protruding from the side of her head.

David spun toward me. "Let's go, Charley. Unlike *some* people, we've got real work to do."

"Yes, we do," I answered in what I hoped sounded like a confident and dismissive tone.

Betty locked eyes with me and mouthed: *I'm sorry.*

I gave her a slight shake of my head and mouthed back: *It's okay.* I hoped she could tell how grateful we were. She'd done so much for us before Hilda the Hun stepped in.

David and I rushed out of the birthing center without looking back. We'd gotten what we came for—and I had a feeling it would turn out to be more than we'd imagined.

CHAPTER NINE

WE HEADED BACK to the station and went straight to Marika's lab. She was hunched over her workscreen, hair pulled back in a loose twist, wearing glasses and a look of deep focus. She gazed up as we entered and a ringlet of hair fell over her left eyebrow. She quickly blew it away with a puff of air, then removed her glasses and set them on the table.

"I've been reading about rats and moles," she said with a laugh. "Did you know that Japanese spiny rats and mole voles have lost their Y chromosomes entirely?"

"Whiptail lizards too," I said.

I rushed to fill Marika in on what Betty had told us about the ongoing research studies into parthenogenesis and the attempts to find a way to reproduce using two eggs. I could see the wheels turning in her mind as she listened. Her eyebrows scrunched up and she gnawed on her lip in the adorable way she always did when she was thinking hard.

She speculated, "If there was a call for research, someone *had* to have known about this. And they must have known for quite a while."

"Our thoughts exactly. Did you get ahold of Simon?"

She shook her head. "Apparently he went off the grid for a research study a few months ago. His colleagues don't know when, or if, he'll be back. But they did give me the name of someone who might be able to help: Wanda Stilson. She did quite a bit of work with Simon before he left."

Marika touched her screen and pulled up a photo of a woman with shoulder-length pink hair, icy blue eyes, and a large but attractive mole above her lip. Her dark bushy eyebrows and silver nose ring made her look like a rock star.

Below her photo was her public profile:

```
Name: Wanda Stilson
Age: 28
Education: PhD in Structural
    Biology & Biophysics; Bachelor
    of Science in Computational
    Biology and GSFS (Gender,
    Sexuality, and Feminist
    Studies)
Internships: Food and Drug
    Administration. Biomedical
    Engineer 1, Inova Health
    System.
Published Work >>
```

Marika clicked on the link to her published work. "Check it out, one of the articles she wrote is titled 'The Gender Evolution: Did the Rise of Woman Lead to the Fall of Man?'"

David and I took a seat on the stools at the tall table across from Marika and listened as she read the essay aloud:

Since the dawn of humanity, males have been viewed as the 'dominant' sex in most civilized cultures. Toward the middle of the twentieth century, America entered a new era which ushered in the first inklings of change.

It began during World War II, when sixteen million American men went off to fight. Women rose to fill the gaps left behind, becoming factory workers, farmers, code breakers, and baseball players. Once the war ended, it became clear that women could contribute just as much to the U.S. economy as men could. Cultural icons like Rosie the Riveter sparked advances for equal rights. The gender evolution had begun.

The feminist movement gained new momentum in the 1960s, with icons like Gloria Steinem and Betty Friedan paving the way toward female empowerment. By the 1990s, 'girl power' was a growing cultural phenomenon. Inspiring messages reminded girls they could do anything boys could do. Women were encouraged to become leaders at work, and popular books and mass media created a community that drove women to achieve their greatest ambitions.

Meanwhile, the workplace was changing. High-tech employers viewed 'soft skills' like collaboration and open communication to be far more valuable than physical strength and stamina. By the time we ushered in our first female president, most women were making higher salaries than their male counterparts. Women were now the primary caretakers as well as the providers—in historical terms, they were the hunters and the gatherers.

So where did that leave American men? Young males began to suffer a crisis of purpose. If women could do it all on their own, what value did men add to society? Little girls were encouraged to learn engineering, math, construction—and they became well-rounded, independent beings who did not feel constrained by their gender. Boys, on the other hand, were not given a place in this new world.

By and large, little boys were not encouraged to play with dolls and care for babies. They were not taught to become more nurturing, emotionally vulnerable, and communicative. Males lost their previous familial and societal roles without being balanced out and encouraged to adopt new roles. As a result, they took what they knew, the place where they held a distinct advantage—physical strength, battle, combat—and they began using it in a misguided attempt to maintain their position of power. They began killing.

I got a chill as Marika read the last line. I frowned, realizing all of it sounded eerily familiar.

"This sounds a lot like a Sentient preview I heard yesterday," I said. "Sloane was interviewing some sociologist who claimed modern males are a threat to society. Some of the phrases she used were almost identical. She said males are suffering a 'crisis of purpose.' That they're seeking power by killing, and that independent women no longer need men to thrive."

"So much for equality," David said sarcastically. He slid off his stool and paced, face flushed with frustration.

"Sorry," he said, "but sometimes it just feels like the pendulum is swinging too far the other direction. If the future is female, who needs men at all? I mean, part of me *gets* it.

What the hell is driving these young boys to violence? Whether it's MPV or something else causing it, it's obvious that something, somewhere, has gone terribly wrong."

Marika nodded and another ringlet of hair fell loose from her twist. This time she left it hovering over her left eye.

She said, "Let's take that frustration and put it into our research. A lot of this comes back to nature versus nurture. Both Wanda and that woman Sloane interviewed were focused on societal factors. That means we have a chance to focus on biology. And given what we know about the dramatic drop in the sex ratio, we should definitely look closer at evolutionary forces as the driver for something like this."

Marika tapped her workscreen and a picture of a large whale appeared, water spewing from its blowhole as it crested the ocean's surface.

"Earlier I was reading about the evolution of whales. Did you know they started out as land animals? As the mammal evolved to live an increasingly aquatic lifestyle, their nostrils moved further and further back on their skulls until it became a blowhole, a quality that helped the whale thrive because it didn't have to go to the surface for air."

She glanced at me and I lifted an eyebrow.

"Go on," I said, though I could already tell the science was about to bore me to tears.

"What if the Y chromosome is disappearing because it's somehow beneficial to the continuation of our species? What if it will help us thrive and evolve in some new way?"

David crossed his arms. "So you're saying an all-female species would be an improvement?"

Marika held up her hands, palms facing David as if in surrender.

"I'm just saying, when you think about a defective Y chromosome being at the root of these attacks, you can't help but take the next logical step and wonder what the world might be like if females were running the show. When's the last time you heard about a woman killing a bunch of people?"

I looked back and forth between them, uncomfortable about the direction the conversation was headed.

"All right, let's just address the elephant in the room," I intervened. "This story is going to bring up some uncomfortable issues of gender roles. It would be all too easy for this entire thing to get twisted into a battle of sexes. But having another thing to fight about isn't going to help anyone. We have to go back to what really matters."

Marika and David watched me intently, waiting for me to continue. A golf ball of emotion rose in my throat as I felt a glimmer of the woman I used to be. The confident reporter I'd been before my dad had been killed, before my hope and faith in humanity had been destroyed. I was buoyed by the strength that came from having something to say—something that mattered more than the fear.

I continued, "If we can uncover what's causing these attacks...whether it's a mutation in the Y chromosome, or sociological influences, or a bunch of different things mixed together...we might be able to change things. Maybe we can even prevent someone else from going through what we have."

I paused and looked at David, knowing he'd understand in a way Marika couldn't, no matter how much she'd loved my dad.

"Is it crazy to think this story might somehow give us peace?" I asked.

He shook his head. "It's not crazy. In fact, I think it's the only part of this whole thing that actually makes sense."

"It makes total sense," Marika agreed. "Let's do this for Papa Tennyson."

"And Stefania," David said.

Memories of the past floated through the space around us, heavy with love and pain. After a while, Marika spoke.

"Listen, before I forget, Frida dropped by earlier. She wanted me to remind you to share the play-by-play as we dig into this. I think she's getting worried about corporate. You may or may not have realized by now that they're real jerks. We have to get approval for every little thing to make sure the story direction matches their brand."

I rolled my eyes. I could only imagine the spin they'd put on the story, the lines they'd feed me.

David tapped his Surge and brought up a virtual videocam recorder. "Why don't we get Frida started with some of that heartfelt commentary? Tell us, Charley: Based on your research into the Y chromosome and its connection to violence, what could the end of men mean for society?"

I laughed nervously. I hated giving off-the-cuff commentary, had always preferred planning out what I was going to say ahead of time. I glanced at Marika and she nodded in encouragement. I reminded myself we could edit it later, then took a deep breath and spoke.

"Well, there are two big areas to investigate. One is the CDC's discovery of MPV and how violence might be connected to the Y chromosome. The other is the alarming decline in male births. And of course, the really big question is: are these two phenomenon connected?"

I paused and ran a hand through my hair, already imagining the critics pointing fingers and poking holes. The truth was, I didn't have the answers to any of those questions, and the idea of diving into genetics and evolution left me wanting to pass the whole thing off to someone else. What really mattered to me was finding a way to stop the violence. How could I get people to care about this story the same way I did?

An image of my dad flashed in my mind, the way he'd looked when we visited the lighthouse on the Outer Banks. He'd been wearing shorts and sandals with tall socks pulled up his calves, which I'd teased him about incessantly. He'd been so young then, with just a few silver grays poking into his dark brown hair, his wrinkles and worry lines eased by the freedom of vacation.

I took a shaky breath and continued.

"To borrow a phrase: I have a dream. My dream is of a future where our families can be families again, where we can leave our homes without wearing bulletproof vests, say goodbye to our loved ones without worrying whether they'll make it back alive. It's a dream where kids can swing on park swings and run barefoot through green grass. Where any of us can board an airplane and discover what's across the ocean, or stand on a distant shore and find out if the birds glide through the air in the same way. Where we can gather to feel the excitement and energy of a live crowd cheering their team to victory. I dream of a world where we can live each day together, without fear of dying. What if what's happening right now—this thing that feels like falling apart—is actually the beginning of fixing whatever's gone wrong? What if it leads to us coming back together to make that dream a reality?"

I gave David the sign to cut. My heart was pounding. "Did I sound too sentimental?"

David shook his head. "What you sounded like was a Fear Fighter."

I gave him a small smile. "Takes one to know one."

David glanced nervously at Marika. Her eyes widened.

"Are you a Fear Fighter?" she whispered.

She glanced around the lab even though the entire fourth floor was empty. Then she held up a hand.

"Don't answer that. If you are, I don't want to know. And if

I were you, I wouldn't go spreading that around. If corporate finds out, you can say goodbye to your job. Unless you can help them find Vanyala Dawson, of course. Then you can count on a nice fat bonus."

David avoided Marika's gaze and tapped his Surge.

"All right, Tennyson, I just transmitted your commentary to Frida. Should be enough to keep her happy for now."

My cheeks burned as I realized I shouldn't have mentioned David's identity, even to Marika. I followed his lead and avoided the subject.

"Great, now we need to focus on getting ahold of Simon. I'm sure he'll have a theory about why this is happening so quickly."

Marika assured me, "I know we can dig up some leads in your dad's files. I brought his hard drive, we can use my private setup instead of hooking into the corporate network. You ready to go beastmode?"

"Huh?" David asked in confusion. "You guys are about to turn into animals?"

I laughed. "Beastmode is what we call it when we go into problem-solving mode," I explained. "There's not much more we can do before the next interview, so we'll probably spend the rest of the day trying to track down Simon and learning everything we can about sex ratios, genetics, and the latest medical studies."

The research wasn't my favorite part of the job, but working side-by-side with Marika made it better. Hours and days could pass as we immersed ourselves in an investigation. Depending on the story and time sensitivity, we'd sometimes pull all-nighters, piles of junk food and energy drinks scattered around us, taking breaks to share notes and hypotheses.

David frowned at his Surge. "Looks like Frida is having

some kind of a problem with the file I just transmitted. I'd better go help her out. I'll catch up with you beasts later."

David left and I moved my stool closer to Marika. She opened her satchel and pulled out my dad's hard drive, then connected it to a small holographic screen and keyboard. The machine whirred to life and her fingers flew across the keyboard. After a few moments, she stopped typing and looked at me.

"Listen, Charley...I didn't mention it when David was here, but your dad left an encoded message for me in his files. I decrypted it last night. It was short and sweet."

She turned the screen so I could read it.

```
Work  with  Charley  when  the  time  is
right. Keep her safe.
```

CHAPTER TEN

THE NEXT MORNING, I woke to the scream of sirens. It was the alarm announcing my front door had been opened. I jolted upright and prepared to bolt for the bathroom, where I would barricade the door and escape from the window.

"Sorry," Marika yelled.

I sighed with relief and rubbed my eyes. I'd been in the middle of a vivid dream where I was running at a track event, my legs soaring over hurdles with an easy exhilaration I'd never experienced in real life.

Marika rushed into my dark bedroom, grabbed my hand, and pulled me out of bed.

"What's wrong?" I asked with a mix of worry and annoyance.

"The story's gone viral."

"Oh my God, who broke it?" I was instantly wide awake.

"We did. Vanessa, turn on the Hub."

My bedroom wall lit up and squares of various news streams appeared in a grid. Every headline screamed the same thing: *The end of men is near.* I spotted myself in one of the streams, the rough footage we'd shot in the maternity lab at Duke. I tapped my square to magnify it. My face took over the majority of the screen, reducing the other reporters to thumbnails along the bottom.

My image said, "I'm Charley Tennyson, reporting for Clarion. We're here in the newborn nursery at Duke University Hospital, where a baby girl named Alesia was born just a few hours ago. And she's not the only one..."

"What the hell?" I burst out. "Why would Frida do this?"

"She said it couldn't wait. She tried to call."

I looked down at my wrist and realized it was bare. I'd been unable to sleep last night, continually searching for information while my mind spun. Finally I'd stripped off my Surge and taken a pill to calm my anxiety. Now I rushed to the bathroom and saw my Surge lying on the counter, red light flashing. I tapped it and saw fourteen missed calls and three voicemails. I played the last one, my finger shaking as I hit play.

"Charley, we've got to day-turn this story," Frida said. "I know you're going to tell me you need more information, but it's only a matter of time before someone else breaks the news. We gotta get it out there first. Call me."

I rushed back to the bedroom, where Marika was perched on the edge of the bed watching the story unfold. "I guarantee you, every person in America has seen your face this morning. This is crazy."

I slapped my Surge back onto my wrist and sat down beside her. The "End of Men," as the story had been dubbed, was the leading feature on every media stream. I compared my short segment at the nursery with the other streams, many of which were broadcasting graphs, charts, and insights from experts. My cheeks burned with anger and embarrassment. Instead of delivering a thoughtful piece of journalism, the story looked shallow. I looked no better than Sloane—

concerned with luring viewers rather than uncovering the truth.

My Surge vibrated and I jolted as if I'd been shocked. *Keep her safe,* my dad had warned. I looked down at my wrist and my fear intensified. It was my mother. The fact that she was reaching out this early meant only one thing: she'd seen the story.

"Hi, Mom," I answered, trying to sound casual.

"Charlene! Thank God you're okay. I just saw you all over the Hub and heard the news. Have you been getting my messages?"

I sighed. The only thing worse than being outshined by other reporters or harassed by evil trolls had to be enduring my mother's guilt.

"Yes, Mom, I got your messages, but I've been a little busy."

"I can see that you've been *very* busy. What I don't understand is *why.*"

As usual, talking to my mother made me feel like a foolish, troublesome five-year-old. She'd always tended to be pessimistic and judgmental, but my dad had balanced her out with his optimism and lightness. Together they were like yin and yang—she brought practicality to his passionate obsessions, and he brought her hope and a sense of wonder. But since he'd died, there was no balance.

"What do you mean, *why,* Mom? It's my job."

"It doesn't have to be your job, Charlene. We have plenty of money. You should just come to Vista Haven where you'll be safe. I couldn't bear it if something happened to you too."

If there was a class in mom guilt, my mother had earned her master's. I imagined her alone in her sparkling chef's kitchen, baking loaves of pumpkin bread and stocking the wine cellar with my favorite red, pacing the empty halls as she awaited my return.

My Surge vibrated with a call from Frida.

"Mom, my boss is calling. I have to go."

I hung up without waiting for her response and answered.

"Frida, what the hell?" I blurted out. My guilt and shame exploded in anger and I paced the room.

"*Excuse* me?" she snapped back. "Where have you been, Charley?"

"I was sleeping. You know, that thing people do in the middle of the night?"

I sank onto the bed and dropped my head into my hands.

"The story wasn't ready to run, Frida. That was just a rough cut to keep you looped in."

"Charley, I'm sorry," she said.

I lifted my head and squinted suspiciously. In the three years I'd known her, I'd never heard her utter those words—and she'd done plenty that she should've apologized for.

She continued, "Listen, I wanted to give you more time, but corporate informed me that another reporter was asking the NCHS about the same birth data we were. With stories like this, you're first or you're last. You've still got the momentum, the glory of being first. Seize it."

Next to me, Marika did a fist pump. I flexed my fingers.

"Corporate has a connection at the NCHS?" I asked.

"Yes, I talked to him for almost an hour last night when I couldn't get ahold of you. He has some very interesting intel. He's hidden away up north, in the Blue Ridge Mountains outside Luray. He agreed to meet tonight. But it must be in person and he refuses to be named."

I chewed my thumbnail. "Which station was asking about the data?"

"It was Sentient. Sloane."

A bitter laugh escaped my lips. "Of *course* it was. She must have been thrilled to hear the news. After all, she's an independent woman who hasn't needed to date a man for two years."

Frida laughed. "Your take on the story will be much more genuine and intriguing, Charley. It will be a real-time investigation, and you're way ahead of everyone else. Corporate has even agreed to get you extra protection. A Deflector Dot will be here for you by tomorrow morning."

"They're willing to invest that much in this?"

I was both calmed that I'd have the device and unnerved that I needed it.

Deflector Dots were a brand new cutting-edge protective device that cost nearly fifty thousand dollars. The small dots attached to your Surge and could be activated within seconds, surrounding you in an impenetrable Tesla shield.

"Whatever you need, it's yours," Frida replied. "This has been classified as a Tier 1 story, alongside the hunt for Vanyala Dawson."

"All right, sync me the source's location. I'll call you with an update after I talk to him."

I ended the call and looked back at the Hub. My gaze zeroed in on the bottom right square, where Sloane stood in a hospital nursery, a sea of infants behind her. She wore a clingy black dress that fit like a second skin. I could just imagine her brushing off any compliments she received: *Oh, this old sack? I just threw it on.*

I used my middle finger to tap Sloane's face, expanding her small square to the main window while my coverage shrank to the lower right.

"Authorities have confirmed that over the last 74 hours, every live birth across America has been female," Sloane announced in her most dramatic voice. "Doctor Kobayashi, do you have any reason to believe this will stop?"

The view switched to the doctor Sloane was interviewing,

an Asian woman with long, blunt bangs that nearly touched her eyelashes.

"On the contrary, Ms. Steele. We have every reason to believe it will continue. Thirty minutes ago, the government issued a mandate requiring that chromosome analysis be performed on unborn fetuses to determine their gender. Thousands of fetuses have been analyzed since then, and each one has proven to be female."

A line of text flashed at the bottom of the screen:

```
Learn the sex of your fetus in seconds!
All at no cost to you!
```

Sloane patted her impossibly flat stomach and smiled. "All you mommies-to-be out there are about to discover a modern medical miracle. A ground-breaking new test called Sequenom will let you detect and report the sex of your fetus in seconds! While the old gender tests required a full eight weeks to discover the sex of the fetus, Sequenom uses cutting-edge technology to find out whether you're expecting a boy or a girl as soon as twenty-two days after fertilization. Can you explain how the test works, Dr. Kobayashi?"

The screen switched to B-roll of an animated DNA sequence, narrated by Dr. Kobayashi.

"The Sequenom test enables us to perform an analysis of DNA from fetal cells in maternal blood samples. With just a small drop of blood, we're able to detect Y chromosome-specific DNA with 99.7% accuracy."

The doctor's tone had lightened and changed rhythm as if she were emulating Sloane. She now sounded more like a salesperson than a physician. The DNA animation switched to a view of her smiling and holding up a white, pen-like lancing device.

"The test poses no risk to the mother or fetus, and it can be completed in less than 90 seconds. Even better, the cost is fully covered by the government. Simply visit any medical facility and you'll be on your way! Ms. Steele has agreed to demonstrate."

The doctor took Sloane's hand and lifted it in front of the camera, then pressed her pointer finger to the tip of the device. An instant later, Sloane waved her hands like a magician to show it was all done, flashing her perfect smile. A tiny red dot of blood glistened on her peachy flesh. The doctor pulled a bright red Band-Aid from her lab coat's pocket, but Sloane snatched her finger away and sucked the blood through pursed lips.

"Wow, that really *was* painless!" she gushed a moment later. "We highly encourage all women to complete the test, even if you're not sure if you're pregnant. In fact, Sentient is running a special contest for our viewers. Women who complete the test and share their results with us by next Friday will be entered for a chance to win free iCar rides for life! We're especially interested in hearing from women who have given birth to a son in the last two years."

I looked at Marika in disbelief. "How could all this have happened already?"

Marika shook her head in disgust. "Seriously. Since when did the government ever work so fast? And leave it to Sloane and Sentient to turn this into a circus."

I quickly flipped through the other stations to evaluate their coverage. Sloane might be right on my heels, but no one else was talking about the story in relation to MPV. At least, not yet. Now that the news was out there, my desire to find out why all of it was happening felt even more pressing. Amid the many questions circling through my mind, I was certain of only one thing: all the answers were buried in the Y chromosome.

CHAPTER ELEVEN

DAVID and I spent the afternoon driving to Luray. I gazed out the window as we drove, watching as the cityscape was replaced by the rolling Blue Ridge Mountains. The pine trees were all dead, their gray bark cracked and peeling from beetle outbreaks. The warmer winters had encouraged the bugs to spread, moving northward in a hungry death march. They covered the mountains in a timeline of carnage, an ugly reminder of everything we'd lost, all the problems we'd been unable to fix.

After a while, David took a left and pulled down a narrow dirt road. The scenery around us shifted as we changed elevations, the scattered mix of pine trees and oaks slowly replaced with dense spruce-fir forests. A red dot appeared on the Mule's navigation screen, indicating our destination was just ahead.

"Is this right?" I asked, glancing around. It looked like we were in the middle of nowhere.

David frowned and tapped the screen. "Looks right according to this. Let's go see."

He pulled off to the side of the road, which was really more of a pathway, not even wide enough to turn around. We got out of the Mule and walked deeper into the quiet.

A thud came from ahead and I jumped. A shadow emerged, a hunched-over man dressed in black with a red ballcap pulled low over his face. As he got closer, I could see that he was limping. David protectively stepped in front of me and puffed out his chest.

The man kept his eyes on me as he approached.

"You the one?"

His voice was raspy and he had an accent I couldn't quite place. Georgia, maybe, or Alabama.

I took a deep breath and tried not to look afraid.

"Frida Demir sent us," I replied, not answering his question but hoping my response was good enough.

He stopped and met my gaze. "You the one," he repeated. This time it wasn't a question. He turned back toward the road he'd just hobbled down and motioned for us to follow him.

David and I walked two steps behind him in silence. The sun was beginning to set and the sky was a bluish gray. As shadows floated around us, I had the sudden realization that whatever lay at the end of this road would change everything. It wasn't a guess; it was a knowing, a hunch I felt deep in my gut. We were about to uncover an answer that—despite my eagerness—I was afraid to find.

The man stopped at the foot of an enormous hemlock tree. It towered two hundred feet above us, its branches heavy with green needles, sloping downward as if to shelter us. The man got down on his knees and began rustling through the dirt, sweeping aside branches, fallen pinecones, and dead needles and leaves. A moment later he pulled open a trapdoor to reveal a ladder that descended into the dark earth.

"We're going off the grid," he informed us. "Your devices

won't work down here. Ready?"

I wished I could say I trusted the situation because I trusted Frida, but that was far from the truth. And yet, stepping down into the mysterious pit was the only way forward.

I glanced at David and he nodded as if to tell me it'd be okay. Did he feel as composed as he looked, or was his heart racing in his chest like mine? If only my Deflector Dot had arrived this morning instead of tomorrow. On the list of scenarios where extra protection would come in handy, following a stranger into a cave in a remote forest seemed pretty high.

The man stepped onto the ladder and gestured for us to follow him.

"I'll be right behind you," David whispered.

We climbed down the ladder, David following so close I was worried he'd step on my fingers. I reached the bottom, stepped off the ladder, and looked around in awe.

We were in a cathedral-sized cavern with soaring ceilings and glowing light. Limestone stalactite dangled from above like icicles. Scarves of powdery calcite lined the walls in delicate snowflake patterns, and columns of stalagmite rose up from the ground in jagged stone formations. Across the room was a plush white couch, an oversized armchair, and a bright orange area rug. Twinkling lights lined the space and gave it a magical, otherworldly glow.

"How long have you been down here?" I asked, looking at the man in shock.

"Twenty-two months. I got one of the first and only unmapped underground Havens, the ones they released before all those new Luxury Havens started popping up."

A thud came from above and echoed through the space. I peered up, eyes wide with fear.

"Don't worry, that's just the cavern door. Got it on an

automatic setup, even added some wiring to replace the shrubbery. You can never be too careful."

The man's muddled accent was gone. He turned and led us to the sitting room and I noticed his former limp had been replaced by a straight back and confident steps. He sank into the armchair and gestured to the couch.

I eased down onto the left side of the sofa. David sat close beside me, his chest puffed out as if he were my bodyguard instead of my production assistant.

I smiled at the man. "My first question is, how in the world did you get this sofa down that ladder?"

He chuckled and put on a pair of horn-rimmed eyeglasses. His eyes appeared magnified and bulging behind the thick glass.

I pointed at my Surge. "Do you mind if I take a voice sync? We'll keep your identity confidential, but it's important for us to have a record of the details."

He shook his head. "I told you, your devices won't work down here. No recording."

The man stood and walked to a cabinet across the room and shuffled through one of the drawers. He grabbed something, then walked back to the sitting area and handed it to me. It was a pen and paper. I laughed uncomfortably and took them. I hadn't written by hand since seventh grade.

The man laughed back. "Just gotta do things the old-fashioned way."

I clicked the pen and ran it across the paper. It worked. It gave me the same feeling as when a flower I'd been watering for weeks finally blossomed, or when the first tomatoes appeared on the vine. Even though it was exactly what was supposed to happen, it felt surprising and unexpected. My hand tingled with a strange sensation as I made blue swirls across the paper. I felt like a kid and a wizard at the same time.

"The old-fashioned way it is," I said. I wrote the date at the top of the paper just like I had in middle school, then added a smiley face for good measure.

I looked up at the man. "So you work at the NCHS?"

"Used to," he corrected. "I was a datakeeper there for twenty-three years. That might sound boring to you, but it was the only thing I ever wanted to do. I love numbers, the way they line up and make patterns. Did you know that every series of numbers has a pattern in it? I've always been good at spotting patterns before anyone else. Numbers just make sense to me, you know?"

He crossed his left leg onto his thigh. I was surprised by how freely he talked. I'd expected to have to pry details from him, but it was as if he'd been waiting for us for years, yearning to share his story with the world. He pulled off his red cap and ran a hand over his bald head, then replaced the cap and lifted the bill. I decided his alias would be Cardinal.

Cardinal continued, "My job at NCHS was to record all the live births across the United States. We used a system called Gatekeeper. The hospitals would send in their records daily, and I would record them in our master system. We tracked the baby's sex, race, blood type, and form of delivery, along with the age of the parents and any genetic birth defects."

He ticked off the categories on his fingers as he listed them, nodding with satisfaction when he landed at six. My hand scribbled across the paper, all too aware that whatever I didn't get down on paper would be lost forever. Unless David's memory was better than mine. I snuck a glance over at him; he was watching the man intently.

"So, it was around three years ago when I first noticed an odd pattern occurring with the sex ratio. You know what that is, right?"

"Yes, the ratio of male babies to female babies."

"Correct," he answered. "About three years ago, I started noticing the ratio was doing some weird stuff. It's always been real stable, like you could bet on it, but there was this one week when the number of boys born dropped like crazy. The following week, it happened again. I showed my boss and she told me to keep an eye on it, but she didn't seem too concerned. The next week, it went down again. That's when I went on our website and noticed our public data didn't match up with what I was recording. I went back to my boss and this time, she seemed worried too. The next day, she called me into her office and told me not to mention it to anyone. She said it was a matter of national security."

Cardinal uncrossed his legs and leaned toward me, his magnified eyes bulging so wide they looked as if they might pop out of his head and roll away. His words took on a frenzied pace as he continued.

"You know when you get that feeling in your gut like something's not right? Well, I got that big time, and I didn't know what to do. I took an oath when I started working for the government. I had a responsibility to do what was right. National security trumps all, but how could I do a good job if my work was being tampered with? And what was the point of keeping data if they were going to change it? I spent a lot of sleepless nights wondering if I should quit. That's around the time when I started to feel like I was being watched."

I asked, "Were there any indications that was in fact the case?"

He glanced around the empty room as if he were being watched at that very moment, then nodded fervently.

"I'd be making coffee and the new neighbor across the street would stare at me through the kitchen window. They hired this new guy, Ted, and I'd catch him looking at my screen. My iCar seemed to always show up just a little too soon, like it had been waiting for me. One day I noticed a tear in the carpet in the back, and I started checking the carpet every time I got in. Guess what? It was always the same iCar."

"That must have been very scary."

I rubbed the goosebumps on my arms. The cave was cool and humid, and Cardinal's prickly paranoia was contagious.

He nodded. "It was terrifying, until I made a home for myself down here."

He gestured around the cavern and his entire demeanor brightened, like a cloud moving away from the sun. "You'd be surprised how refreshing and peaceful it is down here. Being off the grid, I can finally think without the craziness of the world mucking it up. I remember this one time..."

Cardinal abruptly stopped talking and leapt to his feet.

"Did you hear that?" he asked. I paused and listened. The cavern felt quieter than anywhere I'd been in a long time. With no Surge service, there wasn't even that tingle of anxiety to check what was happening elsewhere. We were in our own world.

"I didn't hear anything," I responded.

"Me neither," David said.

Cardinal walked over to the entrance and gazed up, worry lining his face. "Someone's up there."

I felt equal parts fear and doubt. Was he some lunatic who thought everyone was after him? But then I heard it. A rustling from up above. Like someone was running something across the dirt. A hand or a shovel. Digging. Searching for the door.

"They're coming for me," Cardinal said. "I'll be back."

He rushed to the back of the Haven and slipped through a small sliding door hidden in the cave wall. Was he going to get a gun? I looked at David, who had approached the ladder and was looking up, craning his neck as if he could see what was on the other side of the door.

"Be careful," I whispered.

I wrapped my arms around my body and peeked back at the door Cardinal had disappeared behind. I could imagine him bursting out with a machine gun, ready to defend his home.

"I'm pretty sure it was just the wind," David replied, still peering upward.

Did he not realize that was what they said in horror movies before everyone got killed?

I glanced back at the spot where Cardinal had disappeared and had a sudden realization. I jumped up and went to the hidden door, running my hand across the rock. The door slid open. It wasn't a room on the other side, but a long empty corridor.

I ran forward without waiting to see if David followed me, certain that if Cardinal disappeared now, we'd never see him again, never hear the rest of his story. I raced through the steep, rocky tunnel until I stood face to face with a wall. I pressed both hands against the limestone, frantically searching for another hidden door. Nothing.

I spun around to see David behind me. "He's gone," I said.

"Don't worry, we'll find him." David replied unconvincingly.

We crept back to the Haven, listening for footsteps and running our hands along the cave walls as we went. It was so quiet, the silence echoed. The white lights were still aglow when we reentered the cavern, but now they felt eerie instead of magical.

"Let's get back to the station and check some of the stuff Cardinal told us," I said. "Maybe we can track down his boss, make a visit to the CDC."

"Cardinal?" David lifted an eyebrow.

"Oh...yeah. I kind of nicknamed him that. The red hat?"

"I like it, Tennyson."

I grabbed my satchel from the couch and reached for the notes I'd taken. My stomach flipped as I realized they were gone.

"Did you grab the notes?" I whispered.

He shook his head and beelined to the cave's north wall. He ran a hand across it and another hidden door slid open.

"I've seen this kind of grid before," he said. "There's a whole system of passageways down here. I bet Cardinal looped back and grabbed them."

"You've seen grids like this before?" I arched an eyebrow.

He cleared his throat. "Remember when I said I had a very unusual childhood?"

I frowned, my curiosity about David deepening. There was so much I wanted to ask him, but this was no time for twenty questions. Maybe the noise we'd heard had been the wind, but it had been enough to spook Cardinal. My skin itched with a need to get out of there, fast. I looked up at the ladder, trying to convince myself no one was up there.

"I'll go first," David said, as if reading my mind. "Just stay close."

As we climbed, I counted the rungs and watched the tread on the bottom of David's shoes to calm my nerves. When we got to the top, he wedged his feet into the sides of the ladder to balance himself, then put both hands on the trap door and shoved.

We scurried out into the dark forest and looked around. The sun had set while we were in the cave and everything was dark except the stars above. A gust of warm wind blew by and sent a spiral of leaves and pine needles swirling.

David gestured around at the empty forest. "See? I told you we were alone."

I craned my neck, peering into the shadows in every

direction. The cavern door boomed shut and I spun around to see a pile of branches sweep across the ground to conceal the door, just as Cardinal had described.

David grabbed my arm and pointed up at the sky, where a canopy of stars peeked through a clearing in the trees.

"Look, there's the Big Dipper! Let's sit down and enjoy the view for a few minutes."

"Are you crazy?" I whispered. "What if Cardinal was right and someone else is out here? What if they're watching us right now?"

"What if they're not?" David asked, holding my gaze. "What if we're alone and Cardinal's just a scared, paranoid guy who spent the last two years of his life hiding and running?"

David went to the massive pine tree and sat down, leaning against its trunk and bending one leg up in a casual, relaxed pose. He picked up a dead leaf from the ground and twirled it around, then gazed up at the sky.

"We can get in the Mule and race home and hide," he said. "Or we can sit here and look at the stars."

I stared at him in disbelief. "It's official. You're crazy."

"Your VT has you do breathing exercises, right, Tennyson? Mine told me that fear is just excitement without breath. If you breathe into the fear, it transforms it. Try it."

David inhaled a deep audible breath, and then blew it out.

I could hear my VT's voice in my head. *One, two, three. Breathe, breathe, breathe.* I glanced back and forth between David and the Mule. In seventy-nine steps, I could be back inside, locking the doors, turning on the air conditioning, and pulling the harness tight around my chest. But then what? I'd just end up sitting there alone while I waited for David to finish his little stargazing session.

I reached up to touch Marika's necklace, running my finger over the flower petal etchings. *You're stronger than you think.* I sighed and sat down next to David, hugging both legs to my chest.

The tree felt solid against my back, balancing out the vast sky above. The ground was hard and cold. I switched to a cross-legged position and ran my fingers through the dried leaves, then dug my nails into the moist dirt. I filled my lungs with as much air as I could, then let it go.

David and I sat side by side in the dark, breathing deeply and looking up at the stars. It was the closest I'd been to another human being besides Marika in months. By the third breath, I realized David was right. Deep in my gut, fear and excitement felt almost the same.

"That was weird," I said, disbelieving what I'd felt. "Almost like magic."

"Do you believe in magic?" he asked.

I pondered his question before replying. "I think I stopped believing in a lot of things when my dad died."

He continued twirling the leaf in his fingers, spinning it round and round like a carousel.

"Some of that probably won't ever stop," he said. "But there's a point in your recovery where you'll stop wishing you could go back to when he was alive, and start looking at the best way to go forward without him. And then, you just might start believing in magic again."

He pointed up at the sky, where one star was shining brighter than the rest. "North Star. Make a wish."

I laughed. "That's not a thing. Shooting stars, yes. First star you see, yes. But North Star? I've never heard of that calling for a wish."

"I say, anytime you have a chance to make a wish, why not take it?"

David had the naïveté of a child—and the charm of one too. "That's quite hopeful of you," I told him.

"You may say I'm a dreamer...." he sang.

If anyone else said the kinds of things David said, I would've written them off as innocent and gullible. But when he said them, my heart sprang to life. He was like a cool breeze after a sweaty run. He woke me up. Reminded me to pay attention. I met his gaze and smiled. He had that look in his eyes again—like he knew me better than I realized, like he believed in me, admired me. Our faces were close, our arms and hips almost touching. A wish suddenly floated through my mind: *Kiss me.*

Crap. Where the hell did that come from? Was it possible to take back wishes? Kissing David was a terrible idea. We'd be working side by side, day in and day out. I needed to focus on the story. I needed to find my footing again—find myself again, for that matter. I quickly turned away and stared up at the sky, cheeks burning. Had he felt that strange connection too? My mind raced to conjure a take-back wish and erase the crazy idea of kissing David from my brain.

The star I'd wished on blinked green and moved slowly across the sky. I laughed. If that wasn't a sign, I didn't know what was.

"I think I just wished on a satellite," I told David.

"I think you're right," he replied, and gave me a wink. "But you're not the only one."

A rustling in the leaves caught my attention. David extended a stiff arm to shield me, looking alert and ready to jump to his feet. A white-tailed deer emerged from a grouping of trees and sniffed the ground. Its ears stiffened and it paused mid-step, hoof poised as it jerked its head to look at us with wide eyes. A buck strode out behind it, taller and bulkier than the doe, its twisted antlers curving up toward the stars.

The two deer stood side by side, staring at us as we stared back. Four sets of eyes entranced—two human, two animal, two male, two female. The doe set down her raised hoof and flinched as the leaves crackled. They bounded away into the forest.

"I guess we're not alone after all," David whispered.

Something stirred in me as I looked around—an urgent desire to do something. The story felt suddenly urgent, as if someone else might put the missing pieces together at any moment. Time was so short and countless things were out of my control: Cardinal getting spooked, my notes disappearing, Sloane at my heels, the world's violence worsening. Only one thing was in my control: that moment.

I stood up and brushed the damp soil and leaves off my butt. "Do you have a night cam? What if we did a cut right now?"

David lifted an eyebrow in surprise.

"Frida said this should be a real-time investigation," I said. "At this point, we have the story no one else does. Who knows how long that'll last? So let's tell the story."

David grinned and jumped to his feet. He reached into his pocket and pulled out a flat recording device the size of a cracker.

"Allow me to present the Night Owl Model S, featuring 16K resolution, 600 feet of night vision, and the capability to transform dark images into scenery that is clear as day."

"Well, aren't you prepared?" I said with a laugh. I reached down to grab my satchel and pulled out my lipstick.

"You should leave it off," David said. He gestured around at the forest. "Look around—it's so natural, and so beautiful. You look like you're part of it—face bare, cheeks flushed, hair windblown. I promise, you'll agree once you see it."

I'd only gone on the air once without my signature lipstick. It had been one of my earliest stories as a new reporter, a short interview with a local governor who was running for office. The plan was for me to hit hair and makeup before our interview, but a last-minute change in the politician's campaign schedule left me running to catch her three minutes before she left town. I'd been so embarrassed by how plain I looked in the interview that I didn't show anyone the clip or even add it to my portfolio.

"All right," I said.

I positioned myself in front of the tree and scrunched my hair to give it volume. David nodded and I began.

"I'm Charley Tennyson, reporting for Clarion. We're here in the mountains outside Luray, where we've uncovered breaking new information about the End of Men. Previous reports cited the dramatic drop in male births as a sudden event, but we now have reason to believe that government officials have known about the plummeting sex ratio for some time. An anonymous source claims that the nation's official birth records have been forged over the past few years in an attempt to hide the phenomenon. The question is: why?"

I recapped as much as I could about our interview with Cardinal while maintaining his anonymity. Finally, I gave David the sign to cut.

I gazed up at the canopy of glittering sparkles above us. One star streaked across the sky, flashing bright before disappearing into black space.

"Let's sync the recording to Marika," I said. "Maybe she can get a head start and check out the data Cardinal gave us while we drive back. I have no idea how I'm going to sleep tonight."

David took a long last look at the stars, then turned to me. "Tennyson, I don't think any of us will be getting much sleep for a while."

CHAPTER TWELVE

Six hours later, we took the elevator up to the 3rd floor and headed for Frida's office.

It was well past midnight, but the pit was a flurry of activity, with every screen screaming the latest speculations on the End of Men. A small tracking counter was displayed in the bottom right corner of each news stream: *134 hours since a male birth.* Soon we'd be counting in days, then weeks, then months and years. How long before we began counting down the number of men left?

David and I paused at the big screen in the center of the pit, watching the coverage. On one stream, dozens of men stood in line outside Cryos, the nation's leading sperm bank. Apparently the going rate for a vial of sperm had shot up from $1,000 to $5,000 since news of the phenomenon broke, with an even higher premium paid for top quality specimens. A silver-haired economist predicted sperm would become more valuable than gold within the week.

On another screen, a flashing red "FBI most wanted" bulletin showed a front and side view of Vanyala Dawson's avatar without acknowledging the irony. A voiceover intoned, "The search for Vanyala Dawson continues. She is wanted for questioning related to her involvement in several flash peace gatherings and other unlawful activities. Anyone with information regarding her whereabouts is urged to contact the authorities as soon as possible."

My gaze drifted to the video in the center, where Sloane stood in a hot pink dress—a wardrobe she and her producers had no doubt selected with glee. It was a replay of a spot she'd covered late last night, when an impromptu women's march had formed by a feminist faction that split out from the Fear Fighters.

Behind Sloane, hundreds of women marched, brandishing signs like blazing torches. "The Rise of Women!" one sign read. "Girl Power!" another proclaimed in pink block letters. Another bore an illustrated globe alongside the speculation: "Mother Earth is female. What's she telling us?"

The crowds at both the women's rally and at Cryos far exceeded the public capacity limits. It was as if the Fear Fighters attack that happened just a few days ago had already been forgotten, buried in excitement and speculation over the End of Men. But maybe that wasn't such a bad thing. The screens buzzed with energy and the promise of change. History was unfolding before our eyes—and for the first time in months, I was an active participant instead of a spectator.

The counter at the bottom of the news feeds ticked forward: 135 *hours since a male birth.*

I nudged David's arm and we hurried to Frida's office. The door was cracked open and we rushed inside. Frida sat reclined in her desk chair, arms crossed behind her head, feet propped up on her desk. The emerald Louboutin heel on her right foot dangled.

Marika sat across from her, and they both jumped to their

feet as we entered. I hurriedly filled them in on everything we'd learned from Cardinal.

"The good news is, he had a ton of information. He claimed the government has known about the dipping sex ratio for years, and that he was asked to forge the public birth records."

"Asked by whom?" Frida questioned, arching her right eyebrow.

"His boss, the head of the CDC," I answered.

"You said that was the good news," Marika said. "So what's the bad news?"

"We couldn't get the whole story, because just when things were getting somewhere, he got spooked and disappeared. And the notes I took during our interview disappeared right along with him. Either he or someone else took them."

"I'm sure it was him," David interjected. I glanced at him with curiosity. Was he trying to convince us or himself?

"Let's hope no one else got their hands on them," I said. "At this point, the government's potential involvement is one of the biggest advantages we have over the competition."

Frida paced the room in long strides.

"The Y chromosome is what's going to blow this whole thing open. The more I look at the research Marika's been compiling, the more convinced I am that MPV and the End of Men have to be connected. And Charley, the stuff your dad was working on? My God, we should have had him on staff."

Marika pulled up a hologram with two line graphs plotted out next to each other. "I located some hidden data files on the secret web. Raw birth records. They seem to back up what Cardinal told you. The red line is the sex ratio based on the hidden records I found, and the blue line is what was reported on the public NCHS site."

David leaned over and pointed to two distinct blips on the red line. "And these dips are what Cardinal told us about."

"Yep, it looks like they align with the dates he gave you," Marika confirmed. "I've been reaching out to the CDC non-stop to question them about the discrepancy in the birth data, and you would not believe the runaround they're giving me. Actually, you probably *would* believe it—it's the government, after all."

"Did you find anyone who'll talk to us? Or get any leads on Simon?" I asked.

"Nothing on Simon, but I did track down Wanda and she's willing to talk. You're meeting her tomorrow at Duke."

Frida clasped her hands and nodded in approval.

"Splendid. Pull together as much research and background as you can today, then interview Wanda tomorrow. I'll continue my discussions with corporate, see if we can get someone else from NCHS to talk. The cut you sent from Luray was excellent, but I'm sure you know we can't air our suspicions about the government's involvement without solid proof."

She strode to her desk and pulled a small box from the top drawer. "Before I forget, I have your Deflector Dot. Give me your Surge, I'll set it up for you."

I passed over my Surge and watched as Frida peeled the backing off the small plastic dot and attached it to the side. She went through a short setup with a series of taps, then passed it back to me. "There you go. If you're in danger, just press the dot twice and a deflector shield will encapsulate you and the 10-foot radius around you. It goes without saying, this is for emergency use only. They run about ten grand for every two minutes they're activated."

"Hope you don't mind close-ups, Tennyson," David said with a grin. "I'll be staying within ten feet of you at all times."

I laughed. "Sounds like a wise plan."

My cheeks flushed as I remembered the sudden rush of

chemistry I'd felt as we sat together in the forest. That stupid wish I'd made on the star—er, satellite. I knew it was childish, but when David called me Tennyson, it made me feel like we were some kind of famous duo. Tennyson and Vine. It had a ring to it, like Woodward and Bernstein, or Lewis and Clark.

"Come to the lab with me," Marika interjected. "I have some other stuff to show you, and we can keep working on finding Simon."

Frida grabbed David's arm as the three of us turned to leave. "Hold up a minute. I need to talk with you."

David glanced at me and flashed another dimpled grin. "See you later, Tennyson. Great work today."

Marika and I chattered excitedly about the story as we took the elevator up to the empty fourth floor. She was the only one who bothered to come in anymore. The rest of the research team worked remotely, logging into the station's database while safe and sound from their homes.

Marika beeped us into her lab. The instant the door closed behind us, she turned to face me, hands on her hips.

"Ummmm, what was *that?*"

"What was *what?*" I asked.

"What's going on with you and Mr. Wonderful? You guys were totally flirting."

"You mean David?"

Marika laughed. "Do you know any other men who fit that description?"

"Not really," I admitted, laughing back.

"So? Spill it. What's going on?"

"We're just colleagues," I assured her unconvincingly.

"Actually, you're not colleagues. He's your *assistant.*"

"Okay, fine. We're just friends then."

"And that's it?"

"That's it."

"Then why are you blushing?"

I unzipped my vest and hung it by the door. "I'm always blushing. These damn vests are too hot."

There was no sense trying to keep anything from her. The perks and drawbacks of a best friend—she always called me out on my stuff.

"Fine, you're right. I'm blushing. We had kind of a... moment in the forest. Nothing happened, I just felt some chemistry. He's sweet. And he's a good reporter too. He's really smart."

"And hot," Marika added.

"Sure, he's good looking," I admitted in a low voice. "But that's not what matters."

"Oh yeah? And what is it that matters?"

"What are you, jealous?" I teased.

"Of you or him?" Marika asked.

"Don't worry, I won't let a little crush get in the way of my work. David and I are totally focused on the story."

"So you admit that you have a crush."

I turned and walked to the large workstation in the center of the room, then flipped on the computer and sat down on one of the stools.

Marika could be judgmental when it came to men, especially when she felt threatened. I thought back to the last boyfriend I'd had, which seemed like eons ago. He'd been an investigative reporter for another station, and I'd loved the feeling of passionately talking about our craft, exploring ideas, learning from him. But day by day, Marika and I had drifted a little further apart. From the minute I fell in love, I got the distinct feeling she didn't approve. Of course, in that case, she was right. He'd turned out to be a self-centered jerk who disappeared the minute my career began to take off.

Marika perched on the stool next to me. "I'm just saying,

now's not the time to get swept away by some romance. You need to be careful—especially if he's a Fear Fighter."

"I'll be fine. I've got the Deflector Dot," I joked.

"That won't protect your heart."

I sighed with irritation. "Okay, Mom—I got it."

My Surge vibrated and I looked down to see a new message from David. *Pick you up tomorrow at 7am sharp. What's your home address?"*

I flicked the message away and looked back at Marika.

"This reminds me—you never told me how your speed date went."

Her face lit up. "Oh my gosh, it was a blast! Unsurprisingly, I wound up with zero love interests and three new girlfriends. We're planning a wine night soon, are you in?"

I laughed. "You know I'm always in for wine."

Marika and I researched for a few more hours. As we worked, thoughts of David floated into my mind. Us looking up at the stars. The way he'd instinctively moved to protect me on the couch and in the forest. The prayer beads he'd given me, his advice on moving through grief. The idea of him picking me up at home the next morning filled me with anxiety that had nothing to do with my safety. I was suddenly worrying about what to wear, how my hair would look, whether he'd come inside, if I should offer him coffee or tea.

Marika was right—love should be the last thing on my mind. I had a job to do, and a big one. But despite my promise, I couldn't help wondering whether David felt the same way I did. And for the first time in a long time, I couldn't wait to see what tomorrow would bring.

CHAPTER THIRTEEN

THE NEXT MORNING, David picked me up and we hit the road. It felt like the beginning of a routine, like he was slipping into the role that Marika had filled since my dad died. It was all starting to seem like a dream: Cardinal, David, the unfolding story. Any moment now, I'd wake up in my bed, hazy from too much wine the night before.

But it was all real—and that morning, instead of waking up with the usual hole of grief in my chest, I'd woken up full of purpose.

As we drove out to the e-university, I distracted myself with research to prep for our interview with Wanda. To be more accurate, I *tried* to research. Every link I clicked led to an error page.

"Something's wrong with my Surge," I finally told David. "Can I try yours?"

"Yeah, sure." He unclasped the Surge from his wrist and held it out without looking at me. I took it, noticing the band was still warm with his body heat.

"You okay?" I asked. "You seem quiet today."

"Just tired."

I waited for more, but apparently that was all he had to say. I tapped the Surge's screen and a beautiful woman appeared, hovering in hologram form above the passenger side dashboard. She had long glistening blonde hair, bright blue eyes, and a huge smile with slightly crooked canine teeth. David answered the question before I could ask.

"That's Stefania. Today would have been our anniversary."

"Oh," I replied lamely. "She's beautiful."

It was hard for me to discern the tone in David's voice—whether he wanted to talk more, or if I should let it be. It felt like he and I were doing a strange waltz of grief. When one of us was strong, the other was weak, and then we'd switch, spin around, switch again.

I tried to focus on the story as we drove, but my mind kept spiraling back to Stefania. Did he still drink coffee from her favorite mug? Sleep with her old t-shirt or pillow? Did he cry over her, dream of her, wake up and forget she wasn't still sleeping beside him? Losing a parent was one thing, but losing someone you thought you'd spend your life with must be haunting in a completely different way.

David slammed on the brakes and my chest harness locked in a quick compression that left me breathless. I looked up and saw a cluster of blue iCars ahead. Sirens screamed by in the emergency lane to our left, first three cop cars, then a firetruck and ambulance.

I knew the truth in an instant: there had been another attack. I gave our coordinates to David's Surge and the information came back in seconds.

Who: Nineteen-year-old Marc Fisher.

What: Set off a bomb at a flash Fear Fighters gathering.

When: Twelve minutes ago.

Where: Chapel Hill, in front of the old football stadium.

Why:

In the distance, wisps of gray smoke snaked into the sky. I watched them turn in a widening gyre as the unanswered question circled through my mind: *Why, why, why?*

"Damn it," David yelled.

He slammed the dashboard with the heel of his hand and jerked the wheel to take us down a side street. He pulled onto the side of the road and punched the wheel with a clenched fist. His face was cherry red, dripping with sweat.

CDC warnings raced through my mind: *symptoms include sudden bursts of rage, unusual mood swings, increased aggression.* But the truth was, I wanted to hit something too. The idea of another attack so soon after the last one tore me apart. What was happening to our people and our world?

I turned away from David and leaned my head against the window. The glass was cool on my hot forehead and I pressed harder, imagined it cracking in a jagged split. Sirens wailed in the distance. A few iCars drove by, seeking alternate routes to their destinations or perhaps just an escape. Anger gave way to grief as I imagined the people back there, killed for fighting for what they believed in. I lifted my head, which suddenly felt so very heavy and tired, and craned my neck to look out the window. The sky was black with smoke.

I looked back at David. A tear snaked down his right cheek and I felt a sudden urge to reach over and wipe it away. It was the first time I'd ever seen a man cry, really cry. I wanted to smooth down his hair, tell him everything would be okay, even as I myself wondered whether it would be.

"Do you want to call some of your friends?" I asked. "Wait —didn't you say your mom is a Fear Fighter too?"

I held out his Surge and he took it, still not looking at me.

"She wasn't there. That wasn't even a Fear Fighters gathering, there's another group..."

He wiped the tears and sweat from his face and took a deep, shaky breath, visibly trying to pull himself together. "Can I tell you about it later? I just need some time to process. I was already upset about Stefania and now..."

"Of course. Should we postpone the interview with Wanda? Maybe this is a sign..."

He adamantly shook his head. "No, let's get to Duke. We can't let this distract us. If anything, it's a sign of how much we need to find answers."

David punched a button and the Mule sputtered back to life. He pulled away from the curb and we made our way through quiet side streets of shuttered homes, shades pulled tight like eyes afraid to look at the truth. We sat in silence, each of us lost in our own thoughts.

Behind my grief, anger sparked like a firecracker—not just at the nineteen-year-old bomber, but at the people who had gathered to protest. Why had they taken the chance? It was no wonder people were fleeing to Havens, why they hid away and gave up fighting.

I tapped out a message to my mother. I needed to reassure her that I was okay, that I would come visit soon, that I loved her and understood why she worried.

At the moment, being brave and finding answers didn't seem like such a good thing. I was just a lost kid who wanted to go home.

CHAPTER FOURTEEN

THIRTY MINUTES LATER, we rushed across Duke's west campus toward the Fitzpatrick Center. Less than a year ago, the campus had been buzzing with students and life. Now the desolate brick building had an eerie melancholy feeling, its dark windows empty and hollow. The lush green grass that had once given the entrance prestige and dignity was now a field of straw and scorched earth.

After the Harvard University massacre, the government had issued a mandate to shut down all public schools. Many of the buildings had been demolished, others left abandoned. The ones that were lucky enough to have private funding, like this one, became centers for e-university courses. Students completed their coursework via video conference and were permitted to come on site for one-on-one meetings with instructors. No more than five people were allowed in one room at a time.

As we approached the building, a young acne-faced boy with sandy brown hair scurried out, eyes downcast, a black satchel strapped across his shoulder. I instinctively checked my vest. What was in his satchel, and why did he look so shut-off and hurried? What if we opened the front door and the whole building exploded? At some point, being male had become cause for suspicion. It wasn't fair, but it was reality.

Just before we reached the door, I glanced back over my shoulder. The boy was now just a silhouette in the distance, shoulders hunched, head down as he hurried across the lawn. *He's just a kid,* I told myself. A kid who was probably as scared and sad as I was.

David caught my eye. "It's okay. We'll be okay."

"Are you trying to convince me or yourself?" I asked.

He pulled open the heavy oak door and held it for me.

"M'lady," he said with a sweeping, gallant gesture that made me laugh.

"Goofball," I said. "But thanks. I needed that."

I stepped into the foyer and glanced around before spotting a sign for the research wing. I led the way and David shortened his steps to match my pace, walking so close we kept bumping hands. I remembered what he'd said earlier: *Guess I'll be staying within 10 feet of you at all times.* The station had upgraded us both to military-grade ceramic body armor, plus we had the Deflector Dot. And yet, the bombing and the sight of the boy had reminded me that all of it was a false sense of security. No shield was impenetrable.

We approached Lab 45B, where we'd been instructed to meet Wanda. The door was cracked open and it was dark inside. I lifted my hand to knock, but before my knuckles hit the metal, the door swung open and Wanda looked back at us. She was even more fierce than in her picture, pink hair buzzed around the sides, one long bunch flipping down across her right eye in a deflated mohawk.

"Hi, you must be Wanda," I said with a bright smile. "I'm

Charley Tennyson, and this is my production assistant, David Vine."

"I know," she replied as if I were an idiot. "I've seen you all over the Hub. And Simon told me about you."

My skin prickled at his name. "Have you been in touch with Sykes recently?"

"Come in," she instructed, ignoring my question. "And shut the door behind you."

She spun on her heel and marched across the dark room. David and I lifted our eyebrows at each other and stepped inside. As soon as the door shut behind us, Wanda flipped on the lights and I realized we were not alone. Simon Sykes sat in the far corner by the windows, his arms wrapped around himself as if he were freezing and trying to keep warm.

"Hello, Charley Tennyson," he said quietly.

His voice was raspy and he looked emaciated and frail, at least twenty pounds lighter than he had in the holograph. Most of his hair was gone, with just a few wisps of black scattered in odd patches along the sides.

"Mr. Sykes! What a pleasant surprise. I believe you knew my dad, Gabriel?"

"Your father spoke of you often," he answered in a thick Indian accent. He paused and winced, then burst into a fit of coughing, a horrible sound that wracked his entire body. When he finally stopped, he pulled a deep red handkerchief from his pants pocket and wiped his mouth and eyes.

"Are you okay?" I asked.

"I am okay. Just a touch of cancer." He returned the handkerchief to his pocket.

"I'm so sorry," I replied, cringing at the hollow platitude.

Simon waved his hand dismissively. "That is not what we are here to talk about. Please, come, have a seat." He gestured to the chair positioned across from him, then looked at David and frowned.

"I'm fine to stand," David assured him. "Pleasure to meet you, Mr. Sykes. I'm David Vine, Charley's production assistant. Your research sounds brilliant."

Simon's dark eyes glowed with pride. "Thank you, young man. I am pleased to meet you also. Please, both of you, call me Simon."

I sat down across from Simon. He crossed his hands and placed them on his lap, looking formal even in his frailty. He wore the same silk tie he had in the hologram—green and orange paisley, spotted with bursts of pink. Wanda hovered at Simon's side, and it was obvious they were very close.

"You have met my wife?" Simon asked, gesturing to Wanda.

"Oh! I didn't realize. Yes, yes—we've met."

Now that I knew, I could see hints of their partnership. The way their bodies tilted slightly toward each other, how she protectively hovered in front of him, how his soft gaze fluttered to glance at her every few sentences. Their demeanors were very different, though—one was soft and warm, the other steely and cold. Maybe that's why it worked.

"I apologize for the mystery surrounding my whereabouts," Simon explained. "Your father and I discussed this very moment many times, and I vowed to make myself accessible to you when the time came. Unfortunately, it has been a difficult season physically as well as emotionally. It is not only the cancer I am speaking of. Someone found out about my work on The Y Factor and warned me against pursuing the matter. They sent messages, threats to myself and my family. However, I know this is nothing compared to your suffering."

Simon's voice wavered and he paused, tears welling up in

his eyes. "I am so very sorry about your father, my dear. I cannot help but feel responsible."

Wanda rested her hand on his shoulder.

"It wasn't your fault," she said. The insistence in her tone made it clear they'd had this conversation many times before.

Simon nodded, but his face remained strained.

"This person—or persons—they were displeased with the claims in my research. They spread lies to the school board, accused me of horrible things. It never ceases to amaze me how disturbed people become by thoughts and ideas that are outside their realm of comfort. The purpose of a university is to educate, to challenge, to question—is it not? And yet, the school wanted to avoid any notion of a controversy. They insisted I take a sabbatical to ensure my safety. Of course, they were more worried about the safety of their precious funding than my personal well-being. It always comes back to money in one way or another."

"It sure does," David interjected. I glanced at him and he shrugged. "It does," he repeated.

Simon burst into another fit of coughs, his frail shoulders hunched and shaking. Wanda began to rub his back and he relaxed almost instantly. As cold as her demeanor was toward me and David, I could tell she gave her husband immeasurable comfort. He pulled the handkerchief from his pocket and twisted it in his hands.

"I do not have much time left. I am glad you are here today. In my attempts to defend my work, I uncovered a number of facts that are intricately connected to what is happening. However, before we continue, I want to emphasize something to both of you."

Simon looked back and forth between me and David, his eyes solemn and focused. "There is grave danger ahead. Many powerful people do not want the world to know the truth about what has been happening. Are you both certain you want to proceed?"

"We're certain," I replied. "I owe it to my dad to finish what he started. And this isn't just a story anymore. This is our future."

David added, "Besides, there's grave danger around us every day. There was just another bombing in Chapel Hill, a stupid pointless attack that killed more people. It's our duty to stop this madness."

"A bombing?" Simon stroked his chin. "I had not yet heard the news, but it does not surprise me. They are seeking a distraction. They do not want us to uncover the truth."

"Who's *they*?" I asked, frowning. "It was a nineteen-year-old boy behind the bombing."

"I apologize, I am getting ahead of myself. Let us begin and you will see. Please start your recording."

David tapped his Surge and began taking a holograph recording.

"Simon, why don't you begin by introducing yourself?" I prompted.

"My name is Simon Sykes. I am the Professor of Human Genetics at Duke E-University."

Simon must have gone through interview training at some point in his career. Most people had to be instructed to answer in full sentences, a small trick that sped up editing tenfold.

"Thank you, Simon. You were working with Gabriel Tennyson on an unfinished study that explored controversial research on the Y chromosome. Can you please give us a brief recap of your key findings?"

"Our study was called 'The Y Factor.' We were conducting research on the Y chromosome's inherent characteristics and flaws, with a focus on exploring its connection to violence and aggression. Your viewers are most likely familiar with Darwin's theory of natural selection. There is a special form of natural selection called sexual selection, which enhances the traits within one sex in order to help its members win against sexual rivals. For example, human males were designed by nature for higher performance in aggressive, physically demanding action. In more primitive days, this strength helped them win the attention of the female while also enabling them to fight off their competition."

"Are you saying that men were 'designed by nature' to be more aggressive?" I asked.

"In many ways, yes. Aggression is programmed by our DNA. It was a necessary trait in the Paleolithic Era, when men were required to hunt and kill in order to survive and feed their families. Aggression is not all bad—that is an important fact worth underscoring. It can be a helpful trait for soldiers and military members, policemen, fathers defending their families, even sports players. However, over the last few decades, a distinct form of hyper-aggression has affected the male population. You do not need me to give you examples of this. We see it every day in the headlines, in senseless acts of terror that seem to have no reason or explanation. Upon closer examination, it becomes clear that there *is* often an explanation. The answer lies in our genes."

I moved on to the first of my planned questions. "President Hatcher recently announced that the CDC is considering 'male-pattern violence' to be an emerging epidemic. Can you please explain the phenomenon in your own terms?"

"I developed the term 'male-pattern violence' during my work on the Y Factor. I realized the verbiage could help to underscore the connection between masculinity and violence while removing offensive absolutes from the discussion. Consider the well-understood phenomenon of 'male-pattern baldness.' The phrase does not imply that all males are bald, nor does it purport that women never experience baldness or thinning hair. It simply points to a pattern that occurs more frequently within males."

I nodded thoughtfully. "So by saying 'male-pattern violence,' you make it clear that you're not implying *all* men are violent, or that women can *never* be violent."

"Precisely. With that distinction, we may remove the emotional reactions which accompany this discussion and begin to objectively observe the facts."

Simon patted his chest as if searching for something.

"Need a pen?" David chimed in.

Simon chuckled. "You are a shrewd observer, young man. I am not used to being here without my lab coat and teaching devices. Anyhow, everything I have discussed up until now is not revelatory information. Much of this has actually been incorporated into the CDC's findings, and I am thrilled to see they are at last giving this phenomenon the attention it deserves. Today, I would like to share with you new information I have recently discovered—information that has been discreetly hidden."

Simon leaned forward in his chair and I did the same. My palms were sweaty and I wiped them on my pants, then flexed my fingers to air them out. Behind Simon, a ray of morning sun sliced through the window. It shone on him like a spotlight, and particles of glistening dust swirled through the air around him.

He continued, "Many years ago a research team in Berkeley was commissioned to perform experiments on the DNA of criminals convicted of malicious acts of violence. The scientific community has long been aware of two specific genes which are associated with aggressive behavior. One of these is CDH13, which is involved in signaling between cells and has been linked to disorders such as ADHD, autism, and bipolar disorder. More notably is MAOA, a mutation of CDH13 that short-circuits how dopamine is processed. An excess of dopamine can promote aggression, especially when it is combined with certain other triggers. The researchers in Berkeley were able to identify a very powerful trigger—a specific combination of genetic factors they coined the 'Warrior Gene'—which was connected to particularly extreme acts of aggression. After the Warrior Gene was uncovered, a group of genetic engineers began working on a treatment to eliminate it."

The Warrior Gene. Just the sound of it gave me chills.

"What kind of treatment?" I asked.

"That is where you come in, Charlene Tennyson. I have formulated a hypothesis about the scientific research conducted at Berkeley. Their study was backed by extremely deep pockets, I might add. My access to data has been limited after my dismissal and I am unable to substantiate my hypotheses. Wanda is the only reason I am able to be here on campus today —we decided that talking to you was a calculated risk we were willing to take. My hope is that you will have the resources necessary to prove my theories."

Outside, a cloud drifted over the sun and the light in the room shifted. Simon's face was now only half illuminated, giving him a strange Jekyll-and-Hyde appearance.

"What's your hypothesis?" I asked Simon.

"I believe those Berkeley researchers successfully engineered a formula that would eradicate the Warrior Gene— a simple shot that would prevent carriers from passing on the gene to their offspring. Let us imagine, for a moment, that this anti-aggression treatment was covertly issued alongside one of the many annual vaccinations and immunity boosters that are now required by the government. Let us also imagine that, instead of simply rendering males incapable of passing along the Warrior Gene to their offspring, this shot left males incapable of passing along the Y chromosome altogether."

I frowned. "How could the researchers not have realized the impacts of the treatment?"

"Perhaps they *did* realize it. Based upon my analysis of the timeline of events, it was around this point in time when several research teams were commissioned to begin working on another research project: a project to create an asexual reproductive process which would enable two eggs to produce an embryo."

I flashed back to the hospital and our conversation with Nurse Betty. "We heard about that. When we visited Duke to verify the drop in the sex ratio, they had a team working on it. Apparently there was a nationwide call for research."

David cleared his throat. "I'm sorry to interrupt, but are you implying that the government not only covered up data indicating the sex ratio was dropping—but that they were actually *behind* its decline in the first place? I don't mean any disrespect, Simon, but I have a hard time believing our government would knowingly allow or encourage the extinction of males."

"I understand your skepticism, young man. At first the prospect may sound extraordinary, like something out of science fiction. But I believe the government and medical community was following the course that they believed to be in our best interest. Consider the fact that thousands of innocent citizens are slaughtered daily in mass attacks. As uncomfortable as the truth may be, we cannot deny that these killings almost always occur at the hands of men. Might these scientists view their work as a way to save lives and ensure the continuation of mankind?"

"Womankind," Wanda corrected.

Simon's lips turned up in a slight smile. "Yes, darling, that is right. Womankind. And one must note—"

Simon's words were cut off as a burst of gunfire erupted from outside. He jerked his head to look back at the window and it exploded in a crashing of glass.

"Get down!" David yelled and dove for the floor.

A scream strangled in my throat and I groped for my Deflector Dot, fingers shaking as I pressed the button twice. Panic swept over me as I realized I'd never even tested it, too worried about the stupid activation cost. Miraculously, it worked. A Tesla shield appeared around me and my immediate perimeter, capturing David at the far edge. I flattened myself on the cold linoleum and covered my head, unable to trust that the shield would block the danger.

The shots stopped. Somehow the silence was even more terrifying. Was the gunman—or gun*men*—on the way in? I flashed back to the acne-faced boy, the satchel strapped across his shoulder. Why had I talked myself out of my instincts?

I lifted my head and surveyed the room. David lay unmoving at the edge of the Tesla shield. Wanda and Simon were sprawled in a pool of blood and shattered glass. The tips of Simon's brown leather shoes pointed in opposite directions, his legs twisted at an odd angle. Vomit rose in my throat and I was floating, watching the scene from somewhere far away.

"David?" I asked in a strangled voice. "Simon? Wanda?"

The metallic smell of blood filled the room. I forced my mind to focus and make a plan. Should I keep lying there? Call for help? Yes, call for help. I tapped my Surge and connected to the emergency line, hitting "locate me" to instantly transfer our whereabouts to emergency rescue teams. Sirens sounded in the distance—they were far, too far. *Hurry.*

"David?" I called again. He didn't move. I closed my eyes and Stefania floated before me, wearing a flowing white gown, her arms outstretched to David. "Welcome home, honey," she said. They embraced and waltzed across pink clouds.

I was getting dizzy. My tongue tingled with a metallic taste. I lifted my heavy eyelids and looked down to see that my arm was covered in blood. Whose blood? Another image flashed before me, this time of Sloane, the drop of glistening red on her finger after her pregnancy test. "Perfectly painless!" she said with a smile.

Sunlight sliced through the room and I wished for darkness. The awareness that the gunman could be on his way in buzzed through my mind like an angry bee. How long would the Tesla shield last?

"David?" I whispered. I wanted to shout but my voice was strangled like in a nightmare.

And then, thank God, he moved. He rolled over onto his back and pulled a bullet from where it had lodged into his vest, just above his heart.

"Ow. Wind...knocked out."

He struggled to move but was clearly still reeling from the impact of the bullet. The sirens outside blared louder, inching closer.

"Help is on the way," I choked out. I tried to sound hopeful, but I'd become immune to the sound of sirens. I just wanted to close my eyes and disappear. I couldn't feel my legs or my arms, could only feel spinning in my stomach and a strange rushing in my head. I looked toward Simon and Wanda, searching for movement. A faraway voice narrated an all too familiar story. *Two people were killed in an attack today...*

I summoned the energy to army-crawl to David and wrapped an arm around him. His skin was warm and I pulled him closer. Simon and Wanda were dead, but all I could think was: thank God it wasn't us. Thank God David and I were alive.

The sirens pierced the air, flashing red and blue lights just outside the window. I didn't care that help was there, didn't want to move, didn't want to let go of David. The minute we rose from that spot on the floor we were stepping into the aftermath, and I knew all too well what that entailed.

I closed my eyes. Maybe David and I could escape to the mountains. We could build our own commune. Or a goat farm. That's it. We'd make goat cheese and drink goat milk and read books and make love. Who needed anything else?

I was starting to feel woozy. Were we on the goat farm?

"Charley, you're bleeding."

"I'm not pregnant," I said.

"Huh? Charley, stay with me."

I closed my eyes. I just wanted to stay in our dream world, our goat farm.

Then I slipped into blackness.

CHAPTER FIFTEEN

EVEN BEFORE I opened my eyes, I knew from the whirring and beeping of the machines that I was in the hospital. Cot springs poked into my back and fuzzy red squiggles floated across the backs of my eyelids. I opened my eyes and squinted against the harsh fluorescent light. An IV protruded from the top of my left hand, hastily secured with a crooked piece of blue tape. My head throbbed and I felt the tingle of watching eyes.

"Hey you, welcome back."

David was perched in a white chair beside my bed, his face scratched and caked with blood.

"Hey," I answered. My voice was rough and my throat burned, fire on sandpaper.

David picked up a glass of water from the side table and handed it to me, angling the brown paper straw to meet my lips. I guzzled it down. The cool wetness washed away the heat and scratchiness, but a lump remained wedged in my throat. I examined the needle protruding from the thin skin on my hand. Whatever they were giving me, it needed to be stronger. Reality was swimming back.

David took my right hand, slipped it gently into his.

"You're going to be just fine, Tennyson. The police caught the guy, it was an old student of Simon's. Apparently he's had some kind of vendetta against him ever since flunking his genetics class. We just happened to be in the wrong place at the wrong time."

"Bullshit," I replied in a scratchy voice that didn't sound like mine.

"Yeah. I keep thinking about what Simon said—about the bombing being a distraction? It's starting to feel like maybe these attacks aren't so random at all. It's getting bad out there. Things are starting to fall apart. The station's shut down until further notice. Most public places are, except the hospitals."

I was too tired and achy to ask what it all meant. David was still holding my hand and it felt good. It made me feel anchored and safe in a world that could slip away at any moment. A wave of wooziness hit and I closed my eyes. Simon joined me in the darkness—his twisted brown loafers pointing crookedly at the ceiling. My eyes snapped open.

"Is Simon okay? Wanda?" I knew the answer but asked anyway.

"They didn't make it."

Guilt washed over me. If it weren't for me, Simon and Wanda might be sitting somewhere on a beach, sipping Coronas and living out Simon's last days in peace. David bowed his head and hunched his shoulders. I wondered if the guilt was smothering him too. What had we done?

The wall behind David flickered to life and a blonde woman in green scrubs appeared. The image was so lifelike, it was as if she was in the room with us. She had thick-rimmed glasses and pointy features, and her hair was pulled back in a slick bun. Everything about her looked pinched. Her only redeeming quality was a shiny gold-plated brooch clipped to

her right lapel: a beautiful lizard with green crystals down its
back and tail. It was so out of place, I wondered if she was
wearing it to support a cause or as some sort of dare.

"Mrs. Tennyson?" she asked in a tight voice. "I'm Doctor
Morrison."

"Miss," I corrected. Her eyes flickered to David, down to
our hands, and then back to me.

"I'm sorry, *Miss.* You woke up sooner than we expected.
How are you feeling?"

"Thirsty," I said.

David let go of my hand and took the empty glass at my
bedside into the adjoining restroom. I wiped my sweaty palm
on the stiff white sheet. David returned and held the full glass
in front of me, once again angling the straw to my lips so I could
drink without straining myself.

"Thank you," Lizard Woman answered before I could.

"Thank you," I echoed in my eighty-year-old smoker voice.
I didn't feel like myself, didn't sound like myself—God could
only imagine what I looked like. My left hand was numb and
my arm was aching. I wanted to rip the scratchy tape off my
hand and pull out the needle.

"How bad is it?" I asked.

"It's not bad at all. The bullet missed your brachial artery
and made a clean exit without hitting any bones. We were able
to remove all the debris. You'll need to take antibiotics and
change the bandages daily, but I anticipate a full recovery. You
were very lucky."

Lucky. The word echoed through my mind. Despite
everything we'd been through, somehow I *did* feel lucky. I'd
faced the horrors of life and crawled out, shaking but alive.

"When can she leave?" David asked.

"We would like to keep her overnight to ensure that her
vitals are stable. If all goes well, she could go home as soon as

tomorrow. The police will want to talk with both of you, of course, but the first priority should be healing. A nurse will bring you a sling for your arm, and you'll need to be careful not to get the area wet for a few weeks. Is there anyone you'd like to call?"

I thought of my mom. She could sit at my side and wipe my sweaty forehead, feed me yogurt and chicken soup from a bowl, tell me stories about when I'd been a child. But I knew she wouldn't leave her Haven, not even for this. I probably shouldn't tell her what had happened. She'd only worry.

"I already called Marika," David said. "She should be here any minute."

"There's no one else," I replied.

Lizard Woman finished checking my vitals. A tap of her tablet sent the in-room machines whirring and pumping through various tasks. She assured me everything looked wonderful and flickered away. The virtual screen switched to a sparkling lake surrounded by tall aspens and golden leaves. I watched the leaves fall until Marika rushed into the room.

"Charley!"

Her curly hair was wet and wild and she wore yellow athletic gear and sneakers, an oversized gym bag slung over her shoulder. She rushed to my bedside and David stepped back to give her more room, like a changing of the guard.

She scrunched her face in concern. "Thank God you're okay. I mean, my God, are you okay? Can I hug you?" She turned to David before I could answer. "Can I hug her?"

"Of course. Just be careful with her left arm."

Marika wrapped her arms around me and gratitude surged through my heart.

"You have no idea how happy I am to see you," I choked out.

She sat at the foot of my bed, gently rubbing my legs as if I were a child waking up from a bad nightmare. "Tell me everything."

I toyed with the tape on my IV as I recounted what had happened at the university: the window exploding, the sound of gunfire, Simon and Wanda lying dead on the ground. My voice was hollow and distant. Surely I was describing something that had happened to someone else, reporting on a story about the death of strangers.

I squeezed my eyes shut and the horror once again followed me into the darkness. I looked back at David and Marika—my friends, my protectors. Thank God for them. At that moment, everything I cared about was right there in front of me. Lucky.

"You may want to avoid turning on the Hub for a while," Marika told me. "It's crazy out there. You need to rest and clear your head. The story can wait."

"Can it?" I asked. I wasn't so sure. It felt like time and opportunity were slipping through my fingers. But how could I finish the story without Simon? All I had left were his hypotheses and a lot of unanswered questions. A sob escaped me as the reality of his and Wanda's death sunk in. They had been right there talking to us, and now they were dead. Grief and horror flooded through my blood and whirled through my mind, stronger than any drugs they could pump into me.

Marika picked up a plastic bag from the nightstand and turned it over in her hands. It contained my personal belongings: my Surge, wallet, lipstick, necklace. It was surreal to see my belongings gathered like that. I could imagine a stranger's hands plucking the items from my body and dropping them into the bag as if they were nothing more than objects to be collected. But they were more than objects—they were pieces of me and my life, proof that I existed, that I mattered.

I pointed to my necklace. "Help me put it on?" I asked Marika.

She pulled it from the bag and gently lifted it around my neck, fingernails tickling the back of my head as she fastened the clasp. She patted the pendant against my white hospital gown. "There you go, good as new."

I flashed her a tired smile. "I don't know what I'd do without you."

She reached for my hand and squeezed it.

"Let's not ever find out."

CHAPTER SIXTEEN

Two days later, the hospital discharged me. The police came and went, full of probing questions and orders. We'd need to visit the station for a full debrief, provide a statement, turn over our recordings. Miraculously, there were no media inquiries. Between the morning's bombing and all the other craziness, our attack had somehow slipped under the radar. The nurses encouraged us to talk to our VTs about what had happened, warned us of the trauma that victims could suffer after an attack. As if I needed reminding.

By the time David and I pulled up to my house, night was falling. He'd offered to take me home and I accepted, grateful for his companionship in a world that felt increasingly dangerous. He came around to the passenger side of the Mule and helped me out, encouraging me to lean on him for support.

I gazed down the street, where two bodyguards sat in an unmarked black vehicle—a new layer of protection assigned by Frida and the station. They were ready to jump into action the minute anything suspicious happened.

"Hi, lady!" a voice rang out from across the street.

The little neighbor boy was perched on his stone pillar, wearing another superhero costume. A red and yellow "S" blazed from the chest of his blue shirt, and a bright red cape was tied around his neck.

"Hello, Superman," I called back.

He leapt down from the pillar and ran to the edge of their property, arms outstretched, red cape flowing behind him. His arms fell from flight position and he pointed to my sling.

"Are you hurt?"

"Just a little boo-boo." I cringed. The term *boo-boo* was far more appropriate for a three-year-old than a boy his age.

He looked both ways and darted across the street, stopping just an inch or two away from me. He pulled a sheet of stickers from his pocket and gingerly placed one on my sling, then looked up at me with a big smile.

"It's magic. It will protect you."

I ran a finger over the sticker. It was a classic red and yellow comic book bubble with the word "Pow!" inside.

The boy pushed his glasses up on his nose and then spun around. He looked both ways before lifting his arms back into flight position and rushing across the street, cape fluttering.

David carefully guided me inside and eased me into bed. He was far more gentle than necessary, pulling off my shoes, helping me lay down, and delicately tucking the white comforter around me. I closed my eyes for what felt like a few seconds and when I opened them, he was returning with a cup of tea. The comforting smell of chamomile wafted over me as he set the blue mug on the nightstand.

"All right then, get some sleep." He stood to leave.

My heart twisted at the thought of being alone, of the darkness closing in, the empty space around me. The two bodyguards outside gave me about as much comfort as the sticker on my sling.

"Will you stay?" I asked. "I don't want to be alone."

He nodded and slipped off his shoes, then lay down next to me, positioning himself awkwardly on top of the comforter.

"How are you feeling? Arm okay?"

"Arm's fine. The first question's a little tougher to answer."

I searched for words to describe the swirl of emotions inside. "I feel...different," I whispered.

"Me too," he whispered back.

There were no words to do justice to what we'd been through, but I knew the experience had opened up something new in both of us. Showed us the face of our humanity. Stripped away our fears and our dreams, left us with nothing but the raw knowledge that it could all be gone in an instant.

"Why were we so lucky and they weren't?" I asked.

I didn't just mean Simon and Wanda. I meant my dad and Stefania, and the millions of others who had been killed before us, and the millions who would be killed after. Every day, so many people were lost, people just like us. People who were just trying to do their jobs, provide for their families, make a difference, fall in love, reach their goals, make it from day to day. Why should I be so lucky to still get to wake up, to inhale and fill my lungs with air, to look into David's eyes and feel the pillow under my head and the covers wrapped around me? Eventually, death would come for us all. But why had it chosen to pass over me?

"I don't think we'll ever know why," David said. He paused before asking the next question. "Do you believe in God, Charley?"

"I used to, when I was a kid. I used to pray and believe there was someone listening. But then... I just couldn't. Especially after my dad was killed. How can you believe in God when you look at all the terrible things that happen in our world?"

"How can you not?" he asked softly.

He stroked my forearm, fingers soft as a ghost. "I mean, I felt that same swelling of doubt after Stefania died. Of course I did. My grief swallowed my faith in those first few weeks afterward. But then, I'd remember looking into her eyes, or watching her sleep, or the first time we said, 'I love you.' The thing about love is it's so big, so powerful, so wondrous, it can only come from God. If it was just us, we'd never come up with anything as good. The way I look at it, we can focus on the bad in the world and wonder why it happens. Or we can look at the good, and wonder how it could all be possible. And when I ask that question, the only answer I've ever been able to come up with is God."

We lay in silence for a few moments. Hearing David talk about his wife and his faith was like hearing laughter when you're alone. It reminded me of all the things I wanted. Things that felt so close yet so far away. He moved his hand from my arm to my head and began running his fingers through my hair.

"My dad used to do that when I was a kid," I whispered. "He used to tell me bedtime stories every night. Sometimes he read from books, but most of them he made up on the spot. He'd tell me about magical monkeys swinging on licorice vines, and create these amazing fantasy worlds where people were happy and free."

I didn't usually like to talk about myself, had always felt much more comfortable telling other people's stories. But something had broken in me earlier, and I didn't want to hold anything back.

"He was always trying to get me to see the good in the world, and in people," I said. "Once when I was ten, he took me to Disney World—planned the whole thing as a surprise. My heart was bursting with joy as we drove through the entrance gate and I saw the castle towers stretching up to the sky, bright flags waving in the wind. 'Where dreams come true,' the sign said. And I wanted to believe it."

David gave me a soft smile and I realized something about his eyes reminded me of my dad. It was a certain expression— the way his eyes glimmered with compassion and curiosity, the way they looked at me like I was someone special. Someone worth loving. He stopped running his fingers through my hair and reached down to grab my hand. It felt warm and safe, like an anchor, so I kept talking.

"I'd never seen anything like it. There were crowds of people, so much energy and excitement. My mom had always homeschooled me, and my world was very, very small. That day at Disney was my chance to see the world."

"It sounds magical," David said softly.

"It was...until it wasn't. We were standing in front of the castle before the parade. My dad was humming 'It's a Small World,' totally off pitch as usual. There were so many people, so many noises, so much to take in. People were crowding around us, pushing and shoving, and my lungs started to feel tight. The energy balled up inside me, tighter and tighter, and then there was an explosion. It was just fireworks, but I was terrified. People cheered, trumpets blared, the parade began— and all I wanted was to run. I put my hands over my ears and started crying, begging my dad to take me home."

David pulled the covers tighter around us. Why was I telling him all this? But then I realized it didn't matter. All my life, I'd spent so much time and energy worrying what people thought—choosing my words carefully, putting on the perfect face for all to see. Back at the university, I'd heard the whisper of death and realized its judgment was the only one that mattered. I'd watched bullets tear through the air around me, smelled and tasted my own blood, wondered whether my next breath would be my last. All the things I'd spent so much time worrying about didn't even matter. All that mattered was whether I'd leave something important behind after I was gone.

"Do you think you can inherit fear?" I asked. "I always wondered if my mom gave me her anxiety the same way I got her brown eyes."

David ran a finger across my cheek. "What I think is that we can change who we are at any moment. And I think that you, Charley Tennyson, are very brave."

Admiration shone in his eyes and it stung. If he only knew the truth about me, he wouldn't admire me. I couldn't bring myself to tell him about the despair and guilt I felt every day just pulling myself out of bed. Couldn't bear to see that look of wonder replaced by the judgment and shame I saw every time I looked in the mirror.

I said, "We just do what we have to do, right? You wake up, open your eyes, take another breath, and hope that the next day, life won't hurt quite so much."

"That's true in some ways, but you always have a choice. Some people seek safety, hide themselves away and hope someone else will deal with the mess. You choose to fight. You take your pain and let it make you stronger."

"Okay, Nietzsche," I said with a slight smile. Talking to him like this, my whole body and soul felt shaky. I only knew of one way to ease that shakiness.

"Do you want a drink?" I asked.

"I guess we've earned it, haven't we?"

We got up quietly, our eyes adjusting to the darkness, and walked into the kitchen. I got the bottle of bourbon and pulled shot glasses from the cupboard. He placed them side by side, so close their rims were touching, then picked up the bottle and poured slowly. I watched the amber liquid spill out, could already taste its sweetness on my lips. Could already feel the warmth spreading through me, dulling my jagged edges, lightening the burden of my own mortality.

He set the bottle down and handed me my shot glass. Our eyes locked as we lifted our glasses toward each other.

"To Simon and Wanda," he said.

I looked down at the liquor. "I feel selfish. Do you know what I mean?"

"I do. But this is life. Would they want us to act as if we were dead too? I think they'd want us to live every moment with every ounce of spirit we have left."

"You're right. To Simon and Wanda."

I kept my eyes on him as I lifted the glass to my lips. The bourbon slid down my throat, warm at first, then hotter.

"Another?" he asked.

But he was already pouring before I could say yes. We drank again and there it was slipping into me—that floating liberation of letting go, sharpness burned smooth with alcohol's powerful flame. The throbbing in my arm subsided. I thought of my body, my heart still beating, and then of Simon, Wanda, and my dad. Life was so short, so precious, so beautiful and horrific. What did it all mean? I met David's eyes and we drank again, and again, and again.

The hours slipped by as we drank and talked. David told me about his family, how he'd never known his father, how the distance between him and his mother had grown over the years, cold and vast as the Atlantic. He confessed that sometimes, it felt like she cared more about the Fear Fighters than about him, and that he worried if he ever stopped fighting, her love might stop too. We shared stories from our childhoods—favorite songs, embarrassing moments, first kisses. Once in a while something like joy slipped into my heart and struggled to spread its delicate wings.

Finally, as the first rays of sun crept through the blinds, my emotions turned dark with anger and a need to do something, to make someone pay.

"This might sound crazy, but I want to watch the footage. From the university," I said.

"It doesn't sound crazy," he replied. "I've been thinking the same thing, but I didn't think you'd be ready yet."

"I need to do something with all this..." I motioned to my chest, swirling my hand in a circular motion to indicate the turbulence inside. "Let's use my study, I have a whole holograph setup. We can edit at the same time."

We settled into my workstation, side by side on two small chairs, and connected David's Surge to my holograph player. He pressed a button and my image appeared on the wall like a third presence. But it wasn't the footage from the university—it was the footage from Luray, right after we'd interviewed Cardinal. My hair was windblown and my lips were bare, the usual red lipstick replaced with naked pink flesh. Behind me, the empty brown hills stretched into the horizon. Moonlight filtered between the crackling branches of a tree.

David sucked in a breath of air. "Look at you," he said.

And I saw it too. For the first time ever, I thought I looked beautiful.

He turned to look at me. There was half an inch of space between our faces. Half an inch between me and my fantasies coming true. No, fantasies was the wrong word. David was everything I'd been afraid to dream of, everything that seemed too good to exist in our horrible, hate-filled world. The air between us was electric, alive.

Suddenly the half inch of space was gone.

He grabbed me and kissed me, his tongue wet with the taste of bourbon. Desire rushed through me and one word echoed in my mind: more. I wanted more to drink, more of him, more of life. I never knew a craving could feel so good. I'd only ever loved the satisfaction of indulgence, had forgotten to savor the sweetness of longing. A little voice warned me not to love him, told me I'd get hurt, that danger loomed ahead. But whether it was the alcohol or everything we'd shared, something drowned out that voice, stopped the questions from swirling and replaced them with pleasure. Pure pleasure.

He pulled me closer, let his hand drift up under my shirt to touch my bare skin. His fingers found their way to my wound and he paused.

"Does it hurt?" he asked, fingers tracing the edges of the bandage.

My arm throbbed as if in response. "Hurts like crazy. But don't you dare stop."

He smiled and we pulled off my shirt together in a series of careful, awkward maneuvers.

He laughed. "This isn't quite how I pictured this going."

"So you pictured this?"

Instead of answering, he unclasped my bra. I let it fall off my shoulders, drinking in the feel of his eyes on my skin.

"You're beautiful," he said. It wasn't a line. He was stating a fact. Like saying the sky was blue, or life was mysterious. Every extra ounce of fat, wrinkle, or scar I'd ever worried about didn't matter. It was part of me, and I was beautiful.

"So are you," I said, and kissed him hard.

We stood and moved away from the desk, found our way to the floor. I wanted his hands all over me, discovering things no one else had. I wanted his tongue in my mouth, on my neck, down my chest and stomach and thighs, tasting every part of my body. I wanted his chest pressed against mine, holding me so tight I couldn't question or worry.

Outside, the world was changing. Things were falling apart. It didn't matter. None of it mattered. All I cared about was that moment, and David's hands on my body.

I lay on my back and he hovered over me in a push-up position, biceps hardening. I ran a finger over one, admiring how the muscle's curve was defined yet soft. He smiled the tiniest smile, a crooked half smile that said we knew what no one else knew. I pulled him back down toward me and kissed him hungrily. Even as his tongue explored my mouth, I wanted him to be deeper, closer.

I clumsily used my right arm to pull his t-shirt up toward his head, my left arm lying useless at my side. It was still throbbing but I ignored it. The pain was nothing compared to the other feelings swirling through me. David finished what I'd started, pulling off his shirt and tossing it aside. His chest was sweaty. It turned me on even more, knowing I'd made him feel hot enough to sweat. Me, only me. Him, only him.

He reached his hand down my pants to touch me. His hands were rough and calloused, fingers exploring new land. There was no shyness in his touch, no fear or hesitation. He knelt at my feet and pulled down my pants, tossed them across the room before removing his own. He returned to me and I opened myself to him, wet, ready. When he finally entered, the feel of him inside was intoxicating, like a first drink after a long day. I was torn between wanting to savor it slowly and wanting to take it all in an instant—craving another drink even as I was still enjoying the first. He held my gaze as he thrust against me, gently, slowly at first, then harder as he watched the reaction in my eyes.

Making love to David was different than every other man I'd been with. I trusted him completely. Felt like I could let go of every fear and worry and lingering doubt I had and rush forward, like a kid running into the waves without knowing there was such a thing as drowning. I gave him everything and he gave it right back to me. The world outside disappeared and the only story that mattered was ours. There was no him and no me, just an us, a newly found us. With his hands on my body, my brokenness felt less jagged.

Afterward we lay next to each other on the floor, our chests rising and falling, the smell of sweat and sex in the air. With other men I wanted to cuddle afterward, looking for reassurance in the touch of a hand, an intertwined leg. Not him. We lay there not touching, and I had never felt so content just lying next to someone. The distance between us was like a comfortable silence with an old friend. The insecurities that usually swam through my head were gone. I didn't care if my hair was a mess or my stomach looked fat or my armpits stank. I felt free, and complete, and alive.

A vibration came from the hall. It took a moment before I realized it was my Surge, still swathed in the plastic bag and sitting on the entry table. I sat up and looked down at David.

"Duty calls," he said, resting his right arm over his forehead as if blocking the sun. His left hand reached for me, fingers casually grazing my arm for an instant before letting his arm fall back to his side. His bare chest was still glistening with sweat. He gave me that little half smile again and I knew. It was over, but it was just beginning.

With effort, I pulled myself to my feet, not bothering to put on any clothes. I retrieved my Surge from the bag and checked the caller identification. It was Frida, probably calling to check on me and make sure the bodyguards had arrived. I reattached the Surge to my wrist and wandered toward the bathroom.

With effort, I pulled on a lush gray bathrobe and left it hanging open, unable to tie the belt with just one hand. I clutched the side with my good hand and answered in voice-only mode.

"Hi, Frida."

"Are you somewhere safe? I have news."

And just like that, the rest of the world came rushing back.

I felt like I'd reached the top of the roller coaster ascent and no longer wanted to ride. I was afraid of the fall but there was nowhere to go but forward.

"I'm home," I said. That didn't answer whether I was "somewhere safe," but the truth was increasingly clear: nowhere was safe.

"You know the source you talked to in Luray?"

"Cardinal." I knew the next words before she said them.

"He's dead."

I squeezed my eyes shut. Falling, falling.

"Are you sure?" Panic rose in my throat.

"I'm sure. His real name was Rylan Dorrier. He was killed in an iCar crash off Highway 6. Some kind of glitch in the circuit."

We both knew it was a lie. There was no need to ask questions, no need to protest.

"Listen, Charley..." Frida continued. "This is much more dangerous than I'd imagined. We got a call warning us off the story, and corporate wants us to listen. They want us to drop it."

"What?" I burst out in anger. "We can't drop it now. If we do, it'll all be for nothing. I know we're close to answers—I know it."

"I agree, and I told corporate as much. But I get the feeling there's something they're not telling me, something bigger than the anonymous threat. They asked a lot of questions about your sources, want copies of all the footage. I'll keep fighting for you, but I don't have much hope they'll listen. I need you to send over your files and then...just forget about all this for a while. Take some time to heal and rest. Lay low and stay safe."

We hung up with no goodbyes. I sank onto the side of the bathtub and David appeared in the doorway. His chest was bare, unbuttoned jeans hanging loosely at his hips.

I held back tears. "Cardinal's dead, and now corporate's spooked. Everyone's dying, and for what?"

David perched next to me on the tub and wrapped his arm around me. My arm was blazing with pain but I didn't care. His lips were warm as he kissed my cheek, then my forehead and the moist and wrinkled corners of my eyes.

"Shhhh," he whispered, smoothing down my hair. "We'll be okay."

And because he said "we," I believed him.

PART II

―――――――

89 DAYS SINCE A MALE BIRTH

Now all we need is to continue to speak the truth fearlessly, and we shall add to our number those who will turn the scale to the side of equal and full justice in all things.

– Lucy Stone

———

What does the midwife tell us to do? Breathe. And then? Push.

—Valarie Kaur

CHAPTER SEVENTEEN

SOME STORIES UNFOLD SLOWLY, taking months and years for their implications to be felt. Others bring change in an instant. The End of Men was like that.

Hour by hour, the world changed around us. The government began an aggressive donation draft, encouraging men to do their part to help humanity survive by becoming sperm donors. A premium payout would go to any man whose sperm contained a healthy Y chromosome. Floods of men left their jobs for a chance to cash in, gutting the broken economy. Farmers abandoned their crops and already scarce agricultural yields were further diminished. Fires raged, fueled by higher temperatures, drought, and a lack of firefighters. Bridges and roads crumbled without construction workers to maintain them. New builds came to a grinding stop.

After weeks of battles with corporate, David and I made the difficult decision to let go of our investigation into the Y Factor. Not that we had much choice. Marika and all our best fact-checkers had invested countless hours looking into Simon's hypotheses and reached a dead end. None of it added up—the timing was wrong, the science was wrong. We had no more sources, no more leads. Finally, corporate issued a ban on the story and demanded we move on.

The art of surrender didn't come easy. How do you wave the white flag when you've been fighting for so long? How do you pull back, recoup your losses, and forge a new path? It was the words of a dead man that finally drove me to embrace the power of letting go. My VT told me the story of Holocaust survivor Viktor Frankl, who said: "When we are no longer able to change a situation, we are challenged to change ourselves."

The truth was, I was tired of fighting. It seemed all of us were. More than a quarter of the population had fled to Havens, jittery from the crowds and rising chaos. Even the Fear Fighters had gone dark. There had been no flash peace gatherings since early March—no more rallies, no more messages broadcast from Vanyala. David cut off ties with the group after our attack at Duke, though he refused to tell me why. "It's for your own protection," he insisted whenever the topic came up. "The less you know, the safer you'll be."

The strange part was: it was the happiest time of my life. With the world changing around us, there was no shortage of stories to pursue. We left Simon's ideas about the Y Factor behind and plunged into hypotheses and predictions on the End of Men. My career was thriving and it felt like I'd finally found my place. I'd made it through my dad's birthday and even found a way to celebrate. David and I baked blueberry pie and spent the day meandering through photos, holograph videos, and stories. Sharing the pain with him changed it somehow, made it less jagged and raw. We hadn't yet said "I love you," but I felt it growing in my heart. A tiny seed ready to spring from the surface.

One sunny Saturday morning, we were lying in bed, sheets crumpled around us, my hair a tangled mess. We'd woken up early to take a hot, steamy shower, only to find our way back to bed, stumbling and kissing amidst the hazy aroma of coconut shampoo and vanilla body wash. I was scheduled to moderate a big panel discussion on Monday and had piles of work to get done, but none of it seemed as important as the work of exploring each other's bodies, discovering new birthmarks, scars, and stories as the hours lazily rolled by.

Just after noon, a call came into my private work line. I reached for my Surge on the nightstand, where it sat vibrating next to the cup of coffee David had brought me earlier.

"Sounds like another hot lead coming in, Tennyson," David said lightheartedly. When we were in work mode, he called me Tennyson. Outside work, I was Charley or "darling" or sometimes "my love." No matter what he called me, I liked it. My name rolled off his tongue in a way that made me feel like he was meant to say it.

"A woman's work is never done," I replied.

I kissed his forehead and snapped my Surge onto my wrist before rolling out of bed. I'd been fielding calls for the panel for weeks and was eager for it all to be done. Maybe David and I could plan a getaway next weekend. Maybe we'd even visit my mom. She'd been reaching out non-stop, asking if I wanted to go through my dad's old things before she gave them away.

"This is Charley," I answered.

"Charlene Tennyson?" The voice was gruff and muffled.

"Yes, how can I help you?"

"I have something that belongs to you."

I froze. "And what's that?"

"An old colleague of mine gave me some notes you took after speaking with him. I need to tell you what I know. There's not much time."

I stopped in my tracks and spun around. David sat up in bed, eyes wide, chest bare.

"Who is this?" I choked out.

"Go to your door and look for the sign." The line went silent.

I grabbed my rumpled clothes from the floor and told David about the call. We rushed to the front door, David hobbling as he zipped his jeans along the way. In the entryway, I asked Vanessa to view the exterior surveillance video. The security screen lit up with a live feed of the front porch. I pinched the touchscreen to zoom and zip around the periphery, examining every corner, window, brick, and tree branch within a 75-foot vicinity. The street was empty and quiet. The day's threat alert level was green. There was nothing left to do but open the front door.

"Wait," David said.

He reached over me and pressed the vest retrieval button on the wall. Two sets of deluxe body armor sprang down from the ceiling. After our big bonuses, we'd splurged on matching camouflage Kevlar vests, in a trendy new hoodie design with big pockets and an integrated cooling system.

David yanked my vest off the bungie and handed it to me, then secured his own.

"I'm going out there first, like it or not," he informed me.

I zipped up my vest and felt a splitting inside, indignation tumbling with gratitude. I could do it myself, but it felt good to be protected. To have someone willing to lead the way, someone to follow.

I said, "Fine. Vanessa, please open the front door and alert us of any nearby movement."

The front door slid open and David stepped onto the front porch, hovering protectively in front of me. He bent forward and craned his neck to look in every direction before flashing a thumbs up over his shoulder.

I stepped outside and the bright sun glowed on my face.

The sky was sea blue, dotted with puffy clouds, and the air was warm but not stifling. Spring would arrive any day now—the birds were already chirping from the trees. In the tiny garden bed beside the porch, the crocuses my mother and I had planted last summer were blooming in a sudden cluster, just as she'd promised. Three hungry bees zipped around the purple petals, buzzing with joy. An Eastern bluebird soared past us, a worm dangling from its beak, then darted into the flowering pink cherry tree across the street.

It was a beautiful day and we'd almost missed it.

David pointed to the ground beside my feet, where a small gold trinket glimmered. I picked it up and held it in an open, outstretched hand. It was a tiny lizard with green crystals running down its back and tail.

"I've seen this before," I said with a gasp. "The doctor who treated me at Duke was wearing one on her lab coat."

David plucked the trinket from my hand and fingered it, then wiggled the pin on the lizard's gold belly.

"I think it might be a container of some sort," he said, pointing to a tiny crevice at the end of its tail.

I grabbed it back from him and slid my fingernail into the crack. A message lit up beneath the pin: *5 a.m. tomorrow @ Triangle Town Center. Go to the horses. No Surge.*

Across the street, a door slammed. The neighbor boy ran into the yard in a ripped yellow baseball jersey and sullied white pants. His face was red and he dragged a metal baseball bat behind him. His mother flung open the door and rushed after him.

"Milbert, calm down!" she yelled.

"I want Daddy!" he screamed, face red, shoulders trembling. He flung the bat over his shoulder and took off running down the street.

She ran after him. "Milbert, honey, come back!"

We watched them grow smaller until they disappeared into the horizon. My vest's cooling system kicked in and I felt a rush of air across my chest and back. I grabbed David's arm and stepped backward, pulling him inside with me.

The door slid shut. Cool air swept around us as we stood in the secured entryway. The air was too icy, an overbearing attempt at comfort, and the walls were squeezing in like a trash compactor. A heavy weight settled in my chest and I recognized it immediately, though I hadn't seen its face for weeks. Fear.

"What should we do?" David asked, giving words to the question hanging in the air.

"Triangle Town Center is the old shopping center off Highway 1," I said. "My dad used to take me there to ride the carousel."

"What if it's a trap?" he asked.

"What if it's not?" I countered.

I looked down at the lizard and ran a finger down its jagged spine and tail. Tiny jewels pricked my skin. I clenched my fist around the brooch, squeezing so tight that the prickly sensation verged on pain.

The only way for us to stay safe would be to ignore the message. We'd tuck the lizard into a dark drawer and go back to bed, or maybe head to the kitchen to scramble eggs and brew coffee. We could watch a movie, read a book, have a bubbly mimosa and prepare for Monday's big show. Corporate would be very happy.

I loosened my grip on the lizard and the brooch came unhinged. The pin pricked my pointer finger and I instinctively stuck my finger in my mouth to suck away the blood, grimacing at the metallic taste. In that moment, I realized our survival didn't depend on this decision alone. No matter what we did, we were far more fragile than we wanted to believe.

CHAPTER EIGHTEEN

THE NEXT MORNING BEFORE DAWN, we pulled into the mall's old parking lot. It was nearly impossible to make out the faded yellow lines in the asphalt, so David parked the Mule crookedly across two spots. Not that it mattered. The shopping center had been shut down for more than a decade and the entire area was desolate. They'd been talking about demolishing the old building since the '20s, but no one could agree on what to do with the massive lot. Now it sat in decay, an aching reminder of bustling shopping trips, aroma-filled food courts, and magical carousel rides stilled forever.

David turned off the Mule and swiveled to face me.

"You're *sure* you want to do this?" he asked for the millionth time.

I held out an open palm. "I'm sure. Now give it to me."

David sighed before handing over the device he'd jimmy-rigged for me. Insisting I needed extra protection, he stayed up all night wiring together a handmade bracelet that could activate my Detector Dot without my Surge. It eased his worries, but I knew the bracelet was just like my vest—a precaution that could mean nothing or everything.

"Don't forget: tap, tap, hold," he said, reminding me of the activation sequence.

I slid open the door and hopped out. The asphalt at my feet was split and I jumped over the jagged crack. My mother would kill me if she knew I was there, but I couldn't ignore this call of urgency. I owed it to my dad to find answers. More than that, I owed it to myself and the world.

I strode toward the entrance, David hovering close at my side. The sun hadn't yet risen and the hint of dawn sparkled in the sky. Up ahead, the shopping center's once proud arches were now faded and crumbling like a sagging tent with broken poles. I stopped at the gray sculpture in the front courtyard, happy to see it was still intact. It was a circle perched atop a curlicue line and an upside down triangle, designed to look like a silhouette with playful, running arms.

"The carousel is on the second floor," I told David.

"Tap, tap, hold," he reminded me yet again.

David yanked open the glass entry door and held it for me. I stepped inside and scrunched my nose at the stench of must and mold. The marble floor was covered in grime and dust, and shadows were everywhere. To our left was an old diamond store, its scripted neon sign dark and deteriorating. Next to it, a men's clothing store was strewn with haphazard piles of old hangers. It looked as if a purposeful tornado had torn away every suit jacket and shirt, leaving only hooked plastic behind.

We tiptoed toward the dilapidated escalator. I glanced over my shoulder and realized we were leaving a slight trail of footprints on the dirty floor.

"Be careful," David whispered.

I nodded and crept onward. A flash of movement to the left caught my eye. I startled before realizing it was only a shadowed reflection of myself in the darkened store window, my hunched posture making me look like a thief in the night.

We reached the crumbling escalator.

"Let me go first," I told David. "I have the Deflector Dot."

He reluctantly agreed and we climbed the escalator's motionless steps toward the dark second floor. I remembered the first time my dad had brought me there to ride the carousel. I had clenched his hand as we rode up, looking down at the ridged metal steps. They looked like gnashing teeth and I was terrified of the crack at the end.

"Daddy, what if I don't get off fast enough and it swallows me up?" I'd asked, my palm slick with sweat as I gripped his hand. When we reached the top, he had playfully grabbed my waist and whirled me through the air, twirling me twice before setting me safely onto the marble floor. I'd giggled and rushed back to the escalator, crouching down to squint into the crack where the steps flattened out.

"Where do they go?" I'd asked. He laughed and told me it was magic, then helped me research the mechanics a few weeks later.

Now I lifted my gaze from those same metal steps and looked up toward the second floor. The tall glass ceilings were broken and caked in dirt. The sun was beginning its powerful ascent and a fragmented orange glow swathed the air around us. My out-of-shape thighs burned as I placed my foot on the escalator's final step. Without thinking, I leapt over the crack and spun back to face David. He flashed a boyish dimpled grin and made the same leap, adding a goofy pirouette at the end.

A sudden burst of noise erupted from above and a dark object darted through the air at us. David stepped forward to block me with his body, and I instinctively raised my right arm to shield my face before remembering my bracelet. My fingers groped for the button but the danger was already gone. It was just a blackbird darting toward us in a scurry of wings.

I looked up, squinting against the sun's rays, and saw dozens of the birds silhouetted on an eastern ceiling beam. Their beady black eyes watched us intently, their glistening wings motionless at their sides. I wondered why the flock hadn't been spurred to follow the lone escapee.

"Didn't see that one coming," David said with a nervous laugh.

"Thanks for having my back."

"Technically, I had your front, but I feel comfortable saying I've got your whole body."

"And I'm happy to share it with you," I said with a smile.

I grabbed his hand and we continued side by side. A dramatic voice popped into my head, narrating the scene: *Tennyson and Vine pressed on, unhindered by fearful omens.* Maybe after we solved the Great Mystery and saved the world, we'd become characters in a movie.

Up ahead, the old carousel sat motionless, a sad and dusty remnant of the magical ride it had once been. The horses' hooves hovered in the air, graceful legs poised mid-step.

I went to the white stallion in the front and wiped a layer of dust from its blue and gold saddle. The paint was unchipped despite years of abandonment. Would it still run if coins hadn't gone extinct? I stroked the horse's mane and remembered the joy of riding it as a child, prancing in circles, rising and falling without the need for a new destination. My dad had always stood watch, smiling and waving every time I circled around.

A person stepped out from behind the carousel. Their brown hair was cropped short and they wore a navy neoprene bodysuit and a forest green BulletBlocker vest. I couldn't tell if they were a man or woman, but it didn't matter. Their body language and demeanor was as relaxed and welcoming as if we were old friends stopping by for tea.

"Hi, I'm Finley," they said.

"Finley *Duggan*?"

I recognized the name from one of the dead-end leads we'd abandoned last month, but the person before me looked nothing like the one I'd researched online. The photos I remembered were of an overweight man with a round face and a long, wiry beard. The Finley who stood before me had a defined build, no facial hair, and rosy cheeks. I looked closer and spotted vague similarities: the flat nose, small brown eyes, and pointed ears.

"I'm Charley Tennyson, and this is my partner, David Vine."

Finley bristled. "I assumed you'd come alone. Did you leave your Surges behind like I told you?"

We both nodded and Finley's shoulders relaxed. I sensed that the person before me was like a chameleon, able to become whatever was needed to in order to suit the situation.

Finley pulled a Virtual Torch from a side vest pocket and lit it.

"Follow me."

I held my gaze on the torch as Finley led us around the carousel and down a dim, narrow corridor. Facts scrolled through my mind like a computer running code, racing to dig up the details I'd uncovered in my research months ago. Finley Duggan, twenty-eight. Started at the CDC right out of college. Devoted four years to researching illnesses and vaccines to protect the health of our nation. And then...nothing. Finley Duggan had disappeared from public record, no matter how many threads we'd followed.

Finley stopped at an open door at the end of the dark hallway, standing at the threshold with the Virtual Torch raised like a guard. I peeked inside. The tiny room had no windows and was full of shadows.

"Don't be afraid," Finley said, and swept the torch's beam across the walls and ceiling.

The light illuminated the dark spaces one by one. The bottom halves of the walls were lined with cracked paneling and the top halves were a dingy brown. Against the far wall, a mess of bulky cords and tangled wires covered a metal desk, connecting back to an ancient-looking device. A metal wall cabinet hung open, clustered with old keys that glistened as the light swept over them. Two wooden chairs sat side-by-side in front of the desk, and three tidy stacks of extra seats sat in the dark corner.

I stepped across the threshold. David followed so closely behind me I could feel his body heat. Finley pulled the door shut and flipped on an overhead light. The dim bulb above us buzzed and flickered.

Finley led us to two chairs in front of the desk, then went to the corner and grabbed a third chair. Instead of sitting, I went to the cabinet and ran a hand over the keys. They jangled softly, like old church bells urging everyone to come inside. I examined the desk and realized the ancient-looking device was a cracked monitor. An image popped into my mind of a security guard behind the desk, one hand shoving down a glazed donut, the other hand poised on his gun, both eyes glued to the monitor.

"Let's sit down," Finley said.

The three chairs had been repositioned to form a triangle. We all sat down and I looked at my empty hands—no Surge, no paper, no pen. I had nothing to take notes with except my mind, and that would have to be good enough.

"So...you were colleagues with Rylan Dorrier?" I asked. It still felt strange calling Cardinal by his real name.

Finley nodded. "He was one of the best guys we had. He was my first boss when I started at the CDC out of college. I still can't believe..."

Finley's voice wavered and broke, shaking lips pursed into a tight line. The heavy burden of death's reality was the one thing that could silence us all.

Finley continued, "We met up just before his 'accident.' He gave me a copy of your notes. Said if anything happened to him, I should contact you. I'm sure by now, you've realized his death was no accident."

I nodded, glad we could move swiftly past condolences and talk about what came next.

"He was on edge the day we talked," I recounted. "Just before he disappeared, he claimed 'they' were coming for him. It was hard to tell if his fear was warranted or if it was paranoia."

Finley sat back, legs shifting awkwardly before hooking around the ankles. "Somebody needs to pay for what they did to him. I'm tired of hiding."

"They say the truth shall set you free," I said. "Maybe this time, the truth shall lock some evil bastards up."

Finley laughed and relaxed. "It's definitely time for that to happen. The rest of the world is just now finding out about the declining sex ratio, but the CDC has known about it for a very long time. The sex ratio actually started dropping in 1982."

"1982?" I gasped. "This has been happening for that long, and the government *knew*?"

Finley nodded. "It was actually Rylan's predecessor who first discovered it, a data analyst named Michael Maddox. He crunched some numbers one Wednesday morning in January and noticed the sex ratio in the United States had dropped by .02 since the previous year. That small fluctuation might not sound remarkable, but it is. When things are working right, the sex ratio is incredibly stable, like the rising of the sun or the spinning of the earth. It's a consistent but accepted miracle, something we've come to rely on without a second thought."

I frowned. "But Cardinal...I mean, Rylan...told us he discovered the variance himself. So which is it?"

"Both. Rylan didn't know about Maddox's discovery until after he made his. Then he did some research and found a report Maddox had written once upon a time. It had been buried."

"Why would the government conceal something like that?"

Finley shrugged. "My guess is, it wasn't so much that they concealed it—they just ignored it. That's usually the case when a scientist brings a concern to the White House. Ronald Reagan was president at the time, and he had bigger fish to fry. Violence in the Middle East, the Cold War, threats of nuclear warfare and foreign terrorist attacks—not to mention the AIDS epidemic sweeping the nation. His administration basically sent a polite thank-you note back to the CDC, your standard bureaucratic brush-off. Maddox continued to study the phenomenon, though, and wrote letters of increasing urgency as he watched the sex ratio decline ever so slightly each year. Finally, almost five years later, he got a letter back from the White House with instructions to keep the studies and data hidden while scientists worked on a cure."

"They were already working on a cure way back in the '80s?" I asked.

"Sure were, and one of their funded laboratories found something very promising. I assume you've heard of Ganta?"

"Who hasn't?" I replied. I'd done a story on the pharmaceutical giant once, talking to their CEO about an extraordinary vision she'd had that sparked the company's legendary race to find the Alzheimer's cure.

"Then you don't need me to tell you how much power and

money they have. They used the government's money to develop a cure for the declining sex ratio. Well, not a cure really —more of a treatment. They discovered that an infusion of MAOA and CDH13 would create an excess of dopamine and build resilience in the Y chromosome. It was extremely effective in enabling fathers to produce male sons, allowing us to reverse the decline in male births. There was speculation about some of the dangerous long-term side effects, but that didn't slow down the approvals one bit. If anything, it sped them up."

"What kind of side effects?" I asked.

"Have you heard of something called the Warrior Gene?"

The hairs on my arms stood up. This was it: the link to violence, proof of Simon's hypotheses. Maybe Finley was holding the evidence we'd never been able to find.

I said, "One of our sources told us about it. He believed the plummeting sex ratio was caused by government researchers trying to eliminate the Warrior Gene. Is that true?"

Finley shook his head. "Opposite, actually. Trying to save men was what spawned the Warrior Gene. When the government realized fewer males were being born, they'd have done anything to stop it. They were terrified the U.S. would lose our position of power and strength. Ganta's treatment for making the Y chromosome more resilient was promising, so they ignored the red flags. And there were plenty of them."

"Like what?"

"There were indications that boys who received it would be vulnerable to a variety of disorders as they grew, especially once they hit puberty. ADHD, increased aggression, psychosis...the list goes on and on. The government thought it was better to risk those side effects than to put our nation in a weak global position by letting males sink into decline. Had to save the 'founding fathers,' all that patriarchal crap."

"How many subjects received these treatments?"

"Hundreds of thousands. Low-income families were offered hefty rewards to let their sons become guinea pigs. By the time they stopped issuing the shots, violence was spreading like a wildfire. Technology and post-modern society provided plenty of additional fuel. Kids were becoming more isolated and sucked into alternate realities where blood and death were everywhere."

"The perfect storm," I whispered.

Finley nodded. "The Warrior Gene was quietly passed on from one generation to the next. And the government got their wish—for a little while at least. The sex ratio stabilized and patriarchal America kept its power."

What Finley was describing was unthinkable: a government so focused on saving males that it was willing to accept any consequences. If what he was saying was true, our own government and Ganta were to blame for the violence that had shattered our nation. They were to blame for my dad's death, and Stefania's, and millions of other innocent people.

"So the boys and men who committed seemingly random mass attacks...you're saying it was literally in their genes? But there were mass killings long before this treatment was developed, and terrorism and violence exists all over the world. It's been that way since the earliest days of humanity. How can we possibly point to this as the culprit for MPV?"

Finley fidgeted, leaned forward then backward, then forward again. "Who of us can really say what the final lynchpin is that turns a person into a killer? It's impossible to know how things would've played out if they hadn't issued that treatment. But one thing is certain: this dirty little secret planted the seeds of violent urges in a large mass of American males. You can't just manipulate genetics and think nothing bad is going to happen."

"Do you have any proof?" David interjected. His eyebrows were furrowed and his face was red.

I wondered if he was thinking of Stefania's killer—a fifteen-year-old boy who had grown up in an ordinary suburban household. Was it possible that boy had inherited the Warrior Gene because of a government experiment? If they hadn't tried to play God, would David and Stefania be sleeping soundly in their bed right now? Would my dad be sitting down to black coffee and Sunday omelettes with my mom?

Finley unzipped an inside vest pocket and pulled out a small device. "These are the records I've been able to gather. You'll find copies of Michael Maddox's early reports and correspondence between the government. CDC records are in there too. The last pieces you'll need are from Ganta's medical studies. I have a connection for you, a researcher who worked for them and has access to their files. She wants to come clean too. I'd come with you to talk to her, but I'm almost out of time."

"What do you mean, almost out of time?" I asked.

"Rylan told me what was happening to him before he went into hiding. Let's just say I have the same concerns. I keep hearing strange clicks and echoes from my Surge, feel eyes on me even when no one's around. But it's okay, I'm not scared. When Rylan died, I had to take a hard look at my life and decide what I'm going to leave behind. This is it. This will be my legacy."

I looked down at the tiny device in my hand. Could everything really be hinging on this?

"We'll guard this carefully," I told Finley. "We'll guard it with our lives."

CHAPTER NINETEEN

"Damn, girl, I haven't seen bags this big since my mom threw her cheating ex-boyfriend out."

My makeup artist, Gravitas, squinted at my dark, puffy eyes. She opened a satchel bulging with foundations and powders, then whisked out a brush and stepped back to examine my face as if she were a painter at an easel. Finally she nodded as if satisfied with her vision.

"Don't you worry, I have just the trick," she said.

She spun into her creative flow and I closed my eyes, exhausted. I should have spent the night preparing for our panel discussion, resting for what, up until forty-eight hours ago, was one of the most exciting opportunities of my career. Instead I'd lain awake all night, legs twisting the sheets into a sweaty, rumpled mess as I tossed from one dissatisfying position to another.

I didn't know what to do with the information Finley had given us. I thought about all the scenarios: calling Frida to tell her what happened, cancelling the panel, burying the evidence and taking a nice hot bath. David slept soundly beside me, twitching and grunting intermittently. Of course sleep was easier for him; he wasn't the one with his job and reputation on the line. The night inched forward and dawn arrived, but the clarity I was seeking never came. All I had to show for my restless night was dark circles, puffy eyes, and a brand new pimple on my right cheek.

Gravitas stepped back and made a grand sweeping gesture at the mirror.

"Voila! Told you I had just the thing."

My eyes snapped open and I blinked in shock at the face in the mirror. My painted red lips glistened with vibrancy. My brown eyes were big and beautiful, dark circles replaced with brightness. My red pimple was gone and my flawless skin glowed.

"Gravitas, you're a magician!" I said. "Now can you please create a potion to keep me looking like this all the time?"

"Girl, if I could do that, I certainly wouldn't be working here anymore."

I gave her a spontaneous hug and headed to stage three. As I walked, my giddiness over my appearance dissipated and my mind spun into a black hole of doubt. How was I going to handle the panel discussion?

I'd spent weeks assembling the perfect lineup of experts to discuss the End of Men. First, I'd secured an environmentalist to explain how the plummeting sex ratio was connected to climate change. Next, a fertility doctor and a dietician would talk about how the age and diets of mothers can impact the sex of fetuses. An agricultural researcher from the USDA would highlight problems with food production, and a United Nations reference assistant would share a global perspective on sex ratios in other countries. Finally, we'd round out the discussion with a feminist theologian whose passionate views were sure to spice things up.

It all fell within corporate's approved discussion guidelines. There was nothing on the Y Factor, violence, mass attacks, or the Fear Fighters. But Finley's revelations had changed everything. How could I smile and pretend that a mix of natural factors was responsible for the mess our nation was in? It was all just a lie, a deck of cards waiting to be knocked down by a dangling bracelet charm.

I made my entrance. The stage was abuzz with activity as producers and film crew rushed to assemble the final pieces.

"Three minutes to action!" David hollered from the sidelines.

Corporate had moved him to a new role as general production coordinator after he and I had come clean about our relationship. It wasn't exactly a demotion, but we both missed working in the field together. I glanced at the emergency exit. Was it too late to cancel the whole thing and run away to Never Neverland?

David ambled over and plopped onto the red couch reserved for my panel guests.

"You look beautiful," he said.

I gave him a weak smile. "Wish I could take credit, but it's all Gravitas. That woman's a magician."

"Certainly you deserve at least *partial* credit, Tennyson." He flashed a dimpled smile.

I laughed. "You're right. I look gorgeous! Better?"

"Change 'look' to 'am' and we're getting there. You nervous?"

"More like terrified and enraged."

My fingers found their way to my lotus necklace, and I slid the pendant back and forth on the chain. If Marika were there, she'd know what I should do. It had been over three weeks since we'd seen each other—and for us, that was an eternity. Life had just gotten so busy. When I wasn't working on the

End of Men, I was at home with David, swept away by the bliss and magic of new love. Meanwhile, Marika had been hanging out with a new group of girls she'd met through speed-dating. Luckily she and I had plans to celebrate that night with our favorite old ritual of Taekwondo and Luigi's. I couldn't wait to get her perspective on what Finley had told us.

David leaned over and planted a quick kiss on my cheek.

"You've worked so hard planning today. Forget about Finley for the time being and just enjoy the conversation. There will be a time and a place to tell the real story, but it's not today. Today is your day to shine."

I smiled. "Has anyone ever told you, you're charmingly optimistic?"

He laughed. "I've also been called hopelessly naïve."

A heavy hand dropped on my left shoulder and I turned to see Frida. Her hair was stick straight and she had on a new lipstick, a purple-bluish shade that gave her face a ghoulish look. Her eyes darted around the set as if running through a mental checklist.

"We need to discuss something before showtime."

I fanned my face. The overhead lights were blistering and my perfect makeup was already beginning to melt.

She continued, "Hatcher just sent an executive order to all the media stations. It's going to impact key talking points in your panel discussion. I swear, that woman's timing couldn't be any worse. Luckily, I have faith in your ability to adapt."

My heart leapt in my chest. Frida rarely doled out compliments.

She tapped her Surge and a 3D holograph of President Elizabeth Hatcher appeared inches from my face. She looked stunning in a puff-sleeved gold lamé blouse that spun the light into a glittering mirage. Behind her, the navy curtain with the Great Seal of the United States looked dull and archaic.

Hatcher's image looked directly at me as she spoke, the holograph so lifelike I could smell her breath. It was fresh and minty, with a hint of rich espresso.

She said, "Until today, media coverage has referred to America's declining sex ratio as 'The End of Men.' After careful consideration, it has become clear to me that this must change. I believe the media's tendency to focus on negativity has a detrimental impact on society's views and beliefs. Effective immediately, all media professionals shall refer to the unfolding birth phenomenon as 'The Evolution.' Rather than dredging up fears of what we've lost, your narratives should highlight hope for our new future. America was destined for this moment, and we shall reap countless rewards from this transformation."

She tucked her hair behind her right ear. A smattering of silver appeared amongst the brown, glistening like bits of gold in a riverbank's soil. Her voice picked up speed and volume as she spoke, building into an impassioned tone that beckoned with hope.

"My dear journalists, our words create our reality. The stories you tell today can shape the future! History is being written by your voices and the stories we choose. It is your responsibility to show our people the light, not add to the darkness. We must join together to present The Evolution as a beginning, not an ending. Our country has suffered countless tragedies over the decades. We've become impoverished and fearful. The world now views us as weak, broken, misguided. Our once powerful dream of freedom and opportunity was lost somewhere along the way. But we cannot focus on the past! It is time for our founding forefathers' story to end. Today, the United States government and media must join together to help our nation step into a beautiful new future. Today is our joyous daybreak."

Frida swatted away the executive order. I shook my head and blinked, reorienting to the empty space where Hatcher's image had been.

David burst out, "As if the corporate ban on the Y Factor wasn't enough? Now the government is regulating the actual words we can use to report the news?"

David was right. Somehow, I'd nearly been tricked into listening to Hatcher, lured by the need to join together, to follow. Part of me longed to bury all the dark secrets and finally put grief to rest. I wanted to believe the best in people and humanity, to step into the happier and brighter tomorrow she spoke of. But Finley had provided proof that Hatcher was no better than her predecessors. She was nothing but a coward and a liar. If a bright future awaited, we'd have to create it ourselves.

"Frida, David's right," I said. "What about the First Amendment and freedom of press? As journalists, it's not our responsibility to get the public to feel a certain way because the president wants us to. It's our responsibility to tell the truth."

Frida wrung her hands. "I agree, but we're in a state of national emergency. The normal rules don't apply. Corporate's on board with the directive; they've already sent someone to brief the panelists. I need you to guide the conversation and keep it positive. Can you do that or not?"

I glared at her. She'd promised us that getting a huge budget would help our team pursue quality journalism, but all it had done was make us slaves to someone else's agenda. Was it too late to tell her to take that corporate job and shove it? Then I reminded myself: she didn't know what Finley had revealed. If she knew, she'd do what was right.

Before I could speak, Frida spun on her heel and rejoined the film crew, busying herself with tasks and to-dos. My four panel guests trickled into the studio in a single-file line like cattle being led to slaughter.

David gave my hand a quick squeeze and relinquished his seat on the couch. "You got this, Tennyson. It's your time to shine."

He slipped off the set to join Frida near the cameras and teleprompter. I lifted my elbows and flapped my arms to send gusts of air into my sweaty armpits. The red silk blouse and black neoprene pants the wardrobe team had selected was all wrong. The pants pinched my stomach like a girdle and my silky pits would be darkened with sweat marks any moment now. Not to mention, the stupid heels they gave me were a size too big and slipped off every time I took a step. If I'd felt like a phony before, it was tenfold now.

I smiled warmly at the panelists and searched their eyes, trying to discern their feelings about the new narrative. Did they know they were about to become puppets?

We took our seats. My pants pinched, my armpits dripped, my heart pounded. How was I going to do this? I closed my eyes and a voice piped up, providing the direction I'd been searching for all night, maybe all my life. *Forget the fear. Shine.*

David hollered the final countdown. "Three, two, one...Action!"

My mind raced through the talking points I'd planned so carefully over the last month, scrambling to see what needed adjusting. But it was no use, we were out of time. I'd just have to wing it.

"I'm Charley Tennyson, reporting live for Clarion. I'm joined today by several brilliant minds who have graciously agreed to share their insights on the End of Men...excuse me... the *Evolution*. Thank you all so much for coming."

They nodded and smiled, eyes sparkling in the flashing production lights. I recited the introduction I'd written last week.

"This morning, we'll explore a variety of factors connected to the remarkable phenomenon we're now witnessing. What's causing this transformation? Is it being driven by nature or is it nurture? Is it the hand of God or Mother Earth's urgent cry for salvation? Is it all of these things? You've heard the term 'the perfect storm.' Today we'll explore whether we're in the midst of one right now—and if, perhaps, a glorious rainbow is about to appear."

I cringed as I realized which pieces of my introduction hit the mark and which missed. If Cardinal and Finley hadn't risked their lives to share what they knew, my panel discussion would be playing perfectly into Hatcher's evil plan. But I knew the truth, and there was no going back now.

My guests introduced themselves one by one, and I stole the precious moments to reorganize my questions and thoughts. They each enjoyed their time in the spotlight, then turned eagerly to me.

I smiled. "Thank you all once again for taking the time to join me today. Larissa, I'd like to kick off the discussion with you."

Larissa sat forward, eager. She was a petite brunette with a sweet face and cheeks streaked with rosacea.

"As a fertility doctor, you've done a great deal of work diagnosing and treating conditions that can impact conception. You've speculated that the change in the sex ratio may be related to shifts in women's reproductive patterns. Can you please walk us through your research and insights?"

"Absolutely, Charley. And thank you so much for having me on today's show. I'm sure you won't be surprised by our first data point, which is that the majority of American women are waiting until much later in life to have children. But what you *may* be surprised to learn is that older parents are far more likely to have daughters."

The background screen lit up with a stunning 3D line chart plotting out the age of American mothers.

"Did you know that two-thirds of women over age 40 give birth to daughters? And with each additional year in a mother's age, the odds of her having a son decrease by a staggering two percent."

Larissa's already rosy cheeks flamed with red blotches as she talked, her stiff speech pointing to over-rehearsal and memorization. She turned to the screen behind her, obscuring most of her face from the camera. We'd skimped on media training to rush the broadcast to air, and it showed. It was hard not to spot every imperfection on this type of old-fashioned talk show stage.

Larissa made sweeping gestures at the chart and continued. "The analysis you're seeing here maps the average age of mothers in the United States, which has climbed from 23 years of age in 1960, all the way up to 41 today. This is partially due to the women's liberation movement, which led more women to pursue higher education and powerful careers. Many put off starting families until later in life, if they had children at all. I like to think of the correlation between a mother's age and the sex ratio like a see-saw: as the age of mothers rises, the percentage of male births falls."

The chart switched to a 3D animated graphic illustrating the see-saw effect Larissa described. I watched the display for a moment as the rectangle tottered off balance, one side rising as the other dropped to the ground. I moved on to my next question.

"That is fascinating, Larissa, but how do you explain such an extreme drop in male births? Why wouldn't we see a more subtle shift over the years instead of the sudden obliteration of male births that began in February?"

"Excellent   question.   As   you   mentioned   in   your introduction, it's a perfect storm. We can't look at the rising age of mothers as *the* cause for the Evolution. It's merely one factor among many."

I turned to Krystal, one of the USDA's top dieticians. "Krystal, you've made some intriguing discoveries about the impact of women's diets upon the sex of their fetuses. Can you please speak to that?"

Krystal shifted forward on the couch. She wore gray joggers and a casual orange neoprene shirt, the armholes big enough that her green sports bra peeked out from underneath.

"Women's diets in the early stages of pregnancy can play a key role in the sex and health of their unborn child. Research shows that the high-carbohydrate diets—which are all the rage right now—can actually cause mothers to birth more females than males. And we've seen that mother rodents given diets high in processed ingredients tend to produce small, female-biased litters."

A pie chart of the nation's food production soared onto the screen in a dramatic whirling animation. Slices of neon green, turquoise, and cherry red illustrated the percentage of U.S. foods that were naturally produced, mass manufactured, and genetically modified. I squinted at the tiny green sliver of naturally produced foods. They comprised less than one percent of the pie.

Krystal continued, "In busy working households, healthy home-cooked meals have fallen to the wayside, replaced with quick and affordable processed and genetically modified foods. A well-balanced nutritional diet with fruits, vegetables, and lean proteins is out of reach for many families, and it greatly impacts today's busy working women. For example, what did you have for dinner last night and breakfast this morning?"

I flashed back to that morning's three cups of black coffee

and my late-night binge on salty golden crackers and sugary peanut butter.

"I plead the fifth," I said.

Krystal laughed and continued, "Trust me, I'm right there with you. But more than our own health is at risk. In addition to female-biased pregnancies, a woman's malnutrition can lead to devastating infertility struggles. And yet, it's incredibly difficult for us to make wise nutritional choices while balancing our day-to-day lives. Healthy options are simply out of reach, either physically, financially, or both."

Her colleague from the USDA, Hansen, cleared his throat. He was an agricultural researcher and the only man on the panel.

He said, "Natural food sources are diminishing across our land. Our farmlands have been overdeveloped, and harsh climate and damaged soil make it nearly impossible to produce viable crops. Farmers have been forced to implement genetic modifications to stimulate production and turn a profit. The government's ban of international trade in the '20s was a crushing blow to an already dire situation, choking off our nation's access to necessary food supplies."

I shook my head. "It really is horrible. Do you remember the days when you could eat an apple and know it grew on a tree? And dear God, do I miss real chocolate."

Krystal said, "Sadly, those old pleasures are now reserved for the elite and wealthy. Our increased reliance on manufactured and genetically modified foods has other negative impacts as well."

"What are some of the side effects you've seen?" I asked.

"Back in the early 2000s, society began to see increasing cases of food illnesses and allergies. Millions of Americans were no longer able to eat foods they'd been able to digest for centuries. Many parents took their children off gluten, created special diets with organic foods, and tried their best to avoid the harmful contaminants they suspected were damaging their children's bodies and minds. Poor diet and inadequate nutrition can not only damage physical health, but also cause mental disorders and behavioral issues. It's worth emphasizing: all of these impacts may transpire in children and adults at any life stage, but they begin in fetuses based on their mother's dietary choices."

And there it was: a chance to change the conversation. I perched my chin on a folded hand as if posing for a glamour shot.

"Could this reliance on unnatural food sources also cause increased violence and aggression? I'm thinking specifically about male-pattern violence—MPV."

Mentioning violence was off-limits, but I didn't care. Hatcher and corporate could issue all the bans they wanted, but I wasn't theirs to control.

"It is possible," Krystal answered. She crossed her legs, then uncrossed them, then recrossed them in the other direction.

I turned to Liesel Kegan, who worked for the United Nations.

"Liesel, so far our discussion has been focused solely on our nation. You keep a keen eye on global trends in your role at the UN. Is the End of Men happening elsewhere?"

A red light flashed in my peripheral near the cameras. I glanced over to see a flashing warning on the teleprompter: VERBIAGE VIOLATION!

Frida stood in a frozen lunge near the teleprompter, one foot forward like a runner at the start of a race. If I kept pushing, I had no doubt she'd rush on stage and shut the live broadcast down.

Liesel bit her lip. Her gaze flickered from the warning to Frida, then back to me.

"Um, yes," she stammered. "The Evolution is most pronounced in America, but we are beginning to see the sex ratio decline in other major cities around the globe. London, Paris, and Barcelona, to name a few. The UN's scientists believe it could be the earth's response to unsustainable population growth. Societies around the world are facing a shortage of resources, environmental degradation, strains on infrastructure—the list goes on and on. Everything has swung out of balance. In the past, localized phenomenon like this could lead to global crises and large-scale transformations. The Evolution could be yet another way we're seeing this pattern play out, a creative new way for Mother Earth to protect herself. Less males means less opportunity to reproduce and less people to inflict damage on the world."

Hansen interjected, "That raises another interesting discussion point on the potential benefits of what's happening. Our team conducted a number of studies in the farmlands of Texas, the largest remaining agricultural region in the U.S. We learned a great deal about precision animal breeding and the new application of qualitative genetic theory. Farmers have discovered that the most economically efficient community of animals has a large number of females and very few males. A herd of cows with a couple bulls, for example, or a flock of hens with one rooster. America's economy has been faltering since the second Great Depression, but I see a distinct possibility for this phenomenon to help turn things around. A female-dominant nation may be just what's needed to regain our position as the thriving and prosperous country we once were."

Patrice, the feminist theologian, burst out of her seat. Fist raised in the air, she took full command of the stage.

"The future is female! Women have been rising for decades now. Our mothers are birthing an America that has never been, and it will be a great land! A place where women are not marginalized, but fearlessly lead the way. Together under President Hatcher, we will create a thriving nation known for peace, collaboration, and opportunity. It is God's will, and Her glory will be done!"

Patrice stopped, fist raised, and looked around as if expecting a burst of cheering. I stared in silence along with the other panelists. She lowered her fist, sat back down, and straightened her shirt, still shaking with excitement.

"As you can see, I'm very passionate about this topic. I find it truly fascinating that the male has been seen as the dominant sex in so many cultures, when females are clearly the more resilient of the two genders."

"How so?" I pressed.

When she spoke again, she was like a different woman. Her religious fervor and fanaticism was smoothed and calmed by a sense of logic and peace.

"God's hand in this Evolution is clear once you look closer at the biological fragility of the Y chromosome. It starts with the male sperm and carries all the way through to life expectancy. Male fetuses are more vulnerable than females in a wide range of mammals, from mice and rats to humans. Male humans have a higher risk of dying than females, both in childhood and in adulthood. Their life expectancy is shorter than that of females, by more than a decade in some regions. Based on biological factors alone, there's no question the human male is far more vulnerable than the female."

Liesel chimed in, "Many societies around the world have actually seen increased success with more females in the population and less males. For example, the Northern Mariana Islands has had a low sex ratio for many years. Not only does it have a thriving economy, but it also boasts one of the lowest rates of violent crimes in the world."

"Amen, Sister!" Patrice smacked the air between her and Liesel in a virtual high five.

Hansen chimed in, "In the animal world and in human societies, males organize themselves in loose 'packs' while women create tight-knit familiar structures. Think of bee colonies and ant hills—highly organized structures run by females where every being has its specific role and contributes to a greater purpose. It could be quite successful."

Patrice leaned forward, glowing with excitement. "Women are ready to reclaim the position of power that has been stolen from us for centuries. Think about witch-hunt hysteria in the 1600s. Men burned us at the stakes because they could not understand our magical powers. Women were actually highly revered in the early Christian church, but that story has been lost. The Gospel of Mary Magdalene was buried in the Egyptian desert after an edict demanded it be destroyed. Women often owned the house churches where congregations gathered to worship, and they were the land owners in hunter-gatherer societies. That's why they had doweries; women were prized."

The conversation was unfolding just as I'd imagined— before talking to Finley. I agreed with so much of it, but the truth about Hatcher changed everything. I imagined her tuning in from the White House's theater room, tossing popcorn into her mouth and licking her buttery fingers with glee. The master plan she'd envisioned all those years ago was becoming a reality, and we were playing right along like actors on a stage.

But I had a chance to change the conversation.

I lifted my elbows to let my sweaty armpits breathe, then turned to Liesel.

"You mentioned lower rates of violence in countries where there are fewer men. My father actually spent several years researching the connection between the Y chromosome and violence in America, and found some fascinating correlations. Are you aware of any studies on that topic?"

Liesel bit her lip and looked nervously at the cameras. I followed her gaze and saw a flashing red light on the prompter: VIOLATION! CUT TO COMMERCIAL!

Frida's face simmered with fury. Liesel looked back and forth between me and the cameras, then brightened and looked back at me.

"Yes, actually, I'm so glad you asked. There's a fascinating correlation between violence and the sex ratio. In places where violence is high, there are lower percentages of male births. One hypothesis is that it's because mothers are under high psychological stress due to the lingering potential of an attack. Extreme stress on the mother can lead them to miscarry male fetuses, which, as we've discussed, are more fragile. Another hypothesis is that of a positive evolutionary phenomenon. As male-pattern violence intensifies, the natural path toward survival is weeding out men."

I had broken Hatcher's rules, yet Liesel had deftly navigated the conversation right back to the preferred narrative. I was going to have to be more direct.

"I recently spoke with someone who claimed MPV was actually a result of genetic manipulation driven by the government. Have you heard of something called the Warrior Gene?"

Liesel's face went still. After a beat, she turned away from me and looked toward the camera.

"Oops! Looks like it's time for a commercial break! Stay tuned to continue the conversation."

The cameras stopped rolling and Frida hollered, "Everyone, take five. Charley, in my office. Now."

I stormed after Frida. I'd crossed the line but for once, I didn't care. I wouldn't be a pawn in Hatcher's game. I was a journalist, and it was my responsibility to uncover the truth. Otherwise I was no better than Sloane, smiling and faking it, spouting off a shallow story to entertain people instead of finding the courage to face reality.

David caught up to me and squeezed my shoulder.

"You're not alone," he told me.

"Thank you, I appreciate that. But I do need to handle Frida on my own. She and I have a history."

I turned from David and followed Frida into her office. She slammed the door behind me, eyes flashing.

"What the hell was that, Charley? You can't just change course on a whim. Now I have the wrath of corporate to deal with and a rogue panel discussion to control. I honestly don't see a way this ends well for you."

"It wasn't a *whim*, Frida. I met yesterday with an informant who worked with Rylan. Turns out, this whole thing is a grand scheme devised by the government. Hatcher's the latest in a string of people who are just manipulating reality—and all of us. I have proof: letters to and from the government, data and records that have been buried."

The anger in Frida's eyes shifted and she began to pace the room. After a few frantic circuits, she came back and stopped in front of me, jaw clenched.

"Listen, Charley, I appreciate your enthusiasm, but following Hatcher's orders is what's best for the network. You have to forget everything that source told you. Give me your word you'll let it go."

I clenched my hands into fists. "So you just want to bury the evidence? Pretend everything is fine? What happened to the woman who said we'd use our unlimited resources to pursue quality journalism? That we'd leverage our new platform to let the truth be heard?"

Frida's shoulders sank and her face fell. Her eyes—once

bright with purpose and hope for justice—were now lined with despair. I'd been so focused on my own journey that I hadn't noticed how much she'd changed over the last six months too.

She sighed. "That woman is tired, Charley. We have to do what's best for the network. This is much bigger than me and you. Can you let it go or not?"

I clenched and unclenched my fists, flexed my fingers to see how far they'd bend and stretch. I glanced at the door. Should I stay or should I go now? Frida watched, waiting for me to speak.

Finally, I shook my head.

"I won't be a slave to you and corporate any longer. Speaking up is terrifying, yes, but I wasn't raised to be a coward. I quit."

I stormed out of her office and stomped toward the exit. The only way to finish this was on my own terms. It was time to find the truth, once and for all.

CHAPTER TWENTY

THAT EVENING, I stepped into Dojang 12 dressed in a white dobok, virtual reality headgear in hand. My Taekwondo date with Marika was the perfect opportunity to tell her what was going on and get her help. She'd been so swamped with research on a new story that she'd missed the live broadcast and only knew that I'd quit.

I arrived at the VR studio first and stood alone in the empty quiet. The mat was sticky on my bare feet and adrenaline prickled in my blood. I still couldn't believe I'd actually quit my job. What was I going to do now? How would I finish the story, make money, get through the days? There was an actual chance I might not survive.

"Please start the warmup sequence," I said.

The virtual simulation flared to life and the west wall lit up with a 3D Fitness Mirror. I limbered up with a short series of stretches: circle hips, torso twists, lunges. My tight muscles sighed with gratitude. It had been months since I'd exercised and I hadn't realized how much my body had missed it. I began arm circles and winced as pain shot up my left arm, a remnant of the bullet that had ripped through my flesh. Last week's doctor's checkup had confirmed that my arm healed as expected, but I knew the deeper healing would take much longer.

I extended my arms in front of me and began jogging with high knees. My heartrate picked up and I flashed back to the first time I'd practiced Taekwondo. Marika had been trying to convince me to join her for months, but I'd been reluctant to change up my beloved yoga practice. After months of stammering excuses about my weak knees and arms, I'd finally decided to give it a try. Gazing in the mirror during that first workout, I'd stared in disbelief at the powerful, confident warrior emerging before me. Now the same warrior woman was rising again. She was older, heavier, bruised, and beaten. But she was alive.

Marika slipped in the side door and I spun away from the mirror.

"I've missed you!" she said, rushing over and wrapping me in a tight hug. "How've you been? How's Mr. Wonderful?"

"He's...wonderful. But I miss you too. Did you change your hair?"

Her dark spirals were pulled back in a ponytail and glimmered with magenta. She twirled a lock with her finger. "It's henna, do you like it?"

I wiped sweat from my brow, already feeling the brief warmup. "It's beautiful."

"Speaking of beautiful, you're glowing! Did you really storm out of Frida's office?"

"It's been a crazy few weeks. I can't wait to tell you everything."

The lights dimmed to indicate it was time for class. All four walls lit up and we were plunged into a complete 3D VR experience. We stood among twenty other students, all women.

In reality, each of the students were tuning in from their own private vault, logging into an identical simulation to create a seamless illusion of togetherness.

Kyo Sah Nim Sullivan glided to the front of the studio, dressed in a black dobok, and began the opening rituals.

"*Cha Ryot!*" he bellowed, calling us to attention.

Marika and I assumed ready stance: arms at our sides, heels together, gazes fixed forward.

"*Kyung Nae!*" he instructed. We bowed to him, then to each other.

He swept his gaze across the room. "Taekwondo helps us develop physical strength, but that is only part of our mission. Today, my students, remember the power of your mind. To master the physical art, a true *haksaeng* must develop courage, patience, integrity, goodness, and above all else, perseverance. Let us begin. *Seijak!*"

We turned right to face the flags and salute them, then moved into a series of dynamic punching and kicking drills. I lifted my fists and moved to right leg position to prepare for a roundhouse kick. I raised my knee, pivoted my bottom foot, and snap kicked, then brought it back in and down. We repeated the move and my gaze flickered to Marika in the mirror. Usually I envied her masterful abilities, but I was pleased to see that my roundhouse kick looked just as strong as hers. Our legs swept the air in unison—separate and distinct, but equal in power.

The minutes flew by as we completed the individual sequence and moved into sparring. For the first time ever, I outperformed Marika, scoring twelve points to her ten. My final winning move was a perfectly placed spinning kick.

We bowed to each other, dripping with sweat.

"Nice match," I told her, beaming with pride and exhilaration.

"All that time with Mr. Wonderful is treating you right. You killed it today! The sex must be good."

I laughed and winked. "A lady never tells."

Kyo Sah Nim Sullivan strode around the room, pausing in front of each student before returning to the front of the studio. His holograph hovered inches from my face as he gave his final remarks.

"Remember, *haksaengs,* a black belt is a white belt who never quit. Strength does not come from what you can do. It comes from overcoming the things you once thought you could not. *Kam sa ham me da.*"

"*Kam sa ham me da,*" we repeated with a bow.

Kyo Sah Nim Sullivan and the other students blipped away. I'd never gotten used to the hollow echo in my chest when the simulation ended. I kept my hands together in prayer pose, then moved spontaneously into tree pose, a harkening to my old yoga days. I could hear my old instructor's voice: *In times of chaos, balance is everything.*

"Ready for some spaghetti and wine?" Marika asked. She grinned and rubbed her hands together.

I impulsively hugged Marika again. "I'm so damn happy to see you! And you know I'm *always* ready for spaghetti and wine."

We exited the vault and stepped out into the night. The air felt cooler than it had in a long time and it smelled like rain. A wind blew from the east, tickling my sweaty skin and sparking goosebumps. I rubbed my arms and looked up at the sky. Heavy silver clouds swirled over the moon, illuminated by its glow.

Marika started across the street toward Luigi's, but I stayed transfixed, looking up at the sky.

She turned back. "You okay?"

I grabbed her arm and pulled her into the alley.

"I need your help," I whispered.

I glanced over my shoulder, remembering Finley and Cardinal's claims of being followed. It was probably crazy for us to talk out in the open, but another voice told me it didn't matter. Whether we were inside or outside, above ground or hiding in a tunnel, it seemed that someone was always listening.

I lowered my voice. "I got a weird call on Sunday. It was Finley Duggan, remember he used to work with Cardinal? We met up yesterday morning and..."

"Wait, you're still working on the Y Factor? You know it's been banned. And what are you doing, talking about this out here?"

Marika glanced around anxiously. I'd never seen her so afraid.

"Just listen," I said. "We're probably safer out here than anywhere inside."

I quickly filled her in on the events of the last few days. Marika chewed her lower lip as I talked, and her dark, worried expression instantly brought back my fears. Once upon a time, I'd have felt unbalanced and out of control by the horrible "what if" scenarios. But Finley's revelations had shown me a glimpse of something far bigger than myself, and I could no longer just go along for the ride.

"We're so close to finding out the truth," I told Marika. "We just need to fact check Finley's claims and talk to the woman from Ganta. Will you help?"

Marika turned away and paced the alley, massaging the left side of her neck the way she did when she'd spent too many hours working. She'd strained a neck muscle years ago when she slipped getting out of the shower, and the injury flared up whenever she was stressed or anxious. When she finally walked back to me, her neck was streaked with angry red marks.

"Charley, I don't know how to say this gently, so I'm just

going to say it. I think Frida's right. Whatever you think you can find by finishing this story...I just don't think it's worth it. It's too dangerous. Your dad wouldn't have wanted you to get yourself killed over this."

"I don't think I have a choice, Marika. I wish I could explain it, but I can't *not* do this. I owe it to my dad to finish what he started. I guess I can see why you wouldn't understand."

Marika's eyes flashed with anger and I instantly realized my mistake.

"Oh, so I don't understand because he wasn't my dad?" she snapped. "It still hurt to see him die, you know. And I'm *very* familiar with how it feels to watch people I love disappear from my life."

She crossed her arms and lifted an eyebrow.

"What's *that* supposed to mean?" I asked defensively.

The marks on her neck had spread. Flaming blotches now covered her skin like poison oak. Somewhere in the distance, a siren screamed. I peered down the empty alleyway and remembered the students blipping away after Taekwondo, like fragile bugs swatted away by an invisible force.

Marika replied, "It means this isn't the first time you've been swept away by some charmer and forgotten all about your friends. And who's there to pick up the pieces when your heart gets broken? I'm sick of it. What do you really know about David, anyway? More importantly: when will you learn you don't need a man to make you whole?"

A rumbling came from above. I glanced up to see a jet soaring overhead, a rare sight since the travel shutdowns. Its red taillight flashed like a warning. But it was too late for warnings, too late for apologies. Marika and I stood just a few inches apart, yet the distance between us felt much wider. All the truths that had been hovering below the surface of our relationship were rising, cracking, splitting us apart. Couldn't we go back to our sparring match in the studio, when we were fighting but on the same side?

"I know a lot about him," I replied, my voice quivering. "You'd see that he's different if you didn't always push yourself away."

The night air stung my eyes, yanking tears from my body as if I'd been chopping onions. This was the side of Marika I hated. Jealousy and fear made her strike out, try to hurt those around her before they could hurt her.

My Surge vibrated. I expected it to be David but it was the hospital. I frowned. Doctors didn't call on Monday evenings to talk about arms that were already healed.

"I have to take this," I replied, grateful for the distraction. I turned away from Marika to face the brick wall and answered.

"This is Charley Tennyson," I said in my work voice.

"Hello, Ms. Tennyson. This is Doctor Morrison from Duke University Hospital. Do you have a moment?"

"Yes, is everything okay?"

Something like a prayer floated into my mind. *Please let me be okay.* I flexed my fingers, hyper-focused on my heartbeat, my breath, my tiny body that was no more than a speck of dust.

Doctor Morrison continued, "Your bloodwork came back from the lab, Ms. Tennyson. Your blood glucose, calcium, and electrolyte levels all look ideal. However, we detected elevated levels of hCG in your blood."

"What does that mean?" I asked.

She paused before answering. "You appear to be about six weeks pregnant."

On the list of things I'd expected her to say, that was at the very bottom.

Her nasally voice asked, "Do you recall when your last menstrual period was?"

"No," I said.

And now that word was echoing through my head: no, no, no. I wanted to stop the world and rewind, run backwards through my argument with Marika, the lizard on my porch, the revelations from Finley, storming out of Frida's office—all of it. I wanted to go back to the moment David and I had decided male birth control would be good enough, back to the moment this spark of life had been lit inside my body. We weren't ready to become parents together. We were just beginning our relationship, hadn't even said "I love you."

I blinked. Doctor Morrison was still talking.

"You'll need to come in to take a Sequenom test. The new statute allows you one week. For your convenience, we've added a reminder to your calendar."

My Surge vibrated and a message appeared: *Complete Sequenom test within 7 days.*

I looked up at the stars. They swam around me in a swirl of chaos, as if a mysterious hand had plucked a snowglobe from the shelf and given it a careless shake. I could do nothing but press my open hands against the curved sides of the dome, outlining invisible boundaries like a mime stuck in a box.

My stomach turned and my mouth filled with saliva. I hung up and bent at the waist as nausea rose in my gut. I felt eyes on me and jolted up, spun around. Marika would know what to do, I'd run to her with open arms and apologies. But she was gone. I was alone in the dark alley.

A gust of wind sent a pile of leaves swirling. I put a hand on my abdomen and poked with my fingers, searching for signs of swelling and growth.

Fear poked back.

CHAPTER TWENTY-ONE

I PLODDED into my kitchen and dropped a box of steaming spaghetti in the trash compactor. The aroma of rich marinara and meatballs rose up and sent nausea swirling through my gut. After the doctor's call, I'd gone into Luigi's to find Marika, peering into one empty booth pod after another. The entire restaurant was empty. It was probably just a matter of days before they shut down too.

David had called three times in the last hour, but I'd ignored it. How could I tell him I was pregnant? What if Marika was right and he turned out to be like the selfish jerks I'd dated in the past? I considered an emergency session with my VT, but I didn't want to talk to her either. I just wanted to crawl in bed and close my eyes, forget that all of this was happening.

The buzzer at the front door sounded. Vanessa announced, "David Vine is here to see you, Charley. Would you like me to grant access?"

"Show me outside," I instructed, not bothering to say please.

A hologram of the exterior appeared. David paced back and forth, head down, shoulders tight and hunched. I felt a flash of guilt—he'd probably been worried when I hadn't answered his calls. What if David and I *could* find a happily ever after? It would simply be three of us instead of two. We'd move to a Haven, raise the baby together, leave behind investigations and conspiracy theories. Hope sparked in my heart as I imagined giving birth to his baby, starting a new life together. Maybe we could even change the world.

"Grant access," I told Vanessa.

I slipped into the bathroom to clean myself up. After sweating my butt off at Taekwondo and then sobbing for hours, I was a wreck. I splashed cold water on my face, dropped whitening potion in my eyes, and yanked open the drawer where I kept my makeup. If only Gravitas were there.

I heard the front door slide open and shut.

"Sorry I missed your calls!" I hollered. "Be out in a second."

I quickly swept foundation, powder, and blush across my face, trading lipstick for a few strokes of honey-flavored Chapstick. I decided not to tell him about the baby—not yet. I'd wait until after my Sequenom test, when there was no chance of a mistake. For now, I'd just hold him and kiss him and forget about the world. Everything would be okay.

I stepped back and looked in the mirror. I wasn't a miracle-worker like Gravitas, but it was definitely an improvement. I swiped deodorant under my armpits, slathered vanilla-scented lotion on my skin, and slid open the bathroom door.

David was hunched on the couch, his face buried in his hands.

I curled up next to him and kissed his cheek. "Sorry if I worried you," I said.

He didn't look up.

"Are you okay?" I asked.

His shoulders heaved with a deep breath. He looked at me with bloodshot eyes, red face streaked with tears.

"Oh my God, what's wrong?" I asked. But the truth was, I didn't want to hear the answer. I was so tired of hearing about all the things that were wrong. I just wanted to stop the world and get off.

David held my gaze and said, "I haven't been honest with you, Charley."

Shhhh. Keep it to yourself, I don't want to hear.

His voice was monotone and faraway. "You deserve someone better, someone less dangerous. I think I should go away for a while."

"What do you mean, someone better? I don't think there's anyone better than you, David Vine."

I reached over and rubbed his knee, tried to make him smile. He slid his leg away.

"I'm part of a crazy, messed up world, Charley."

"Aren't we all?"

He sighed. "Just let me get through this. Me starting at the Verge wasn't an accident. I was on assignment. I was supposed to connect with you, convince you to help us with the Y Factor. My mom orchestrated the whole thing."

"Your mom?" I echoed.

He nodded. "Vanyala Dawson."

An image of the FBI's most wanted list flashed in my mind.

"Vanyala is your *mom*? Why didn't you tell me?"

He shrugged. "I was scared. I didn't know what you'd do. Didn't want to risk messing this up."

"Does anyone know?" I asked.

He nodded. "Frida found out a while ago. She actually...hit on me afterward. Told me if I went along with what she wanted, it could be our little secret. I refused, of course. Now she says my time's up, and she's ready to go public."

"She did *what?* David, that's sexual harassment and blackmail! We won't let her get away with this. I understand why you didn't tell me about your mom. It's okay."

I took his hand. He looked down and clasped his fingers around mine, then ran his thumb over the delicate skin on the dorsal side of my hand. I watched him trace the veins and metacarpals, my thin flesh crinkling like scritta paper.

He let go of my hand. "There's more," he whispered.

My heart pounded as if I were running the final stretch of a race. My arm ached, my knees ached, my lungs spasmed and squeezed. The final bend was just ahead but I couldn't possibly leap over one more hurdle. And yet we raced on.

He choked out the next words. "It wasn't just a boy who killed my wife. It was *our* boy. Beckett."

David's voice was quaky as he continued. "He was such a good kid. He was quiet, sweet, loved to play with blocks and Legos. Instead of building things, he'd sort his toys by color and line them up. A line of blue, a line of green, a line of red. He loved organizing and finding patterns, would spend hours focused on puzzles and interlocking toys. I remember thinking he'd be a scientist when he got older, or maybe an engineer. He'd dissect things too—flowers, Surges, remote controls—just take them apart piece by piece to see how they worked. He was smart, patient, very focused."

He continued, "You're probably wondering why I'm telling you that part. But here's the thing. When these attacks happen, people look at the boys and think they're monsters. They wonder: how could the parents not see? How could they not know? Trust me, I ask myself all these questions too. They haunt me every day and night."

I thought back to how I'd felt after my dad was killed. He was right. I'd thought of the sniper at the marathon as an absolute monster. I couldn't begin to imagine the agony a parent must feel when their own child turned out to be a killer. The guilt they must carry—wishing they'd seen a sign, that they'd done something, anything, differently.

David avoided my gaze. His eyes flickered up and to the left as if retrieving files and data from his brain. I knew he had to get all the memories out, the good and the bad.

He continued, "The day it happened, I knew something was wrong. I woke up with this feeling in my gut, like something wasn't right. But he seemed fine, everything seemed fine. I made breakfast for him and Stefania: birds in a nest, their favorite. I'll never forget cracking the eggs, flipping over the bread, watching it become a buttery brown. I couldn't eat because I felt so queasy. I thought I was getting sick, blamed it on stress at work. Back then, I was an accountant. Can you believe that? It was tax season and I was hating life. What the hell did I know about real problems? I was so stupid, so naïve."

I didn't want to hear the rest, but I knew he had to tell me, had to get it out. It was like watching a horror movie. *Don't go up the stairs*, I wanted to tell the character. *Run out the front door, find a phone.* But of course, some stories just have to play out. We can't change the ending, no matter how desperately we want to.

"I went into the office downtown. I remember Stefania not wanting me to go. She'd been trying to get me to work from home, but I couldn't bring myself to do it. I liked being around people—the energy, the idea of having somewhere to go. I always felt like working from home was giving up. Giving into the fear."

I nodded in understanding. My dad had been the same way, no matter how hard my mom had tried to get him to stay home. It was weird to imagine David with his wife—Stefania— and their son. I wondered what they were like together. They sounded like an ordinary family. Busy and stressed, but happy and in love. At least, that's the picture I painted in my mind. I wondered what picture David had painted in his—if he could still see a happy family or if his memories had been tainted with the knowledge of how it all ended.

"I still wonder if things would have been different if I'd listened to her," he said, eyes glistening with tears. "If I'd been at home, I could have stopped him. I could have saved both of them from all this. I could have..." His face crumpled and he buried his head in his hands.

"It's not your fault," I whispered, but I knew they were only words. People had said those same words to me a million times and I'd never believed them. Instead, I'd tortured myself with "what ifs" and "should haves," replaying the day my dad had been shot over and over in my head. If only I'd run faster, or slower, or said no to the race, or let him sign us up for the early wave, or...

David continued, "That day was the most horrible thing I'll ever live through. I lost everything in an instant. I came home to find Stefania lying dead in the living room. I assumed it was an intruder, that someone snuck in and killed her. I raced around the house calling for Beckett, steeling myself for the moment I'd find him dead too. But he was gone. Even after the police uncovered the truth, it took me months to believe it. Then the nightmares started—recurring dreams that I came home five minutes earlier and stopped Beckett in time."

"Where is your son now?" I asked.

"I don't know. He disappeared. I looked for him for years, even though I had no clue how I'd face him once I found him. My heart told me he probably committed suicide, but now I can't help but wonder if he's in government custody somewhere. Just another lab rat in someone's MPV research."

Word by word, the happily ever after I'd imagined for us slipped away. Between Vanyala and Beckett, David would never be safe to live out his life in peace. And that meant *we'd* never be safe. Having his baby and loving him would mean accepting all of it—his past, his family, his secrets, the danger of being found out at any moment.

It also meant David had the Warrior Gene in his blood. Was he just a ticking time bomb too? How could I step into the world he'd described? Worse, how could I bring an innocent baby into it? She wouldn't be an ordinary little girl. She'd be Vanyala Dawson's grandchild, a killer's sister, and who knew what else? We'd be stuck in a crazy world of fear, fighting, and secrets forever.

David let go of my hand. "These last few months have been wonderful, but I can't pull you into all this. I've been feeling so angry lately. It's like water simmering on a stove. For a long time, my grief had an outlet: finding answers, uncovering a reason for the attacks. Now that we know the truth, I'm angrier than ever. I don't know what I might do. You deserve better than this, better than me."

He stood up. I told myself to stand, too. I should confess that I felt just as angry as he did, furious at the people who had ruined our lives and our world. I should tell him about the baby, ask him not to go, take his hand and assure him that everything would be okay. But I didn't believe it anymore. Reality seemed like nothing more than smoke and mirrors. How could anything be okay ever again?

David turned and walked to the door. I sat and watched him go. He didn't look back, just slipped outside and was gone. I stared at the closed door and imagined him on the other side, open fingers resting on the red wood, searching for a crack in the barrier between us.

I wandered into the kitchen and looked at the wine in the cabinet. The smell of Luigi's wafted up from the garbage and I put a hand to my mouth, reminded of the life forming in my belly. I swallowed and rushed the bathroom. The nausea passed and I stared at the empty bathtub and relaxation crystals. My normal rituals felt pointless and wrong, yet I needed something, anything, to soothe the chaos that was swirling inside me.

I went to the study and pulled my dad's book from the shelf. I flipped it open, traced the shadow of the man in the drawing, heard my dad's voice.

We're going on a bear hunt. I'm not scared.

My tears dropped onto the page like rain, reality and stories blurring into one. Instead of echoing the refrain, my heart whimpered with the truth.

But I AM scared, Daddy, and there's no one here to protect me.

A voice came back, sudden and clear:

My child, you are not alone.

Suddenly I felt eyes on me. The book fell from my hands and I sank to my knees. My shaking hands were pushed together by a strange force, something bigger and far more powerful than me. It was beautiful, mysterious, infinite, undeniable. Suddenly it all made sense. It was all connected, every moment since my first breath. I saw a glimpse of the underside of the tapestry, the tangled jumble necessary to weave the art on the other side. Everything was a mess, but it was a beautiful mess.

I sobbed and gasped for air, feeling smothered. The reality was so clear, I thought it might be my final breath. And then I closed my eyes and did something I never thought I'd do again.

I prayed.

CHAPTER TWENTY-TWO

For two days, I hid from the world. Morning sickness marched in as if summoned by the pinchy-faced Lizard Woman. No one told me pregnancy nausea worked around the clock, but it left me kneeling at the toilet all hours of the day and night.

At least it stopped my mind from whirling. When I wasn't vomiting, I was lying awake in bed, sweating, tossing, turning, coughing with some new sickness that had seized hold of my lungs. I heard voices, felt eyes on me, couldn't tell what was real and what was a sleep-deprived hallucination. My mind spun out one horrible scenario after another on the ceiling. I contemplated abortion, adoption, poverty, homelessness, a psychiatric institution, sleeping pills—anything to stop the fear and pain.

Finally, the sickness broke and I stood, shaking, to see who was left in the mirror. I leaned close to my reflection, fogged the glass with my sour breath and wiped it clean. The familiar eyes of a sad little girl looked back. I splashed cold water on my face, sucked it in and swallowed it in desperate, heaving gulps.

Memories flickered before me: a child scrubbing dark makeup from her face, her best friend beside her, being silly to make her laugh.

It was time to swallow my pride and use a lifeline.

Marika answered on the first ring. "Charley! Are you okay? My God, I've been so worried about you."

"I'm pregnant," I blurted out. "And David left me."

"What? Take a deep breath. I'm here."

I sat on the bathroom floor, curled my knees into my chest, and told her everything. She listened as I rambled, made sense of my babbling, and confidently assured me that—somehow, some way—everything would be okay.

"Can I come over?" I asked. After days holed up in my studio alone, I was desperate to escape. Everywhere I looked was another painful memory or hallucination.

"Of course. I'll be right here waiting for you."

By the time I got to Marika's, the sun was setting. It had been two days since our fight after Taekwondo. Two days since I'd found out I was pregnant. Two days since David had confessed his secrets and walked out the door. How could my entire life break apart in two short days? I thought back to the ticking of the clock at the hospital the day my dad had died, the smell of burned coffee. The reality was, it could all fall apart in two seconds.

I pressed my finger to the identification pad on Marika's front door. A green light flashed and a comforting 'ding' chimed.

"Welcome back, Charley," a warm, feminine voice said.

I stepped inside and was greeted by the smell of chocolate chip cookies.

"Hello?" I called out.

"I'll be right there!" Marika called from the kitchen. "Sit down, relax, have a cookie! I'm making you some tea."

I took off my vest and hung it on a bungee, then dragged myself into the living room. Anxiety had joined my morning sickness and exhaustion, leaving me sleep-deprived and possibly hallucinating. I curled up on the big gray sectional couch and tucked my legs under me. A plate of fresh-baked chocolate chip cookies sat on the table. I snatched one up and took a delicious, gooey bite, closing my eyes to savor its sweet, simple bliss.

And then I was in the kitchen with my mom, baking cookies. I'd always loved the part when I got to sprinkle white sugar atop the lump of brown sugar. I'd shake it gently, pretending it was snow covering a mountain. I always made her crack the eggs, terrified that a stray eggshell would ruin the whole batch. As soon as she turned to put the eggs back in the refrigerator, I'd sneak a hunk of raw dough, ignoring her warnings of salmonella.

"Since when do you bake cookies?" I hollered to Marika, my mouth full of heaven.

"It was wine night with the ladies!" Marika called back. "Gloriana brought them. Aren't they delicious? You can't even tell it's not real chocolate!"

She entered the living room, full glass of wine in one hand, mug of steaming hot tea in the other. She looked casually beautiful, sporting her favorite red tank top and black joggers. She took a big sip of wine and I gazed with envy, imagining how the alcohol would numb everything that hurt. Maybe I could have just one glass to take the edge off. What could one little glass of wine really hurt?

Marika set a white mug of steaming hot tea on the table in front of me. I spun it around to grab the handle and realized it was my Christmas gift to her three years ago. A female silhouette sat cross-legged, hands clasped in prayer. Above her head, scrawled in rugged black script, was the phrase "Namaste, bitches!"

I lifted it to my lips and sipped, but the tea was blistering hot. I set it back down.

"How are you feeling?" Marika asked, rubbing my knee.

I sighed. "It's hard to tell if I'm puking my guts out because I'm pregnant or because my life is falling apart. I might be going crazy or dying."

"Your life is *not* falling apart, and you're not crazy or dying. We've been through worse, and we'll get through this just fine."

She pulled me into a hug and squeezed tight. I hugged her back. The pressure of her embrace made the weak and broken parts inside me tremble like an aftershock, land settling after the big quake.

Marika placed her hands on the sides of my face, forcing me to look her in the eye.

"Charley, everything will be okay. You're not alone. You always have me."

"I know. You're the only person I can trust. I hate it when we fight."

She gave me a soft smile. "I was being an idiot. I just get so protective of you—and of myself too. I think I was just scared."

"Scared of what?" I asked.

She shrugged. "The story, partially, and how dangerous it's become. But more than that—losing you. I guess I was jealous. I hated the idea of you going off and being happy with someone else, and me being alone."

"Are you kidding me? Even if David hadn't turned out to be a liar, that would never happen. You're stuck with me, whether you like it or not."

She laughed and picked up her wine glass, swirling the red liquid before taking a big gulp. "Maybe we just say screw it and move to a Haven. Do yoga, enjoy a controlled climate, raise the baby together."

Her words were slurred, her lips and teeth stained red. My gaze wandered to the glass of wine and she gave a sloppy shrug.

"I may have had a couple glasses before you got here. It was wine night."

"You're such a lightweight," I teased. "And I'm so jealous of that wine right now, you have no idea."

"Well suck it up, buttercup, because I'm about to open another bottle."

I laughed. "One of us may as well enjoy the evening."

She stumbled back to the kitchen and an explosion of clangs and clammers erupted. I grabbed the fuzzy gray afghan from the back of the couch and wrapped it around me like a shawl. I wanted to pretend it was just another ordinary night. That we were hanging out, watching old romantic comedies, gossiping about the characters and drooling over handsome actors. How many times had we done just that? I always fell asleep long before the final credits rolled, sometimes just a few minutes into the show. David always teased me about it too.

Marika came back from the kitchen with a fresh bottle of wine and a plate piled high with cheese, crackers, and salami. She held the wine bottle by the neck and brought it toward the table, making two wobbly misses before landing the fat bottom with a solid *thud*.

"Can we watch a movie tonight?" I asked. "Something funny."

"YES! A movie. Want some crackers?"

She held the plate out to me. Crumbs clung to the corner of her lips and she plopped a golden square into her already full mouth. The smell of red wine and chemicals hit me. Nausea rose in my stomach and I clutched a hand to my mouth. I imagined the tiny embryo inside my belly, a swirl of mysterious cells, waving a hand as if to say: don't you forget about me. I picked up another cookie and gobbled it down, then licked the grease from my fingers and thumb.

Marika set the plate on the table and sank down next to me on the couch. "We were talking at wine night about men becoming extinct. It's all so crazy! And then I started thinking about us. The way we connect. How good I feel when I'm with you. It's like I can let my guard down, just be totally myself."

I smiled, remembering us locking pinkies as seven-year-olds, becoming blood sisters as crazy teens. "Best friends forever!" we sang. That was before we knew that forever didn't always work out the way we'd planned.

Marika chewed her lip and scrunched her face. "What if this is all we need? The hell with the rest of it. The hell with David, the story, everyone. We'll raise the baby together. We can be a family."

"What do you mean?" I asked.

Marika grabbed my hand and squeezed it. Her hand was soft like the cookie—comforting, warm, familiar. She ran the tips of her nails over my skin in the softest and tickliest of touches. Goosebumps sprang up on my arm.

"Just think about how good we would be together, Charley. We can't trust anyone the way we can trust each other. All the women at wine night were saying, if men go extinct, this is our future. Why not just embrace it now?"

I looked down at her red fingernails caressing my skin. My stomach was uneasy and restless, like when I was hungover and couldn't tell if I was hungry or full. I felt like I was sitting next to a stranger, like I'd been plunged into some alternate reality. The news was reporting an increase in same-sex marriages since the phenomenon began, though no one had been able to pin down the correlation. Was Marika's offer based on a genuine feeling or was it simply a new identity to explore and play with, a costume to try on and see how it fit?

My palms began to sweat. I yawned and stretched, a casual excuse to pull my hand away.

"What else did the women say?" I asked.

"It was a fascinating discussion. Gloriana said sexuality isn't like, you're straight or you're gay. It's not that black and white. It's about love. Connection. Intimacy. What the End of Men is making us all realize is that gender is incidental. What matters is people. Souls. No matter what it's wrapped up in, love is love."

I tried to imagine what it might be like, her and I together. But as her words echoed through me—*love is love*—David flashed in my mind. I remembered how good I'd felt when he held me in his arms, opened the door for me, took care of me, called me darling. It was different from when Marika took care of me. They were both love, and maybe on the face of it they were the same, but the underbelly was different.

I nodded. "I do love you, and in a lot of ways, we *are* going to raise this baby together. But I don't think about romantic love like that. I think about love and I think about..."

My voice trailed off. I didn't want to hurt her.

"David," she said.

"Yes. I don't know if we'll end up together, but what I felt for him—what I *feel* for him—it's still there. And he's this baby's father. I can't just run away with you and rob my daughter of the gift of her dad."

A distance wedged itself onto the couch between us, a heavy silence that felt mysterious and uncrossable. I'd always thought I knew Marika as well as I knew myself, yet I hadn't seen any of this coming. How long had she been feeling this way? Was this why she'd exploded the way she had in the alley? Or was all of it just a reaction to what was happening in the world?

"Do you want to watch a movie?" I asked hopefully.

She smiled but it didn't reach her eyes. "I had way too much wine, I might just go to bed. I'll get you a pillow and put on a show."

She stood up and turned away.

"Marika, I'm sorry."

She turned back and swatted a hand. "You have nothing to apologize for. We'll be okay. And if David doesn't realize how lucky he is to have you, he's an idiot."

She brought me a pillow, tucked me in, and turned on the old 1990s version of Romeo and Juliet.

"Sweet dreams," she said, and kissed my forehead.

I watched the movie and cried my eyes out. It all unfolded just like I knew it would—love torn apart because of different families and backgrounds. How could it end in anything but tragedy?

The credits rolled and sleep still hadn't come. I flicked on the Hub, flipping through streams until I spotted Hatcher. A caption at the bottom of the screen informed me it was the replay of an emergency briefing she'd issued earlier. She stood behind a podium in front of a new purple and gold curtain. The Great Seal of the United States was nowhere to be seen. My stomach turned at the sight of her face, but I expanded the screen anyway, too curious not to watch.

Her hair was swept back in a classy updo and sparkling diamond earrings dangled down her neck.

"In light of recent events in which certain members of the media have abused their rights, this administration has decided to establish a Department of Truth," she stated. "This group of highly esteemed individuals shall take on the critical task of monitoring communications and censoring those which are inconsistent with what we believe to be true. Congress shall also introduce legislation authorizing the National Security Agency to monitor communications of known criminal organizations and terrorist organizations. The Department of Truth will be given access to a highly secured database created by the NSA in order to perform monitoring for certain keywords and flag individuals and organizations who are in violation of true reporting."

Hatcher folded her hands and leaned forward, her lips curved upward in a smirk. "The Fear Fighters are hereby declared to be a Civil Terrorist Organization. Vanyala Dawson, Fear Fighters, consider this your final warning. Cease your unlawful activities or expect to be prosecuted to the full extent of the law."

I flipped off the Hub and sat in shock. Just when I thought things couldn't get any worse, they did. She'd mentioned 'certain members of the media' who had abused their rights. Was this because of me and what I'd done at the panel? Had I actually made things worse and put David and the Fear Fighters in even greater danger than they'd been in before?

I shoved three more cookies in my face and polished off the plate of cheese and crackers. None of it soothed the turbulence inside. Finally I stood up and walked to the entry, pulled my vest off the bungee, and tugged it on. I zipped it as high as it would go, then walked out the door into the night. I had no idea where I was going or what I'd do, I just knew I couldn't sit there alone.

Sirens wailed in the distance, but they seemed part of another world, someone else's problem to fix. The air was heavy and wet, streets spotted with puddles. When I was a kid, I used to love splashing in them, kicking the water so it splashed my calves and sprang through the air. I used to run, jump, climb, splash, leap, and twirl. When did I stop? Was it the world that had changed or just me? I wished again we could go backward, undo all the mistakes, heal all the wounds.

A puddle sparkled in the moonlight and I stomped into it. My mother's voice rose up: *Don't get your shoes wet.*

I stood in the cold water, feet immersed, and looked up at the cloudy dark sky. A star glistened in the north, one brighter than the others. I put a hand on my stomach, felt a tug toward something magical, true, and infinite. It was time to use my final lifeline.

CHAPTER TWENTY-THREE

I LIFTED my hand to knock on my mother's majestic arched entry door. It was made of aged bronze and double-glazed iron, with intricately carved lines of sunflowers along the edges.

Traveling to Vista Haven had been surreal; everything they showed in the commercials was true. It was a glistening Utopia overflowing with lush green plants, gorgeous flowers, rolling vistas, and manmade rivers and waterfalls—all nestled in a bulletproof dome with a perfectly controlled climate. The top of the dome was a technological miracle, conveying ever-changing imagery that looked just like a real sky.

I knocked three times and looked up. White clouds floated across a sea of turquoise blue, shifting and changing shape as if brushed by the wind.

My mother swung the door inward, smiling. My breath caught in my chest at the sight of her. She'd somehow grown more beautiful in the four months since I'd seen her. Her skin looked more relaxed, her blue eyes happier, her silvery ash blonde hair shinier.

"Charley! What a wonderful surprise. You should have told

me you were coming, I would have baked pumpkin bread or made a fresh pot of stew!"

"Can I come in?"

She stepped backward and opened her arms in a sweeping gesture. "Of course! Think of this as your home."

I stepped inside and gazed around at the grand entry. It was like no home I'd ever known. The sweeping ceilings were vast and endless, the dark wood floor gleamed and glistened. An elegant spiral staircase with glass railings twirled up toward a bright second floor with skylights and rows of tall windows. Wood trim and abstract oil paintings accented the white walls. A spiral raindrop crystal chandelier hung behind my mother's head, ready to illuminate the space once night came.

"It's beautiful, Mom."

She smiled and waved a hand. "It's coming along. Come in, I'll show you around."

We walked through the foyer and down a wide open hallway. Windows and light were everywhere, bringing in so much sunshine and greenery that it didn't even feel like we were inside. A pale pink runner softened our steps. The left side of the hallway was a stylish wall-length aquarium, where beautiful fish of all shapes and sizes swam amidst streams of bubbles and chunks of multi-colored coral.

The hallway ended at a beautiful chef's kitchen. The dazzling open space had granite countertops, light wood paneling, and a huge island at the center. I ran my hand across the granite and admired the glimmer of the double stove, the sparkle of the copper cookware dangling from a bronze pot rack.

My mother motioned to three brown leather stools at the island.

"Sit down, make yourself at home!"

I perched on the outside stool and rested my elbows on the counter, then sunk my head into my hands.

I expected her to ask what was wrong, but instead she walked around the island so she was directly across from me. She leaned down on her elbows and tipped my chin up with a gentle touch, encouraging me to look up and meet her eyes. I did, and was even more surprised by what I saw. Her eyes sparkled and she looked more girlish than I'd ever seen her, even back when my dad was alive. The anxious, fearful woman I remembered had been replaced by someone light, bright, and full of energy.

"Would you like a glass of champagne?" she asked.

I shook my head and my face crumbled. "I can't. I'm pregnant."

Her face lit up and she clasped her hands together. "Oh, honey! That's amazing!"

She came back around the island and pulled me to my feet, wrapped me in a giant hug, then stood back and placed a hand on my belly.

"How far along are you? Did the morning sickness start yet? Mine was absolutely horrific. But you were worth it."

The joy on her face was heartbreaking. Everything I'd been trying to hold together fell apart and I started crying.

"It's all a mess, Mom. Me, my life, the world. I don't know what to do."

She pulled me to her. "Oh, honey. Come here. Shhhhh."

We stood in the kitchen, her holding me as I sobbed, and I braced myself for what I knew was coming: *Just stay here with me at Vista Haven, it's so beautiful and serene.* But she surprised me again. She brushed my hair from my forehead and gently wiped the tears from my cheeks.

"My darling, you are *not* a mess. You're the furthest thing from it. I was watching you lead that panel discussion the other day, and all I could think of was how proud your father would have been. You've grown up to be just like him, you know. Strong, brave, determined."

I wiped tears from my face. "You think I'm brave?

"You've always been that way. Do you remember when you were five and had surgery for your umbilical hernia?" she asked.

"I remember I got to eat a lot of ice cream."

She laughed. "Well, yes, there was that. But what I remember is that within hours of coming home from the hospital, you were bounding around the house. I had the same surgery when I was a kid and I stayed in bed for a week, crying from the pain, barely able to turn over onto my side. But you—somehow, you recovered almost instantly."

"I think I do remember that. You kept chasing me around the house, trying to get me to go back to bed."

"Exactly, but you wouldn't have it. You had games to play, forts to build. You've always been like that, ready to take on the world. And I've always been the way I am—scared of things beyond my comfort zone."

I sighed, exhaling the worry that had coiled inside me like a snake. "You know, Mom, we're not as different as you think. I'm scared out of my mind ninety-nine percent of the time."

She laughed. "That's the bravest kind of person, honey. The one who feels the fear and does it anyway. You're like one of those people on the Hub, those Fear Fighters. Not everyone has that kind of strength, you know."

I sat in stunned silence, pride cracking through my despair. My mom saw me in a completely different light than I'd imagined. She reached over and took my hand.

"Come with me, let's go sit in the study. I was just going through some of your father's things."

I followed her down another beautiful light-filled hallway

and into a cozy room toward the back of the house. It sparkled with floor-to-ceiling windows and a set of French doors that were flung open to let the fresh air in. A rock courtyard with a waterfall was just outside, surrounded by a flowing river and vistas of rolling green hills.

My mother knelt in front of a wood-burning fireplace, then swung her legs around into a cross-legged position. I plopped down next to her and ran a hand through the silky fibers of the white shag rug. The heat of the fire immediately warmed my cheeks and I leaned in, basking in the glow. She pulled a thick photo album from a pile and flipped it open.

"Your father insisted we print all our pictures instead of keeping them as digital libraries. I always complained about the space these big boxes took up, but now I see how wise it was."

She pointed to a picture of me and my dad standing in our old backyard in Boulder, Colorado. It was back before the Great Separation—before the west had burned and the nation had split apart, before we'd traded our beautiful mountain life for a secured apartment building on the East Coast.

"Remember that time you broke your ankle racing to the fence?" she asked.

I laughed. "That damn bone still hurts every morning."

I gazed down at the photo and traced a finger over my dad's face, then my own. The flatirons rose up behind us and we were leaning on an old wooden fence that served as the only divider between our backyard and miles of open space. My dad and I had raced through that field every weekend for years.

On the day I'd broken my ankle, I was winning—for the first time ever. Just before I got to the fence, I stepped in a hole and felt a snap. As I'd reached forward to brace my fall, my hands had scraped against the wooden fence, palms filling with splinters. I'd landed on the ground bleeding, broken, and fighting to hold back tears. Over the following weeks, I'd been fascinated to watch the cuts and scrapes in my skin heal as my broken bone healed under my cast.

My fingers trailed to the bullet wound on my shoulder. Whether it was a hole in my flesh, scraped palms, or a broken bone, my body had always found a way to heal. I wondered if the heart worked the same way, or if some wounds were too deep.

"I miss that house," I said wistfully. "That life, that world."

"Me too, honey. It was so quiet and peaceful. Something about the city just never felt like home to me. It was always too big and scary. Unfortunately, I think I passed a lot of my fears on to you when you were growing up."

I shrugged. "I think I'd have been scared either way. Being brave came naturally to Dad, but I always had to push for it."

"And push, you did. You might feel like everything's a mess and nothing will ever be okay again, but it will be. You will be just fine. That's how life is. We rise, we struggle, we fall, we rise again."

Tears sprang to my eyes. We'd never talked like this before. Why did everything have to fall apart for us to find a way to come together?

I took a deep, shaky breath. "I'm so scared, Mom. I can't even fathom having a baby right now. Especially in this world. I have no clue how to be a mother."

She glanced down at my belly and her eyes glimmered with excitement. "That's how every new mother has felt, honey, ever since the beginning of time. You'll figure it out. Sometimes you'll feel like it's enough; other times you'll feel like a failure. But I have a feeling you will be wonderful—much better than I ever was."

"You were a great mom," I said.

She laughed. "I know I wasn't the kind of mother you wanted me to be. I was always so torn between encouraging you to follow your dreams and wanting to keep you safe under my wing forever."

We sat in silence and for once, there wasn't an empty void between us. I realized we all just wanted the same thing in life: to feel safe. Some found safety in hiding from the world's violence and pain. They avoided risk, pulled their loved ones close, did whatever they could to shield them from harm. Some found safety in a bottle of wine, a bowl of pasta, a hot bath after a long day. Some found it in protesting injustice and fighting to change things. Some found it in love. Once upon a time, I'd found it in my dad. And my mom, she'd found it in me.

I saw us as if from above, then, two women sitting by a fire, trying to find their way back together after months and years of unspoken hurts. I rested my hand on my stomach, imagined the seed of life growing within. Could becoming a mother help me become the woman I'd always longed to be?

I pulled another album toward me and flipped through photos of my childhood. My mother's eyes had watched me grow from a baby to a young girl to a woman. Her hands had changed my diapers, cooked for me, bandaged my wounds. Her arms had cradled me, embraced me, and then reluctantly released me out into the world to find my own way.

I closed the album and reached for another one I'd never seen before. The outside was adorned in burgundy velvet and gold gilding.

"That's from your dad's college days," my mother said as I cracked it open. "We met just after he graduated. It's amazing to think back to that time. It was truly another world."

The pages felt ancient, thick plastic cracking and breaking. The inside cover bore my dad's handwriting: University of Colorado at Boulder. I flipped through it, amazed to see photos of my father as a young man. He was so handsome—tanned cheeks, buzzed haircut, dark eyebrows, bright eyes. I stopped at a photo of him sitting perched on a large gray boulder, a woman on each side of him.

My mother pointed to the woman on the right. "Recognize her?"

She did look vaguely familiar. I squinted, trying to place her.

"That's Elizabeth Hatcher," my mother said.

My mouth dropped open. "What? How did you guys forget to mention that Dad was friends with the President?"

"Your father swore me to secrecy. I never understood why, he refused to talk about it. He was very disturbed when she got elected, though—and became even more upset during her re-election campaign. He started working around the clock and researching everything he could about those Fear Fighters. I tried to give him space, but it was hard to watch him run himself ragged."

I delicately pulled the photo from its plastic encasing and clutched it to my chest, then leapt to my feet. "Mom, I have to go."

Disappointment splashed across her face. "You just got here! I want to hear about the baby and the lucky man who has your heart."

"I know, I'm so sorry. I promise I'll be back soon. I honestly thought I might stay here forever, but there's something I have to do first."

She climbed slowly to her feet, massaging her knees and circling her ankles as she stood.

"All right, then. Don't worry about me. I'll be here when you get back. Go save the world."

I hugged her and rushed to the front door, the corners of my mouth turning upward as I stepped outside. I stood on the doorstep and tapped my Surge to make a call. As I waited for an answer, I gazed up at the blue sky, searching for shapes in the puffy white clouds. I spotted a dragon, a sleeping baby with its thumb in its mouth, and a giant heart.

"Hello?" a voice answered.

"Mouse ears," I said, using the code phase Finley had provided.

It was time to solve this Great Mystery once and for all.

CHAPTER TWENTY-FOUR

WHEN I ARRIVED at the hospital, it was eerily quiet. David was already there at the security station, hands shoved in his pockets, shoulders slumped. He looked up as I approached, a flicker of hope flashing across his face.

I put a finger to my lips and jerked my head, motioning for him to follow me around the corner to the back of the building. At this point, I was certain that Cardinal and Finley were right. Someone was always listening. I'd gone home and dumped my Surge just in case, bringing only the jimmy-rigged device David had made to activate my Deflector Dot.

We stood against the brick wall and, for a second, I glimpsed a bird's eye view of what we must look like, two small people standing there, lost and alone, desperately wanting to find their way back together. The distance between us shrank, then, and the image of him as a threat to my safety wavered. It was no longer a solidified reality, just one of several possible views.

He asked, "Are you okay? I was surprised to hear from you."

I cleared my throat. "Before you say anything, I have a confession."

Concern flashed in his eyes.

I continued, "When you came over, I had just gotten some unexpected news myself. My doctor called me earlier that night."

His look of concern deepened. "The doctor? What's wrong, are you okay?"

"I'm okay, but...my blood tests discovered something unexpected. I'm pregnant."

Shock spread across his face. Then it slipped away, replaced by a smile. He impulsively grabbed me in a big hug, squeezing so tight I could barely breathe. I pushed him away.

"Hang on, David. I can't just forget about what happened. I understand how you lied in the beginning, but how could you not tell me the truth after that? After everything we went through together? Trust is the most important thing in a relationship. If we don't have that, we don't have anything. You have to be honest with me if we're going to have any shot at making this work."

"You're right. I'm so sorry. The longer it went on, the harder it got to tell you. I told myself I was protecting you, but that's no excuse. What can I do to prove that you can trust me again?"

I shrugged and looked down at my feet. The longer I looked into his eyes, the more I wanted things to be okay, to just forget everything and start over. But I had to balance logic with emotion, had to make sure I didn't get swept away again.

"How do you feel about the baby?" he asked.

I sighed. "Like throwing up. Not just from morning sickness, but all the emotion that goes along with it. It's so scary and surreal. How can we bring a sweet baby girl into this horrible world?"

"How can we not?" he asked.

I looked up and met his eyes. "How do *you* feel about the baby?" I whispered.

Waiting for him to respond, I felt like I was standing there naked. I could only control my part of the equation, put out my heart like an offering made from trembling hands.

"I feel like I want to whisk both of you away from all this. Let's just get a Haven, Charley. We'll raise her in a safe place, show her the love and beauty that's left in the world. I don't want my daughter growing up the way I did—scared, running, lying."

"That sounds wonderful. But first, we need to make sure the world knows the truth about Hatcher and the government's deception. Otherwise, you and your family will never be safe. *We'll* never be safe."

I opened my satchel and pulled out my dad's old college photo. "Look, that's my dad and that's Hatcher. They *knew* each other. I don't know the details yet, but this feels like a big thread we need to pull on."

David took the photo from me and his hand started to shake. He pointed to the other woman in the photo.

"Charley, that's my mom. Vanyala Dawson."

I snatched the photo back and looked at it in shock. "Well, now we've *definitely* got to see where this leads."

He nodded. "You're right. We'll go see my mom and put together the final pieces. Finish this thing once and for all."

"Deal. And remember the researcher Finley told us about, the one from Ganta? We're meeting her in the library in a few minutes."

"What *haven't* you thought of, Tennyson?" He laughed and shook his head, then reached an open hand toward me and bent at the knee in a chivalrous knight's gesture. "Shall we, then?"

I looked down at his hand, contemplating. I shook my head and turned.

"Follow me," I said.

I led the way to the medical center's library and archives, where I'd arranged for us to meet Finley's contact. Her name was Abigail Willington and she'd worked for Ganta throughout her medical studies and in the years afterward. I'd wanted to meet somewhere more private, but Abigail insisted no one ever used the library anymore and all the records we'd need were there. We walked quietly through the medical center's hallways toward the library, glancing furtively over behind us every few seconds.

"We'll be okay," David whispered again and again.

We entered the library and I looked around at the rows of shelves lined with books—real books, made of paper, such a beautiful and ancient thing. The library was empty and quiet and I imagined an old librarian with spectacles greeting us. *Shhhhh*, she'd say, raising a finger to her pursed and wrinkled lips.

Toward the back, a woman sat alone at one of the tables. Her shoulders were hunched, her head hung so low that her hair covered her face. She looked up as we approached and her hair fell away to reveal a pink birthmark splashed across her right cheek. She stood and motioned for us to follow her into one of the private study rooms.

We slipped inside the small space—a dark room with a rectangular birch table and two chairs on each side. She took the seat in the corner. David closed the door and we sat across from her, our knees touching beneath the tiny table.

"I'm Abigail," she said, pulling her hair across her cheek. I wondered how much of her life she'd spent trying to hide from her own face—ashamed of the birthmark that, in some regions, might identify her as a queen or a gifted sage.

She slid a thick manila folder toward us. "This should be everything you need. Hard copies, to prevent anything from being tracked."

I took the folder but refrained from opening it. Nothing this easy could be trusted.

"Why are you doing this?" I asked.

She tucked her hair behind her ear before immediately untucking it and pulling it back across her face.

"I worked at Ganta for five years, all through my medical studies and afterward. At first, it was thrilling—my dream job. We were doing research that truly mattered. Then, several years ago, things started changing. We got a new CEO who didn't follow guidelines. She started pushing the boundaries of our research and ignoring key points in the data. The things they're doing now...they're just not right."

Her eyes darted to David and she gave him a soft, sad smile. She pulled the folder back toward her and opened it, flipping through the pages until she found what she wanted. She turned it so we could see. It was a sketch of a homogenous lineup of blonde and brunette women with lithe bodies, warm smiles, and glowing skin and hair.

"This is what they want the future to be," she explained. "You know they've been mandating sperm donation, right? They've also been filtering and prioritizing the sperm to create the 'best' tomorrow. They're able to weed out genetic diseases and abnormalities, even some mental disorders, in favor of semen that will produce babies with positive, healthy traits. But they don't know where to stop. Who wants to live in a future like this, where everyone's the same? We can't just get rid of the things that make each person unique, judge a life for being 'less than.' That's not our call to make."

"It's very brave of you to come forward," I told her. "I'm sure you're already aware of how dangerous this is."

She nodded. "I finally had to accept that it would be dangerous whether I came forward or not. I don't know if you've heard the latest news, but Hatcher is beginning to order mandatory tests on all boys under eighteen. They're looking for the Warrior Gene and weeding out those who have it before they can do any damage. I have a son. He's six. If he tests positive, he could be locked up for God knows how long— because of something he *might* do in the future. I'm bringing him to an underground haven, somewhere they can't track us. You won't be able to find me either."

She tucked her hair behind her ear again. I tried not to be distracted by her birthmark, tried to hold her gaze. She looked down at the mockup of our "female future" and sighed before closing the folder and pushing it toward me.

"This is my last chance at salvation."

I looked at David. His face was scrunched in worry and I knew he was thinking of his son. The fifteen-year-old boy who had suddenly committed a monstrous act, showing him the worst he feared was inside himself. If they were looking for boys with the Warrior Gene and Beckett was still alive, they'd lock him up, take him away. David wasn't safe either. We were sinking into a dictatorship, watching our nation's structures and systems crumble around us.

I picked up the folder and clutched it to my chest.

"Thank you, Abigail. It may just be the last chance for all of us."

CHAPTER TWENTY-FIVE

DAVID and I left the library and rushed back down the main corridor. My mind spun at the enormity of the task ahead. No matter how much evidence we'd collected, how were we possibly going to make it public? We couldn't trust Frida, Clarion, or any other media outlet. They were all tucked in Hatcher's pocket. Our only hope was to use the promise of an exclusive story with Vanyala as some kind of bargaining chip. But a bargain with who? And would Vanyala be willing to turn herself in for a chance to bring the truth to light?

I stopped at the elevators and pointed to the sign for the birthing center.

"There's one more thing we should do before leaving. I have two days to complete the mandated Sequenom test. If I don't take it, they'll come looking for me. For *us*."

"You're right. Let's take it and then get the hell out of town. I have a plan."

We held hands as we took the elevator up to the birthing center. I remembered our last ride on that same elevator when we'd first begun investigating the End of Men months ago. It was crazy to think of how far we'd come since then—how much we'd gained, how much we'd lost. I thought again of the baby growing inside me—our baby—and a flash of nervous excitement rushed through me. Somewhere along the way, I'd learned how to let go of the fear of uncertainty and look forward to the unexpected twists and turns.

We approached the nurse's station and spotted Betty. Her eyes lit up when she saw us.

"Charley! David!" she exclaimed.

"Betty!" David and I said in unison. I couldn't help but laugh. We sounded as if we were long lost friends rather than people who'd casually met once. But I'd felt a connection with Betty from the moment I set eyes on her and sensed that she'd be an important part of our story somehow.

I lowered my voice out of instinct. "Doctor Morrison told me to come by. I'm here to take the Sequenom test?"

She clasped her hands together in delight, looking like a little girl who'd just been told she was getting a puppy.

"I heard the news! Congratulations! You two are going to have the most beautiful daughter. I just finished up my shift, but follow me—I'll do the test myself. It's the least I can do for Charley Tennyson."

"How exactly did you hear that I was pregnant?" I asked. Apparently HIPAA and medical privacy were out the window too.

She blushed. "I was working the night Doctor Morrison got the lab results and I helped her find your contact information. I wasn't supposed to say anything. I'm sorry."

"We all make mistakes," I said. I couldn't tell her it was okay. None of it was okay. Prickles of anxiety swirled in my blood. Had it been a mistake to go there at all? David and I should be tucked away somewhere safe, somewhere they couldn't find us.

Betty led us down a corridor into a secured medical room, her clogs squeaking each step of the way.

"I still can't believe everything that's been happening over the last few months," she said. "No more boys! I told all my friends I was there the day you found out. This whole thing is so crazy. Do you know what's causing it yet?"

"We're getting closer to answers every day," I replied.

"Well, I can't wait to watch the rest of your panel discussion! I loved how you split it in two segments to keep us all on the edge of our seats."

I smirked. So *that* was how Clarion had spun it. I wondered who they'd get to host the second half, what tall tale they'd weave to explain away all the questions.

We entered Room 509 and Betty closed the door behind us. She gestured to the exam table and I sat down. The stiff white paper itched my thighs and I glanced around at the machines and tubes. The room felt like it was getting smaller. Betty reached into a drawer and pulled out a small device, then presented it with a flourish.

"Okay, you two, this is the test. It's synced with the Sequenom app, so you can test for pregnancy and meet the compliance requirements of the gender test at the same time. We just need you to tap here to sign the HIPAA waiver, which will authorize the results to be shared in the community database."

"Would you mind if I take some footage?" David asked. "This might not be newsworthy, but I'd love to show our daughter one day."

We both nodded and I looked back at Betty, automatically slipping into reporter mode. "How many of these tests have you given so far?" I asked.

"Me, personally? A few dozen. But nationwide? I've heard the latest count is nearing four million. And the results are all the same. Every woman who's pregnant is expecting a girl." A tone of wistfulness slipped into her voice.

"So what do you think about all of this, Betty?" David interjected, playing up to the camera. "How do you feel about the idea of a female-only future?"

She bit her lip. "I have to admit, at first the whole thing was enthralling. No more boys being born! It's wild. And being right there when you discovered it made it all so much more exciting. But now, reality's starting to sink in. It's hard to imagine, isn't it? A world where we're all the same sex?"

Betty shook her head before continuing. "Some of the nurses and doctors think it's a good thing. They talk about how much more peaceful the world will be. No more mass attacks, no more horrific violence, no more ER rooms flooded with victims and crying families. I see their point, but there's a nagging voice in me that says it's not right. We need men, and women, the way God intended. There has to be balance."

"I couldn't agree more," I told her. Her words were a reminder that this wasn't just an investigation; it was a story that impacted all of us. How would the extinction of men shape our society? How would it transform our lives, our beliefs, our futures? We owed it to our future generations to uncover the truth about what was happening, and why, and what it would mean for tomorrow.

Betty glanced at David, blushing. "Men aren't all bad. And women aren't all good. I think we need both sexes to uncover the best inside each of us."

She looked back at me and held up the test. "Should we get this show on the road?"

"No time like the present," I replied.

My heart leapt as I thought about getting the official pregnancy results. Doctor Morrison had told me the blood test had a 99% accuracy rating. With a second test, we'd close the marginal gap and all questions would be answered. In that moment, I realized my deepest fear had done a complete turnaround. Before, I'd been terrified I was pregnant. Now I was terrified of the test being negative, of not having the future I'd started to imagine with David.

"Okay, Charley, all you need to do is press your finger on this pad," Betty instructed. "You'll feel a tiny prick, but don't worry, it doesn't hurt. At least, that's what I'm told."

"You haven't taken one yet?" I asked. They'd encouraged all women to take one, whether or not they thought they were pregnant.

She shook her head and laughed. "If I were pregnant, that'd be your best story yet. A modern-day virgin birth. Hallelujah!"

I laughed. "Stranger things have happened, Betty."

I pressed my finger to the pad and kept talking, playing to the camera.

"All right, let's see if everyone's telling the truth about there being no pain."

I felt a tiny prick, but Betty was right—it didn't hurt. It felt like that first tingle when your leg fell asleep, right before discomfort set in.

"How long does it take to get the results?" David asked.

"Sixty seconds. Pretty amazing, huh? Just a few decades ago, women had to wait months to find out the sex of their babies. Medical technology is a wonder."

"That's one word for it," I said.

My mind drifted to Ganta, to everything Abigail had told us. An old quote drifted through my head: *With great power comes great responsibility.* Unfortunately, with great power also came great abuse. Ganta's first experiments to create a more resilient Y chromosome had cost us dearly; we'd paid with the blood of our fathers, our sons, our daughters. And now they were over-correcting, swinging to the opposite side of the spectrum by eliminating men altogether. Why couldn't people learn from the lessons of the past?

Betty, David, and I sat in silence as the seconds ticked by. We gazed at the device's results screen along with the camera's watchful eye. A minute later, a blue line appeared.

"Oh my God," Betty choked out. She turned to me with eyes full of disbelief and amazement. "It's a boy."

"What?" I asked, even though I'd heard her perfectly clearly.

"Black means you're not pregnant. Pink means it's a girl. Blue means...well, I haven't seen blue yet, but I know what it means. It means it's a boy."

"But...that's impossible. Isn't it?" I looked over at David, then back at Betty, then back at the test. The blue line was still there.

"Holy Jesus, it's a miracle!" Betty whispered, crossing herself. She dropped to her knees and clasped her hands together as if in prayer.

"Ummm...Betty? I don't mean to interrupt, but there must be some mistake. Should we try another test?"

I refused to believe the results. I'd just wrapped my head around the idea of being a mother, but the idea of birthing some kind of miracle was another thing completely.

"You're right, let's take another one." Betty reached into a drawer and pulled out another test.

"You said they've given millions of these and they're all girls?" David asked, still filming as I took the second test. We watched, waited, recorded. Once again, a blue line appeared. Blue like the sky on a clear day, and the color of my mother's eyes, and the ocean on a tropical paradise. I got a strange sense that I was dreaming or watching the scene from afar.

David said, "The test must be flawed."

Betty shook her head. "They said the tests are 99.7%

accurate. And with two of them..." Her voice trailed off before finishing. "It's a boy. I don't know how, I don't know why, but I can tell you: it's a boy."

Of all the things to think of in that moment, President Hatcher's face floated before me. As it did, a jolt of fear rushed through me.

"David, stop filming," I said.

He pressed a button and the hologram disappeared. We stood in silence. Betty started pacing around the room, the squeaking of her shoes breaking the silence. It was almost comedic, the fact that those squeaky orange clogs might become the soundtrack of history's turning point.

A million questions rushed through my mind, but one truth shone through clearly: we were in danger.

"Betty, I need you to promise you won't tell anyone," I said. "People have died because of the questions we're raising about the End of Men. There's a lot more behind all this than anyone knows."

"I won't tell anyone," Betty replied, nodding fervently. "But the results...they're automatically sent to the community database. They're probably being uploaded there right now."

She looked down at the first test on the counter and picked it up, turning it so the screen was facing me.

"Look," she said. The blue line had disappeared and the screen was now flashing red. I imagined a datakeeper in a room somewhere, leaning forward in shock as the results appeared on a screen, pulling a lever to send emergency sirens blaring.

"We have to go."

I grabbed my satchel off the chair. David stood frozen in shock, face pale, eyes wide with disbelief. He shook his head, slowly at first, then harder as if he were coming to consciousness or waking from a dream. He looked at me and the disbelief shifted to fear. I wasn't sure if he was more worried about our safety or the idea of what our son might become.

"Come on, there's a back way," Betty said. "I'm coming too, I want to help!"

She grabbed my hand and pulled me into the hallway, then opened a hidden stairwell door. We stepped inside and the heavy door echoed as it shut behind us. She squeezed my hand, slippery with sweat. I took a deep breath and looked at David.

"Don't worry, Charley. I'll protect you," David said. I knew he'd try, but I couldn't help wondering if it would be enough.

I looked at Betty and a flutter of gratitude rose up in my chest. Despite the fact that I barely knew her, I trusted her. There was no logic or reason to back up my feeling, but maybe when you'd seen enough evil in the world, it was easier to spot the good.

And then we ran.

CHAPTER TWENTY-SIX

We raced down the stairs and burst into the night. I struggled to orient myself as we sprinted toward the Mule and tumbled inside. David slid into the front seat, I leapt in the passenger's seat, and Betty climbed into the back. The Mule roared to life and we peeled away.

"Come back here with me," Betty said, motioning for me to get into the back. She was protecting me too.

I crawled next to her, acutely aware of every nerve in my body. My stomach felt heavy with the weight of what I was carrying. It wasn't even a fetus yet, had no fingertips or toes or eyes. It was nothing more than a blob of cells and a promise of what might be. Yet it meant everything. Not just to me, but to the world.

David merged onto the highway and I realized we were the exact obvious of inconspicuous—a stark white Mule in a sea of blue iCars. As soon as they saw the results from my test, we wouldn't be difficult to find. They probably had trackers on us already. I remembered Cardinal's story about being watched, getting the same iCar every time.

"Where are we going?" I asked. My voice quivered and I hated it.

Betty grabbed my hand. "It'll be okay."

I thought back to the first time I'd met her, the timid nurse with the red scrunchie and orange clogs, the one who backed down the instant Hilda appeared. The crazier and more dangerous things got, the stronger she seemed to become. What was it that made some people crumble under pressure and others turn into jewels?

David pulled something from his pocket and I caught a whiff of lavender. He reached back and handed us two purple prayer bead bracelets.

"Take these and put them on your left wrists. Betty, dump your Surge out the window. This is how we'll communicate from now on. I'll explain how they work later."

Betty bit her lip and nodded as David rolled down the back window. She detached her Surge and stuck her left hand outside, the device dangling between her thumb and middle finger like a soiled diaper. A flash of worry flickered over her face. I knew how uneasy she must feel at the prospect of letting go. Our Surges were no longer just devices: they were extensions of ourselves. They held our most cherished photos, memories, contacts, and ideas, buzzed with the promise of instant access to any question or desire.

Betty closed her eyes. The wind rushed through her hair and her brow unfurrowed as her fingers released their grasp. The Surge fell to the earth and we zoomed ahead. I wondered if she felt its loss the way I had at first—a hollow ache, a sense of being untethered and aimless, like a balloon floating through the sky. She opened her eyes and stuck her head out the window, smiling like a kid. I couldn't help but laugh. It was the look of freedom.

Up front, David held his purple prayer bead bracelet to his lips.

"We need your help," he said. He held his wrist to his ear and listened quietly for a few minutes before replying, "Okay, see you soon."

He jerked the wheel to the right to abruptly exit the highway, then pulled onto a dirt road I'd never been on before. Within minutes, trees lined the sides of the road and hills stretched out on both sides of us. He headed straight for a thick swath of greenery, showing no signs of slowing down.

"Uhhhh, David?"

He jerked the wheel again to send the Mule careening behind the bushes, tires kicking up dust as we spun to a stop in the brush. He killed the power and swiveled to face us.

"Let's go."

He leapt out and Betty and I scrambled after him. He led us to a nearby patch of bushes, where he began tossing aside branches and leaves to uncover some type of transportation device. It was a clear dome with two captain's seats and a joystick between them. I pressed a hand against the glass exterior.

"Is this thing street legal?" I joked.

David grinned. "Tennyson, where we're going, we don't need roads. I call it the Adventurer."

His eyes sparkled with pride in his creation. He pressed a finger to an identity pad and the door swung open. He glanced back at Betty, a sheepish look on his face.

"It'll be a little cramped, I only built it for two. But we'll make do."

He reached under the front seats and pulled, and a rickety platform extended in the small space behind the seats. He pulled two pillows from the ceiling, where they were secured with a green bungee.

"Voila! Room for three."

"I'll lay down in the back," I offered. "Betty, you can ride shotgun."

"Great idea, you should rest. Let's roll," David said.

We piled inside and the pod thrummed to life. Within seconds, we were zipping deep into the woods. We drove in silence, the space between us heavy with the weight of what we weren't saying. No one uttered a word about the tiny embryo I was carrying, what it might mean, or how it could be possible.

I tried to sleep, but my mind was spinning too fast. When I closed my eyes, faces flashed through the darkness. President Hatcher, Cardinal, Finley, Simon, Abigail. How did all the pieces connect? We were a million miles away from everyone, yet I could sense them all in my periphery like players just off the stage. They were woven into our story, a tangled knot I couldn't unravel.

My thoughts drifted to Marika. *We'll raise the baby together,* she'd proposed. *We could be a family.* The idea that she didn't know I was carrying a son made the distance between us seem even more vast. Would he be a monster or a miracle? What made the difference between the two anyway? Sometimes it seemed it was nothing more than chance: the random toss of a coin, a wrong path taken at a fork, a life lesson poorly learned. I pushed thoughts of Beckett away, knowing we'd have to deal with that concern later. There was simply too much to worry about. I could only take it one problem at a time.

Finally, the Adventurer stopped. Bending oak trees hovered on all sides of us.

David twisted around and gave me a tired smile. "We're here."

Betty stirred in her seat, rubbing her eyes and yawning like Goldilocks after a nice nap. I felt a twinge of envy that she could rest amidst all of this. Would I ever get a good night's sleep again?

Branches and leaves scratched at the windows as David swung open the driver's side door. He'd wedged the Adventurer into a tight space between two trees. He jumped out and his feet made a soft thud on the dirt. He reached for my hand and helped me out, holding my arm as gingerly as if I were a senior citizen.

"I won't break," I teased.

I stood in the dark forest and gazed around. Layers of trees and forest rolled out like a photographic backdrop. The air was crisp, the sky was infinite. I sucked in a breath of air and my lungs exploded with joy. It was the deepest, freshest breath I'd taken since...I couldn't remember how long. Maybe ever. I tipped my head backward and gaped in wonder at the Milky Way. The stars looked back, twinkling.

David took my hand and led me and Betty through the woods. There was no trail, but he strolled with confidence, as if he'd traveled these woods many times before. The trees stood watch like silent soldiers protecting us from unknown enemies. We reached a small clearing and David let go of my hand. He knelt down and tossed aside a clump of branches, then pulled open a trap door.

"Told you that cavern in Luray wasn't my first rodeo," he said. "Stay close."

He climbed down the ladder and I followed him, Betty right behind me. We stepped off the ladder and into a cave. It was much more plain than Cardinal's haven had been. Flowstone ran along the top of the walls, while cave popcorn lined the bottom. Framed maps and cave drawings were everywhere. How many more of these places existed, hidden deep in the country's forests and mountains? It seemed there must be whole secret societies interwoven beneath our nation's cities and mountains, underground homes connected by tunnels. Communities of people living in secrecy, hiding from the horrors above.

A thud echoed through the cavern as the entry door snapped shut. David led us down a short tunnel and toward a twinkle of lights. We entered a sitting room, where a woman sat on a plush red armchair. She looked exotic—Israeli, maybe—with deep brown eyes, thick eyebrows, course hair, and chiseled features. She appeared to be a few years older than me, maybe thirty-five.

"Charley, meet my mom," David said.

She took both my hands in hers. "I'm so glad you're here."

I looked back and forth between David and her in surprise.

"You look so...young," I said awkwardly.

She gave me a smile and a wink. "It's the cave water."

"In that case, may I please have a glass of water?" I asked.

She laughed and the melodic sound of it was just like David's. "You don't remember meeting me, do you?" she asked, her eyes twinkling.

I shook my head.

"It was many years ago, when you were just a young girl. At one of the Fear Fighters' first underground gatherings."

I sucked in a deep breath and everything became very still. A faraway memory began to take shape. It was a party...she had on a red dress. And then I remembered. "My God, that's right. You did a poetry reading, right? Something about a caged bird?"

She nodded. "Maya Angelou. The caged bird sings of freedom."

I broke out in a smile and turned to David as a new memory took shape. "You were there too!"

He'd been a cute, impish little boy with endless energy. He'd run in circles during the readings and speeches, grabbing my hand and encouraging me to stop being so serious and play. He'd even given me a peck on the cheek before he left.

"That was the year the Fear Fighters were formed," Vanyala explained, her eyes soft with memories. "Very fledgling beginnings, but a beginning still. That beautiful old poem was our first rally cry. You sat on your father's lap, eyes wide, taking in the whole thing with a child's sense of wonder."

And suddenly memories tore through me, one after another. The room had smelled of hot chocolate and spice cake. I'd sat cross-legged on the floor listening to Vanyala, but the concrete was cold and hard so I'd crawled into my father's lap, thrilled for an excuse to feel his arms wrap around me. Everyone had been there: the old woman in 3B with her pink sweater and gray-blue hair. The man in 4G, with Archie the miniature schnauzer curled up on his lap. And so many other strangers—neighbors we'd never met despite the fact that we all lived under the same roof with just a few thin walls separating us.

It was the first of many weekly gatherings. Residents had set aside Monday evenings to gather in the basements of their apartment buildings and talk, tell stories, share food. The idea was to bring back the things people used to do together, when there were communities and neighbors. When the longing for togetherness was stronger than the fear.

"My father called them Magic Mondays," I remembered.

Vanyala replied, "It was the Fear Fighters' first organized initiative. Those secret meetings sprang up in cities all across the nation. I came to the first one in your building, and that's when I met you. Your dad had told me so much about you, and you were exactly as he described. Beautiful. Sweet. Friendly. When you met me, you curtsied and said, 'Can I get you something to drink, Miss Vala?'"

I laughed at the memory. For me, Magic Mondays had been

truly magical. For a long time before they'd started, I'd been yearning for something I couldn't pinpoint. As an only child who was home-schooled, my childhood was made up of long days inside with my mother. I loved her and our activities, but sometimes a feeling like a dark black hole would rise up in my chest. The hole got bigger at night, when I lay in bed and wondered about the world outside our walls. I didn't yet know that the feeling had a name: loneliness. But that first Monday night, when all those people got together in the same room, I found what I'd been missing. Community. Connection. Purpose.

I wanted her to tell me everything about my father, every moment and memory. For so long, he had been nothing but a jumble of lost love. There was no one to share him with, no one who really understood. My mom didn't like to talk about him—too painful, she said. And now, out of nowhere, this woman appeared who had been his friend. David's mom. Vanyala Dawson. How was it possible?

"Wow, small world," Betty chimed in. I'd been in such shock that I'd forgotten she was standing there, a witness to all the craziness.

David's mother turned to Betty, extended a hand. "Hello, I'm Vanyala."

"I've always thought Vanyala was such a beautiful name," I told her, eager to form a connection. She was no longer 'Vanyala Dawson, wanted fugitive.' She was my love's mother, our child's grandmother, and my father's long lost friend.

"I was named after a warrior princess," she explained. "There was a legend about her while I was growing up. She was one of India's first female rulers. When her country was overtaken by tyrants, she raised up a community of people to fight back, organized an army and fought on the front lines herself. She defied everyone's beliefs about what a woman could and could not do."

"She was basically a badass," David interjected. We laughed and he added, "By the way, you don't have to watch your language around my mom."

Vanyala gestured to the sitting room. "We have so much to talk about. Please, sit, all of you. I'll get us some tea."

She disappeared into the kitchen. Betty sat on the loveseat and David and I settled onto the couch. The red leather was soft on my legs and David was warm next to me. Our thighs touched and he placed a hand on my knee. Dawn was approaching and I had that woozy feeling that came from too many hours without sleep. I rested my head on David's shoulder, drained by the enormity of all that had happened and all that lay ahead.

"Is this where you grew up?" I murmured, my eyes flickering from the stone walls to the dusty floor to the sparse furnishings.

"Someplace like it. Told you my childhood was a little different."

Vanyala came back with a tray and set it on the coffee table, then began pouring our tea. It seemed such an ordinary thing. Sitting down for a cup of tea, getting to know my boyfriend's mom. Meanwhile the whole world was changing, and more change was on the way. But amid change, we hold onto what we can—and so I took the mug from Vanyala, clutched it in both hands, and savored the warm smell of orange and rosemary. I prayed it would stay for a while—not just the smell, but the feeling of warmth and comfort. The feeling of safety.

I cleared my throat. "How long have you been down here alone?"

"Longer than I care to think about," she replied. "I've been getting regular death threats from Hatcher's followers since I can remember. They want the Fear Fighters to stop fighting and just follow the laws. We created a simulated appearance for my broadcasts to keep my identity hidden, but it wasn't enough. The government even put out a bounty for me. Not surprising, really. Elizabeth was always very stubborn. I'm sure you've heard about her latest stunt, declaring the Fear Fighters to be a Civil Terrorist Organization."

"I heard about that. What does it mean, exactly?"

"It's yet another layer of power that increases the government's rights to monitor and prosecute me and other group members. As a 'terrorist organization,' the Fear Fighters will now have significant restrictions imposed on us that could restrict our ability to defend ourselves against prosecution in a court of law. For example, the government can confiscate our bank accounts so we have no money to hire defense attorneys. Even worse, the new Department of Truth is now requiring internet providers to censor any communications of individuals or organizations that do not agree with the official version of truth."

"It's unbelievable that she could do this. How well did you and my father know President Hatcher? She seems truly evil."

Vanyala replied, "We were very close in the beginning. We were part of a university activist group called the Peace Project, which was focused on ending violence around the world. Elizabeth and I were roommates and we were matched with your father for a project that stemmed from Columbine. Our little trifecta quickly became focused on ending gun violence and mass attacks in the United States. Needless to say, we took very different paths after college. Elizabeth went into government, your father went into academia, and I took the entrepreneurial route."

Vanyala paused to add a lump of sugar to her tea. She took

a sip and nodded, then set the mug back down on the side table next to her armchair.

"She and I stayed in touch for a while, but as the world continued to change, it became obvious we had very different beliefs. Elizabeth was adamant about arming women and issuing more controls on public spaces, whereas I proposed strict regulation of gun ownership and was against the idea of public shutdowns. She always leaned toward bureaucracy, while I took a more grassroots approach. Ultimately, these differences caused a big blowout. Now she'd love nothing more than to see me behind bars."

A sad, wistful look crept into her eyes. "It's strange to see what she's become. She's consumed by her convictions. Of course, I suppose she'd say the same about me. I often look back and wonder where things went so astray. Once upon a time, we were fighting for the same thing."

Vanyala picked up her mug, gripping it in both hands the same way I did. It struck me that despite her status as the Fear Fighters' leader, she was just an ordinary woman like me. A woman who had once been a little girl with big dreams, who faced challenges and insecurities, who wondered if she could really trust anyone.

"Will you tell me about my father?" I asked.

I knew I should be focused on the End of Men, but at that moment, nothing seemed more important than learning more about the man who had been the first love of my life. I wanted to capture new stories for my bank of memories, see a glimpse of the young man he'd been before I existed.

Vanyala curled her legs up under her like a teenager, still holding her tea in both hands.

"He led my college orientation and I bumped into him again on the first day of the semester. I got lost looking for a class and felt totally flustered. There were dozens of buildings spread across campus, thousands of students buzzing around. I remember wandering in circles, looking at all the other kids who seemed to know exactly where they were going. I wondered when they'd realize I was really just a poor little girl who lucked out on a scholarship. I was the first one in my family to go to college, and I felt like a total imposter."

I nodded in understanding. "I know the feeling well. In my first year at the station, I had the same feeling every time I went on the air. I'd stand there, heart pounding, palms sweating, wondering when they'd call me out as the amateur that I was."

"Terrible, isn't it, the false stories our minds torture us with? Anyway, I couldn't figure out which building my science class was in and was desperately searching on my phone for a map or instructions. Your father saw me and asked, 'Hey Yala, where ya headed?' I didn't know what building to tell him and blurted out the only thing I could remember—Karen Caroll's biology class. It was ridiculous to expect he'd know where my single class was on that massive campus. He laughed and said, 'Me too. Don't worry, kid—I'll show you the ropes.'"

She smiled, her eyes lighting up at the memory. I wondered if she missed my father the way I did, if she felt the same burning pain when she remembered him.

"He loved helping people," I said.

"Gabriel was very kind. We became friends right away. And your mother, she was beautiful."

"She still is. I always wished I'd gotten her blue eyes."

"You have your father's eyes," Vanyala said. "And from what David has told me, you have his vision too. He was very inspiring."

Vanyala continued, "Your father and I stayed in touch even after graduation. When the mass attacks got worse, he and I would brainstorm ideas and solutions, just like we'd done in the old days of Project Peace. After the Great Separation and the early capacity restrictions, we picked up our efforts. We made a good team. I was the outspoken, emotional activist while he specialized in logic, data, and research."

She paused to take a sip of her tea and I emulated her. She seemed so strong and wise, I wondered why she and David didn't get along. He fidgeted beside me, tugging at a stray strand on his pants.

Vanyala continued, "By the time businesses began shutting down their offices, most employees embraced the idea of working from home. With mass attacks happening daily, staying home was much safer than facing the ongoing risks of being out in public—not to mention easier and more convenient. But I had other ideas, and they didn't involve safe and easy. I never let go of my desire to stop violence and move gun restrictions forward. I found like-minded individuals and formed the Fear Fighters."

Vanyala continued, "When I introduced your dad to the Fear Fighters, he was intrigued but standoffish. It was only later that I found out why. The group made your mother nervous. You were young, Charley, just seven or eight, and your mother desperately wanted to protect you from all the dangers of the world. The thought of your father becoming involved with some group of radicals was extremely unappealing. It's perfectly understandable, given what she'd been through. She just wanted to keep her family safe."

A long-forgotten memory floated back to me. I'd woken up to the sound of yelling, which was unusual in my house. I snuck out of my room and hunched in the hallway, listening outside my parent's bedroom door. I could only hear snippets of their conversation, but I heard enough to know they were arguing about the Fear Fighters. The anger in their voices had given me a knot in my stomach. I didn't understand who the Fear Fighters were or why my parents would be arguing about them.

"I remember that period of time," I said. "I was worried they were going to get a divorce. My dad started working longer hours and he kept missing dinner. But then, all of a sudden the fighting was over, and things went back to normal."

"Your father told me what they'd decided. He would introduce your family slowly to the secret world that lay hidden beyond sensors and fear."

"Why didn't I see you more often, if you and my dad were so close?"

Vanyala shifted in her chair. "I don't think your mother was comfortable with us being friends."

Suspicion shot through my gut. My questions must have been written on my face, because Vanyala quickly continued.

"Charley, I want to assure you, your father and I were only ever friends. More like brother and sister, actually. I was deeply involved in the Fear Fighters movement, and Gabriel was deeply in love with your mother. He would have done anything for her, and for you. For your family."

"Well, almost anything," I said, remembering the only other disagreement I remembered my parents having. "My mom was always trying to get him to work from home. She worried about him every time he left the house. 'What if there's an attack, Gabriel?' she'd ask him again and again. 'What would we do without you?'"

I liked talking to Vanyala about my dad, but it also made me uncomfortable. It reminded me there was a whole side of him I hadn't known. I knew the man who let me sit on his shoulders, tucked me in and told me stories at night. But I knew nothing about the man who went to work for hours on end, whose mysterious conversations with secret people became more important than dinners at home with us. I used to watch him leave in the morning, carrying his tablet as he headed out for the office, and worry that he might not come back.

David squeezed my knee and cleared his throat. "Tell her how this connects to the story, Mom. To the Y Factor and the End of Men."

Vanyala sat up straighter, regaining the sense of stoic strength I'd first noticed in her.

"Charley, long before you started working on the Y Factor, the Fear Fighters were researching the cause of violence. Have you heard of Montag?"

When I shook my head, she explained, "It's part of the secret web, a secured database where every media outlet's stories are logged and monitored. Make no mistake: the Department of Truth may be a new organization in the public's eyes, but freedom of press has been an illusion for a very long time. Three massive corporations basically control everything we see, hear, and read. These media giants are under extreme financial and political pressure to publish stories that fit the desired mold. Producers receive specific instructions from their parent companies, who receive specific instructions from their boards, who are led by wealthy people with political connections. News outlets are 'asked' to tell certain stories, in a certain way—and trust me, they're anything but requests. Your producers may claim their content strategy is driven by public interests and viewership, but that couldn't be further from the truth. The real purpose is to shape the reality and perception that the government wants to be true."

I felt a growing queasiness in my gut. The things I'd built my career on were slipping away. I was beginning to realize how fragile the truth was. How fragile everything was.

David added, "No speech is free. The only voices that get media attention are those that are funded."

Vanyala nodded and continued. "A while back, the Fear Fighters hacked into Montag. Once we obtained an access point, we were able to see logs of all the stories being developed across the nation. The group's intention for accessing the data was good, but we realized immediately how dangerous it was. There was so much sensitive IP—stories, sources, data. And now, the Fear Fighters have become intricately wrapped up in so many secrets and conspiracies. Sometimes I wish I didn't know the things I know. I think back to when I was that young woman stepping onto campus, nervous but determined to change the world. I always believed people were inherently good, but I've come to learn otherwise."

"I still can't quite wrap my head around the government's involvement and intentions. The latest source we talked to claimed they're responsible for the epidemic of violence. That it was an unintended side effect of trying to stop the End of Men."

"It's hard to believe, but it's all true. You must remember, our government used to be much different than it is now. The House and Senate were mostly male controlled, with very few women in positions of power. There was no chance a government like that was going to sit back and allow males to become extinct, even if that was the natural course God or Mother Nature was putting forth. Medical researchers were convinced they could find a way to stop the dramatic deterioration in the Y chromosome. And in a way, they were right."

"Which leads us to Ganta," I said.

"That's right," Vanyala confirmed. "Pretty much any significant medical development over the last century can be traced back to them. They came up with the Alzheimer's cure, the cancer vaccine, and the shot for reversing paralysis."

"That's just the tip of the iceberg," Betty interrupted excitedly. "Ganta also came up with the anti-aging genomic solution and the capability to print replacement organs on 3D printers."

"Yes, they have done some wonderful, life-changing work," Vanyala acknowledged. "And around the turn of the century, they developed a revolutionary gene therapy that repairs faulty genes. The genome-editing technique enabled scientists to clip a specific DNA sequence and replace it with a new one. When the government first discovered the plummeting sex ratio, they turned to Ganta, who figured out how to isolate the Y chromosome and correct the defective gene. The gene repair system made the Y chromosome much more resilient. But there's such a thing as too much resilience, Charley."

Her words sent chills through me. I looked at David, wondering if he was thinking of Beckett. There was still so much I needed to learn about his son, his history, his genes. David continued toying with the loose strand on his pants, while Betty leaned forward in her chair as if she were watching the latest thriller on the Hub.

"To gain the quick results they needed, the researchers had to boost the percentage of cells that had the defective gene replaced. They developed a combined nanoparticle and viral delivery system in order to obtain the high percentage of repair they needed. Whereas the previous Y chromosome had been losing genes, this new 'repaired' form of the Y chromosome gained five new genes. The government rushed FDA approvals and hospitals began issuing the gene repair system in the form of an immunity booster at birth. It seemed they had solved their problem. Until years later, when they realized that one of the new genes had the potential to cause hyper-aggression in boys as they grew older."

"The Warrior Gene," I said, swallowing the lump in my throat.

"Exactly."

I turned to David. "So Finley and Abigail were right, and Simon had it backwards. The government wasn't responsible for the extinction of males. They were trying to correct the problem and ended up creating a hyper-aggressive Y chromosome that drove MPV."

Vanyala said, "Actually, I don't believe they *created* it. I believe they simply intensified what was already there. For the most part, males have always been programmed to be aggressors. But what used to be a subtle difference in genetic makeup was intensified, so that we saw younger and younger males impacted, and impacted in far greater ways. In your panel discussion, you talked about the End of Men being the perfect storm, a result of a number of different factors. Despite what the government did, we can't discount the myriad of other factors. Societal influence, mass media, mental health, a splintering of faith, technology's tendency to drive human isolation—so many things in our society have spun out of control. On its own, the Warrior Gene may not have had such disastrous consequences. But in our world, it was a tipping point."

I frowned. "How are we going to bring all this to light? I think President Hatcher is truly convinced that once men are gone, not only will the violence go away, but the United States will somehow regain our position of economic power. Apparently she wants to create a homogenous future of lovely, powerful, and economically successful women."

Vanyala nodded. "That was her vision back when we were in college. She told your father and I about it, and we tried to explain the dangers of genetic manipulation and ethnic cleansing, but our arguments only seemed to further her convictions. Her administration was the one that issued the national call for research and sparked the medical community to race toward a way for two eggs to form an embryo. And now Ganta is looking at a picture-perfect launch scenario. Their entire marketing campaign is built around the slogan: 'The future is female.' A century from now, we'll have a generation of women who have never seen a live male."

My hand floated down to touch my stomach and I instinctively grabbed David's hand. He met my gaze and gave me a small, tired smile. I realized for the first time how scared he was.

I looked back at Vanyala and asked, "What if it turns out the future isn't female after all?"

She frowned. "What do you mean?"

David put his arm around me and pulled me closer, squeezing protectively. I wanted to relax into his embrace, but I couldn't. My blood was vibrating with energy, as if I'd had too much caffeine. I picked up my mug and took a sip, hoping the tea would calm my nerves, but it was lukewarm and the orange spice was bitter. I put it down and stood, stomach turning.

"Where's your restroom? I think I might be sick." I raised a hand to my mouth, pushing back the nausea that was suddenly swirling through me.

Vanyala sprang to her feet and rushed me to the bathroom, a look of concern on her face. I escaped inside and leaned over the toilet. My stomach turned but nothing happened. For the first time in weeks, it wasn't vomit rising in me. It was anxiety. I went to the sink and looked in the mirror. My eyes were bloodshot, my face lined with tension and fatigue. I heard murmurs from outside the door and wondered if they were talking about me. Whispering about the secret I was carrying. I splashed my face with cold water, patted it dry with a purple hand towel, and returned to the sitting room. They all looked up anxiously.

"Did you tell her?" I asked David.

He shook his head. "I wanted to wait for you."

I sat back down and he took my hand in his. The look of concern on Vanyala's face deepened.

"What's wrong, dear?" Her eyes darted back and forth between David and me.

I gave her a small, shaky smile. "I'm pregnant," I said. The words felt strange, like a shirt that didn't fit right. Two tiny words that changed so much. Vanyala's face lit up with joy and surprise. Before she could respond, I continued with the only three words that could change things even more.

"It's a boy."

Vanyala's hand flew up to her mouth. "Are you sure?" she gasped. Her face was clouded with fear, and seeing this strong woman afraid of the news sent another jolt of anxiety vibrating through me.

Betty interjected, "I gave her two tests, and they both showed the same thing."

Vanyala's expression turned from shock to stone. "No one can know. You don't know these people, what they will do."

David said, "Trust me, Mom, we know all about what these people will do."

He gripped my hand, nails cutting into my skin. I wanted to tell him to let go, but the pain reminded me that I was alive, that all of this was real. That I had something to protect, something worth saving.

"It's okay," I told them. "I can't explain it, but I just know things will be okay. Better than okay. But we have to tell the story, as soon as possible, to everyone."

They looked at me as if I were out of my mind. There was a chance they were right. I didn't feel like myself. I felt stronger and more confident, as if I were being pulled toward something important. I should be worried about the Warrior Gene, especially after hearing about Beckett, but I wasn't. Thinking about our son gave me a strange sense of peace. My dad used to tell me our destinies were written in the stars. Crazy as it seemed, I knew this baby was my destiny.

I said, "The longer we keep the real story a secret, the more danger we're in. Once we release the story and everyone knows, we're no longer a threat."

Everyone was silent, considering.

Betty chimed in, "I'm pretty sure they already know about the baby. The hospital would have reported the test results right away."

I directed my gaze to Vanyala. "Will you show me the evidence you've gathered?"

After a long pause, she said, "You're right. The only way to end all this is to put it out there. It's time to finally show the truth."

David let go of my hand. I looked down to see indentations where his nails had been. Vanyala stood and led us all down a tunnel to a tiny dark room. The walls were bare and a massive workstation sat in the corner, covered in machines and wires. She pressed a button on the wall, and the machines whirled to life.

"We built our own database linking to the research we gathered," she explained. "It's on the dark web, so no one can find it without knowing exactly what they're looking for. It runs on voice command. Just tell it what you need and it will sift through the files and data to find it."

We began to dig. It was stunning, the data that Vanyala and the Fear Fighters had collected and organized. We started reading, sorting, arranging. It was like a puzzle, searching for the right pieces and putting them together to form a concrete narrative. We worked for hours, the four of us, taking breaks only to eat and go to the bathroom. Once in a while we'd share notes, little tidbits of what we'd found. We kept a running log of the questions that came up, things we knew we'd need proof for, and worked through them one at a time.

Thoughts of my dad were with me as we worked. He felt

closer than he had in a long time. I wondered if he could see me
now, working alongside Vanyala and her son. Would he be
happy to know his grandson was on the way? Stunned to hear
that he and his old college friend would now be grandparents to
the same baby? I remembered my mother's words earlier, the
surge of pride I'd felt when she said: *Your father would be so
proud.* The thought gave me the energy I needed to keep
working through the night.

The clock ticked on. It would wait for no one.

CHAPTER TWENTY-SEVEN

VANYALA AND BETTY went to bed sometime around 1 a.m., and David and I worked through the night. The hours slipped by, and before I knew it, the smell of pancakes and bacon wafted around us. My stomach responded with a growl.

David stood and stretched his back and arms. "Let's take a break and get some food."

I followed him down the dark hall into the kitchen.

"Good morning," Vanyala greeted. I hadn't taken her for the homemaker type, but she was standing in the kitchen wearing a green apron, spatula in hand. She flipped a pancake from the pan onto a plate and brought the stack over to the table.

"Thanks, Mom," David said as we sat down. He loaded a plate with pancakes, scrambled eggs, and bacon, then handed it to me and filled his own plate. Betty sat at the table across from us, a cup of hot coffee clutched in both hands. I smiled as I realized her red scrunchie was back, hair pulled into a high, crooked ponytail.

"You didn't sleep at all, did you?" Vanyala asked. She untied her apron and joined us at the table.

I said, "There's so much good stuff, it's hard to pull away from it to sleep. Were you ever a reporter? Your research was meticulous. Every time we thought there was a hole, we found the answer."

"It wasn't all me," she corrected. "The entire group has been working on this for years. We just didn't know what to do with it until now."

Vanyala piled three pancakes onto her plate and doused them in syrup, then picked up her fork. "Unfortunately, we'll still need to figure out how to make the story public," she said, her fork hovering over her plate. "The portal I used to use to hack into the Hub's airwaves has been shut down, and communication in and out is no longer possible. I can't even reach the Fear Fighters now."

She reached over and squeezed my hand.

"But you mustn't concern yourself with that, dear. You need to keep up your strength and remember to rest. This is a marathon, not a sprint."

We smiled at each other, the seeds of a new relationship planted. I hadn't realized it before, but she had the same strong, prominent cheekbones Marika did. *Marika.* Thinking of her almost made me lose my appetite. Was she okay? When would I get to see her again? Things didn't feel real unless she was there. My hand floated up to touch the pendant on my necklace.

"Marika must be so worried," I said to no one in particular. "I have to let her know I'm okay."

Vanyala and David exchanged a glance, then looked back at me.

"It's too dangerous, Charley," David told me gently. "By

now, they know about the baby. They're going to want to find you. They'll be watching her, waiting for you to reach out."

I knew he was right. I could imagine her calling, sending message after message and getting nothing but voicemail. Maybe she'd even been contacted by the government or the hospital. What if she was in danger too?

I thought of her red fingernails delicately brushing my hand, remembered her offer to run away and raise the baby together. Part of me wondered: if all this had happened before I met David, would I have considered her offer? We'd joked about being together a million times. It was always her and me, me and her, through thick and thin, grief and joy. She had a magical way of turning things around and making everything okay. What if the wine women were right and love *was* just love? A beautiful, dying emotion that had become overcomplicated with rules, regulations, and expectations.

"Marika might be able to help us get the story out there," I said, the realization hitting me at once. "She did it before—hijacked the server and built a microsite for an in-depth feature I developed. She nearly got fired, but the story got such good ratings, she ended up getting promoted instead."

After a few moments of silence, Betty said softly, "I could bring it to her."

We all looked over at her.

"I could go," she repeated, her voice stronger this time. "They won't be looking for me. They don't even know that I know you outside of the hospital."

"But will they know that you're the one who gave me the Sequenom test?" I asked.

"Good point. But no, I don't think so. You caught me at the end of my shift, so your name wasn't in my patient logs. And I was so excited about seeing you guys, and about the baby, I didn't even pull up your chart."

She blushed with the admission, looking like a star-struck fan. "For all they know, you snagged a couple tests and ducked into a room to take them yourself."

We were silent, considering. Her idea made sense. David and Vanyala looked at me.

"Would Marika take the risk?" David asked.

"Do you trust her?" Vanyala asked.

I answered them both at once. "Absolutely."

"I'll go with you," Vanyala told Betty. "I need to get word to the Fear Fighters, tell them what's coming. We'll leave tonight."

The rest of the day flew by, and by late afternoon, the story was ready. All the pieces I'd spent months collecting came together and became one clear picture supported by research and evidence. We had everything except the closing.

I took a shower, letting the hot water rush over me as I thought about my sign-off. What could I say to tie it all together and make everything we'd been through worthwhile? I got dressed in the clothes Vanyala gave me and put on Marika's necklace, then wandered into the kitchen. David, Vanyala, and Betty were sitting around the table, drinking chai tea. As I watched them laugh and talk, I could almost imagine it was an ordinary evening, that we were friends and family about to sit down for dinner. My new tribe. Only one thing was missing: Marika.

I lifted a hand to touch the ceramic lotus pendant around my neck. That was my answer for the sign-off.

"David, I'm ready to shoot the end. Let's go outside."

He stood and followed me down the tunnel and up the ladder.

"I know the perfect spot," David said once we were outside. He took my hand and we walked side-by-side through the woods. The ground began to slope and soon we were climbing. The sun was just starting to set and the sky was a swirling mix of color. The hues changed by the second, first blue, then orange, then red and pink. The forest's deep silence enveloped us until we rounded a bend at the top of the hill.

"This is it," David said.

Laid out before us was the most breathtaking vista I'd ever seen. The mountains rolled into eternity, fog hovering over them like an ocean. They looked blue in the light, a stark contrast against the glowing pink clouds and orange sky. Spring flowers burst from bushes in pink, white, and lavender clumps. The oak trees stood tall, thousands of them together. My heart swelled to see so many of them still alive, this section of the forest somehow immune to the beetles that had swallowed up thousands of nearby acres.

I took my position in front of the outlook. I ran a hand through my hair and realized it was still damp from the shower. I didn't have a shred of makeup on, and I didn't care. All the things I'd spent so much time and energy worrying about didn't matter. The only thing that mattered was that moment, and the words I would say. Standing there immersed in the beauty of nature, I could finally see the truth. All the world was a stage and a story. The characters were players, but they did not act alone. We were guided by a beautiful creative force, one that was far too mysterious and vast for our human minds to comprehend.

David signaled that he was ready.

I took a deep breath and began.

"I'm Charley Tennyson, an independent reporter in search of the truth. Not a whitewashed, government-approved version of the truth: the actual truth. The world has been hungry for answers about the End of Men and what it means for our future. I've hounded scientists, doctors, and government officials, asking them why it's happening? Why here? Why now? It's the question we all come back to, like two-year-olds.

Why, why, why? We ask questions like: Why did my father have to die? Why is the sky blue? Why am I alive? Why is all this happening? Instead of asking the more difficult questions like: What will I carry on for my dad now that he's gone? What color would I paint the sky, if I could? What will I do today that matters?

"It's now been more than three months since a male was born. I've done my best to find out why this is happening, and some of the answers are shocking. You won't be able to look at the world in the same way. But I wonder if you'll notice the same thing I did. Despite all the answers I found, I still wasn't satisfied. And I think it's because we've been asking the wrong question. What I've finally realized is, the 'why' is inconsequential. No matter what answer comes back, we'll never be satisfied. Why are males becoming extinct? Why is there violence? Why did that lost boy have to shoot that bullet at the exact spot where my father was standing? It might have been a million things, it might have been nothing. Asking why will always lead to more questions."

I held out my necklace, showing the pendant to the camera.

"This necklace was given to me by a dear friend. It's a lotus flower. She told me the lotus is a symbol of resilience. It grows in muddy water, the dirt falling off its petals as it rises above the murk to achieve beauty. It's a reminder that no matter what we come from, we can rise above it. A reminder that we're stronger than we think. This story is for those of you who want to run toward questions instead of away from them. For those who are willing to do more than ask 'why' while looking for someone to point the finger at. It's for those who have the courage to ask the hardest question of all: *What*. What do we do now? What kind of world do we want to live in? What are we willing to sacrifice in order to create it?

"When I ask questions like that, the same answer keeps

coming back. It's all about love. What do *you* love most in this world? What will you do to honor it? Will you tuck it away in a vault and try to keep it safe from harm, or will you nourish it, share it, help it grow? The world needs you and the love you have to give, now more than ever. If that scares you, it's okay. It *is* scary. But once you lean into the fear instead of running away from it, you'll realize what I did. Love is stronger than fear, and all of us are stronger than we think."

I motioned for David to stop filming. I turned and faced the outlook, watching as the sky's pink and orange shades faded to gray. It was hard to tell if the day was ending or the night was beginning. I'd given all I had to give, said all I had to say. But was it enough? David stepped up behind me and wrapped his arms around me.

"I love you," he whispered in my ear.

"I love me, too," I replied.

And it was enough. More than enough.

CHAPTER TWENTY-EIGHT

DAVID and I walked back in comfortable silence. There were no more questions to ask, no more words to say. Betty and Vanyala were standing by the Adventurer when we got back, leaning against the side with crossed arms.

David handed them a copy of the hologram file with the full story. I hugged them both and said goodbye, smiling at the sight of them together. Betty with her red scrunchie, Vanyala with her strong cheekbones and deer eyes—two women from completely different worlds, brought together for this mission. I wondered if I'd ever see them again. They probably wondered the same thing about me.

As Betty started to climb into the Adventurer, I realized there was one more thing I needed to do.

"Wait," I said, reaching behind my neck to undo the clasp on my necklace. "Will you give this to Marika? And tell her..." I struggled to think of the right words before realizing that only one thing really mattered. "Tell her I love her."

Betty took the necklace and clambered into the passenger's seat. Vanyala climbed into the driver's seat next to her.

"Like mother, like son," I said with a smile.

"Who do you think taught me how to drive?" David replied with a laugh.

David and I waved goodbye, watching as the vehicle disappeared into the forest. We were silent for a moment before David spoke.

"Charley, can I tell you a secret?"

"I hope you'll tell me *all* your secrets."

"I'm scared. Not about the story. About the baby. You heard my mom: there's such a thing as too much resilience. Beckett is proof that I have the Warrior Gene in me. What does it say that my Y chromosome is resilient enough to carry on when no one else's is? The idea of having a baby with you is amazing, but what if we're bringing a monster into the world?"

I paused, weighing my response. How could I assure him of what I knew, what I felt inside?

I gestured to a log. "Let's sit down. This is pretty much your front porch, right?"

The quiet of the forest enveloped us as we sat side-by-side on the log. The knotty wood was hard and uncomfortable, but it felt incredible to be outside—to breathe fresh air, to see the woods, mountains, and sky that had remained unchanged despite all that had happened.

"David, someone very wise once told me that fear is just excitement without breath. If you breathe into the fear, it transforms it. Try it."

We sat in silence, breathing deeply and staring up at the sky. Above us was a galaxy of stars, millions and millions of them. I felt tiny and infinite at the same time. I picked out one bright, glistening star and pointed.

"North Star. Make a wish."

He laughed. "Are you sure that's not a satellite?"

"I'm positive."

I placed my hand on my stomach, searching for movement. I felt nothing but I knew that it was there—the promise of what was to come. Sometimes things are growing quietly below the surface and you don't know, can't see them, until they emerge suddenly like a butterfly from a cocoon. And all those months you spent waiting, wishing for a transformation, working and working and not seeing anything happen, all of it makes sense. It all comes together in one moment, a flash of colored wings taking flight to the sky.

A memory of my dad floated into my mind, of he and I on the roof of our building one Magic Monday night, staring up at a starry sky just like this one. "Share your voice with the world," he had whispered.

I thought of the recording about to land in Marika's hands, wondered what would happen when the world discovered the truth. I thought of the baby growing inside me. I hadn't always wanted to be a mother, but I had always wanted to tell a story that mattered. All the pieces were in place. I had done it. I had finished the story.

And now, finally, it was time for a new one to begin.

AUTHOR'S NOTE

THIS IS A CONFESSION.

I know this book was far from perfect. You may have spotted some flaws, inconsistencies, scientific impossibilities, and (gasp!) a typo or two. Publishing it has been a giant leap in the dark. I could have taken more time to make it better. I could have made more edits, added another round of polish, thought longer and harder about how this world and its characters look, smell, and feel.

But time is short, in the grand scheme of things. The COVID-19 pandemic has reminded me of that fact—with startling, heartbreaking, unavoidable clarity. And for the first time since I started this book fifteen long years ago, I was able to look at what I'd written—and the woman who wrote it—and see the truth. It's flawed, but it's good. It's enough.

Who knows, maybe you'll like my book EVEN MORE because of its mistakes. Maybe you'll spot a crack, a plot hole, or a crappy sentence and say—hey, I could do better than that! And then, maybe you will.

My book and I don't have to be the best. We don't have to

be perfect. We don't have to always be right (even though I still really like to be). But we do always have to show up to the page. We have to try our best to speak our truth—to be honest, and raw, and brave. If you see something of yourself in these pages, I hope you find it beautiful and true. And if you don't, I hope you not only ask yourself "why" but take the leap in the dark to ask: "What would I do instead"?[1]

What can YOU create that speaks to YOUR truth? What will you do with this one precious, beautiful, broken life you've been given? What do you need to turn the page *right now* and begin telling and living the story that's been buried in your heart? When will you listen to the Crazy Idea that whispers in the dark of night (or sometimes in the shower)—that relentless "what if" musing, the thing you bury behind excuses like "if only" and "someday"?

Those are the questions I asked myself during my fifteen-year odyssey of writing this book. And rewriting it. And quitting. And crying, drinking, running, doubting, falling, fighting, learning, growing. And, somehow, believing in my idea and myself enough to stand up and start again.

For most of this journey, I was determined to find an agent and a big, impressive publisher. I wanted someone I could hide behind, someone to give me validation and approval. I figured: If I could find someone who REALLY knew what the hell they were talking about, they could confirm to the world that my book and I were good enough.

The irony is, once I gave up on that need, I became the person I needed to be to finally finish this story and share it with the world. If I pitched this version of my novel, there's a pretty good chance I'd find an agent. I could score a "real" publisher, maybe make some big moolah.

Or I could leap, now, alone, lifted up by the one true

God/Goddess and all the amazing people in my life who have helped make this possible.

Enjoy the read. Our future awaits.

---

1. This sentiment was inspired by the amazing closing speech in Benjamin Button. If you haven't watched it, go watch it. It's really beautiful, and not JUST because it's Brad Pitt.

ACKNOWLEDGMENTS

They say it takes a village to raise a child. It takes a choir of angels to publish a book. At least it did for me.

Thank you to my mom, Dianna Drinnon, for baking cookies and banana nut bread, splitting your Dr. Peppers, taking me to the library, and reading me bedtime stories until I could read them back to you. Most of all, thank you for always making sure I knew how very much I was loved.

Thank you to my dad, Paul Drinnon, for being my math tutor, billiards instructor, joke teller, dream sharer, fan club president, and the most big-hearted man I will ever know.

Thank you to the beautiful spirit that was my co-author—God/Goddess, I don't know your name, but I do know you. Thank you for giving me the courage to push through years of broken rewrites until the true story emerged.

Thank you to Matt Strobel, my husband, my partner, my love. With you by my side, I feel safe to shine.

Thank you to Asher, Harper, and Kaleb, for giving me a glimpse of what it's like to be a mom without birthing a child of my own, and giving me three more reasons to fight for a better tomorrow.

Thank you to my earliest readers for looking beyond the gaping holes to see the potential, especially my big sister Donna Perry and my soul sisters Jeni Miri, Jennifer Holmberg, and Mary Rea.

Thank you to my editor and writing instructor, Eleanor Brown, for your excellent guidance, revisions, and ideas. And to my many writing instructors over the years, especially Doug Kurtz, Jennifer Lauck, and everyone at Lighthouse Writers Workshop.

Thanks to my launch team for believing in me and investing your time and expertise to help make this a success:

Milan Klusacek, my cover artist, for taking my fuzzy ideas and making them clear and beautiful.

Lisa Bongiovanni, my accidental mentor, for rally-time pushes, website development, and existential crisis support.

Maya and Amy, for writing from the heart and laughing till we cried in the Costa Rican jungle. My fear is not my fate.

Thank you to my team at Red Canary for generous support and encouragement of my dream, especially Keith McCammon,

Brian Donohue, Susannah Clark, Brianne Houck, and Kyla Feeney.

My nieces, for sharing opinions and new perspectives. Keep reading, asking questions, and speaking up.

My coach, Sage Hobbs, for showing me how to play big.

And a gigantic thanks to all my fellow writers:

Tamara Palmer, for showing me that real writers show up on the daily. Tami 's Tribe for camaraderie and support, and the Power Goddesses for edits and encouragement. Danny Ferry for pushing me to keep going through the horrible, terrible middle. Mindy Neff for self-publishing advice and wisdom.

Thanks to Bryan Sykes for writing *Adam's Curse*, and Hanna Rosin for her non-fiction work *The End of Men*, both of which provided invaluable research and inspiration for this story.

And to the many other writers who taught and supported me without knowing it: Julia Cameron, Elizabeth Gilbert, Anne Lamott, Natalie Goldberg, Stephen King, Dean Koontz, Linda Sivertsen, Theo Pauline Nestor, and so many more. Words matter, and yours inspired me to believe I could do this. Thank you.

ABOUT THE AUTHOR

Suzanne Strobel has been crafting stories since she was a shy 6-year-old book nerd known as Suzanne Drinnon.

Suzanne earned her Bachelor's in Creative Writing at the University of Colorado Boulder. Her writing career has run the gamut from greeting cards and gift books to cybersecurity blogs, travel articles, and advertising campaigns for new homes and business ventures. END OF MEN is her debut novel.

Suzanne and her husband, Matt, live in Denver with three wonderful boys and a dachshund named Bucca.

Stay up-to-date on book releases and news at suzannestrobel.com.

Made in USA - Kendallville, IN
1195573_9781736134511
11.17.2020 1010